ARCHER AT WAR

Also by Colin Eston

Will Archer Mysteries

Archer Bows in
Archer's Irish Jig
Archer's Home Run
Archer at Court

Saint and Czinner Mysteries

Dying for Love
The Dusk Messenger
The Pepys Memorandum
The Seed of Osiris

COLIN ESTON

Archer at War

The fifth *Will Archer* mystery

Dying

Dead. Or as good as.

Bodies around me, writhing, groaning. Our whole foul environment heaving. No stability, only flux.

Like slow bubbles in mud, lethargic, memories surface and belch.

A twilight London street. A blow to the head.

Was it my *head? Was I the victim, set upon and dragged away, half conscious?*

The lost soul beside me shifts, moaning. The stink of his stale vomit and unwashed body nauseates me.

But I have nowhere to turn. Prone bodies crowd me on every side. And I stink as bad as the rest of them.

The ooze of recollection regurgitates another globule, bursting like a blister in my mind.

My captors plied me with drink. Ramming the bottle between my teeth, forcing me to swallow the fiery liquid or choke.

Then voices:

'Name?'

Silence.

'Can he not speak for himself?'

'Worse for wear, yer honour, but keen to take the King's

shilling.'

'Sign there, or make your mark.'

My hand seized and guided in a rough cross.

An outcry of oaths and curses as one of the lost souls in this purgatory lurches to his feet and attempts to stagger across the carpet of bodies, treading on heads, stumbling across legs and arms.

I lever myself into sitting position. I put my hand to my brow, easing the dull ache of prolonged intoxication, and see him lean across a rail and void his guts over the side.

And suddenly, as the final bubble bursts, I know I am lost.

Enlisted against my will. Separated from friends and family.

I am aboard a troop ship bound for the King's War.

Wrenched away from home and country.

Deprived even of identity.

For, as the fog in my brain clears, I recall a soft, cultured voice in that London street: *'That's the man, sergeant,'* and, as a blow to my temple felled me into unconsciousness, *'his name is - Jack Weaver.'*

Sea

The sea is full of naked bodies. The day is bright but the sun which sets shards of dazzling light glittering from the water has no warmth in it as pink bodies splash and caper, yelping and yawping against the cold.

It is not the weather for bathing but neither I nor my companions, all newly disembarked from the brig which rides at anchor short distance away, have much choice.

The rancid stench of the troop ship must be washed away. The filth, the sweat and the vomit swilled off before we are all born anew as soldiers in the army of King George.

None of us has washed or shaved for a week or more. My unkempt mane is lank with grease and my chin covered in a growth of dark hair, too long to be called stubble but not yet profuse enough to merit the title of beard.

The freezing water is both a torture and a godsend. It enervates, creeping deep into our very bones, making them ache with cold. Yet it also stimulates us to further exertion, to slap pale arms against our bodies, plunge heads beneath the waves, as we scour the muck from our frozen flesh and rub the blood back into our veins.

Just a few hours ago we were huddled together, fearful

and nauseous, as the ship pitched and tossed on the North Sea. Now - no matter that we are frozen to the marrow - we shove and manhandle one another in the sheer relief and exhilaration of being alive.

Most of these men are strangers to me. As are the events of the last few weeks.

I have no clear recollection of anything since I was abducted. All I remember is being knocked half unconscious in a London street on my way back home to Mr Garrick's lodgings. Since then my captors have kept me in a kind of limbo by plying me with strong spirits or rendering me insensible with blows.

It is only since I was half dragged, half carried, aboard the ship now docked at the harbour-side in this unknown port that fragments of memory – or imagined dream? - have started to connect themselves in my brain.

From my present circumstances, it is clear that I have been pressed into the army. Not by chance, but through the agency of someone who bears me ill will.

I do not know who this may be. Only that it is probably someone at Leicester House, the unofficial 'Court' of Frederick, Prince of Wales, set up in opposition to that of his father, King George.

I doubt, however, that my abduction was at the Prince's instigation, or even if he knows of it. As a minor player in

Mr David Garrick's theatre company, I am too small a fry to be any concern of his.

But in recently helping to foil a plot against the King's life, I have incurred the anger of someone who has exacted this revenge.

Someone who is working either for the French or for the Jacobite cause against His Majesty, King George II.

Suddenly I am taken by surprise by a pair òf hands on my shoulders, pushing me beneath the waves. I swallow water, breathe it up my nose, acrid, salty. I thrash about madly, fearful that I am being drowned.

My one thought is that those who kidnapped me are now determined to make an end of me. Having not been considerate enough to die conveniently on the voyage, I am now to perish, unknown and unremarked, in the freezing waters of a foreign shore.

I surface, spluttering and retching, heaving in lungfuls of clean, cold air, determined to fight for my survival.

Only to find myself confronted by a wide grin. I unbunch my fists.

I recognise the open features and fair curly hair of a fellow I briefly encountered some days ago as we both bent double over the ship's rail and voided the contents of our bellies into the churning sea.

'Tom Hooper,' says he, holding out a big, calloused hand.

'Pleased to make your acquaintance, Jack Weaver, specially now we're not heaving our guts into the briny no longer.'

I accept his strong grasp. He has the broad frame of one accustomed to manual labour. Strong, wide shoulders and a barrel of a chest covered in a mat of curly hair which does little to conceal the hard swell of muscle.

A useful lad to have as a friend, I think, in this new world I have been thrust into.

I am on the point of telling him he is mistaken about my real name when a commotion nearby distracts our attention.

The whoops and guffaws of exuberant horseplay are interleaved with yells of protest and then spluttering cries of genuine distress.

I turn to see a group of fellows plunging one of their number repeatedly under the waves. They are burly fellows and he is slight and pale. It is clear he is the butt of their persecution rather than a willing participant in their antics.

My companion, Tom, sees this, too, and together we wade across to rescue him.

'Hold hard, mates,' says Hooper good-humouredly, 'you'll drown the minikin chit if you're not careful.'

'Back off, joskin,' snarls the one who seems to be the chief instigator of the maltreatment. 'This is no business o' yours. We're doin' Jack Sprat 'ere a service, a-washing off 'is malmsey stain, ain't we, lads?' he says, appealing to his fellow ruffians with a cruel laugh.

And now, as their victim surfaces choking and coughing, I see that almost half his face is covered by a dark red or purplish mark that indeed looks like a red wine stain.

'Then you're wasting your labours,' say I. 'You'd as lief try to change the colour of his eyes, for 'tis a kind of birthmark. I have seen its like before.'

Their ringleader scoffs and turns to resume his sport, but I see one or two of the others back off. They are bullies but they are also superstitious.

'Nay,' I hear one murmur to his confederates, 'I'll not mess wi' the devil. Sure 'tis the mark of Satan.'

Mumbling, they disperse.

Roughly, their leader seizes the shivering lad by his arm and, almost wrenching it from the socket, flings him towards Tom and me.

'Here, have him, and much good may he do you!'

Then he wades off to berate his cronies for their cravenness.

Shaking as much from his ordeal as from the cold water, the hapless young man wraps his arms around his thin chest and murmurs, 'Thank you, friends. I feared I was a dead man.' He hunches his shoulders covering the side of his face with his hand. 'It is my curse, this damned deformity.'

His voice, though tremulous, betrays no trace of

coarseness. He is well-spoken and polite.

'Benjamin Woodrow,' he says, detaching a thin arm from around his shivering frame. 'Erstwhile student and would-be lawyer,' he continues despondently, 'yet what client would trust himself to such a countenance as mine?'

'Tom Hooper,' replies my fellow saviour heartily, 'farmhand and carter.' He takes Woodrow's slim hand in his mighty paw.

I, too, extend my hand in friendship. 'Will...' I begin, but then correct myself. 'Jack Weaver, former actor.'

Inwardly, I curse myself for not having the courage to disclose the misrepresentation, but at the moment nothing in my world is as it should be.

The time for explanations must wait till later, when I have come to know them better.

Uniform

Some while after, clasping a rough blanket around myself, I am part of a snaking line being herded towards a series of trestle tables.

At the first I am made to drop my blanket and submit, naked and shivering, to a cursory medical examination.

The doctor - if he is indeed a doctor, for his coat is well-worn and out at elbow and he has a hangdog look as if his work is more a penance than a duty – is flanked by a uniformed soldier who inspects his every move, occasionally interrupting to repeat some operation himself.

I am told to open my mouth wide and stick out my tongue which is apparently deemed satisfactory. Then he raps upon my chest in several places, tests the muscles in my arms and scrutinises my armpits and my groin for swellings or pustules.

I am pronounced clear of infection and allowed to replace my blanket and move on to the next table which is piled high with coarse linen shirts and woollen britches.

The soldier manning the stall casts an eye over my shoulders and chest and asks if I know how tall I am.

'Five foot nine,' I tell him.

He extracts a shirt from one of the piles and holds it

against my chest, then repeats the ritual with a pair of britches held against my waist.

He thrusts them into my arms. 'Courtesy of King George,' he says. 'Take care of 'em. You'd best be good wi' needle and thread, for a replacement'll cost you a month's wages.'

From what I know of a soldier's pay I reckon that to be about thirty shillings. I resolve to perfect my needlework skills. Clutching the first items of my uniform, I shuffle onwards to the next table.

Behind and in front of me, similar shivering, blanket-draped men are slowly filing through the same process.

But some, I note, have fallen at the first hurdle and sit bent double coughing or lie prostrate groaning upon the ground. A few, clearly suffering from the flux, seek the privacy of bushes.

Nearby stands a wagon and horses ready, I guess, to transport them to hospital until they are recovered enough to re-join the regiment – or to escape enlistment in the most final way.

Within half an hour, I am a fully kitted-out as an infantryman. A long shirt whose tails back and front pass between my legs, doing away with the need for under drawers. Knee-length white britches, long black buttoned gaiters and black boots.

After buttoning up the large white waistcoat, I don the high-collared, knee-length red coat and discover it allows of no stance but ramrod straight. As I fasten the pairs of pewter buttons into their worsted-lace framed buttonholes, I am relieved to find that the front skirts can at least be hooked back, presumably for marching. Finally I top it all off with a black tricorn hat.

Despite the unfamiliar roughness of the coarse cloth against my skin, I fancy myself quite the coxcomb and wish that Susan, back at Bow Street, could see me.

But with that thought comes the overwhelming realisation of my situation.

No one in England knows where I am or what has happened to me.

Not Susan, the kitchenmaid with whom I have spent many a pleasant evening of dalliance. Not Charlie, whom I rescued from a life on the streets and who has become almost a younger brother to me. Nor Mr David Garrick, the renowned actor, who took me in when I was in similar straits to Charlie and trained me as an actor in his company.

I may be dead for all they know and my heart aches to think of the distress my unexplained absence must be causing.

And there are others who may not yet even be aware of my disappearance because news will not have reached them

– if, indeed, anyone has thought to send it.

My mother in Yorkshire, together with Nicolas St Anton and his wife Sarah, whom I have left managing the estates which only last year I discovered I am master of.

Man of means though I am, however, that wealth can not help me in my present plight.

Nor can influence from Sir William Hervey, spymaster and head of the King's Secret Service. His last advice to me was to retire to my home in Yorkshire for a time, whilst he worked to find those who sought to exact retribution for my part in foiling their plots.

He cannot be aware that they – whoever they are – have already pre-empted him.

To all of them and to everyone who now surrounds me on this foreign shore – even to myself – Will Archer is lost.

This fellow who now briefly peacocks in his newly-donned military uniform is Jack Weaver - a name plucked out of the blue by those who were set to abduct me.

A name which now resounds in my ears, accompanied by a hearty slap upon my back. 'Jack Weaver! A pox, but ain't we damned fine fellows to be sure!'

Tom Hooper, a broader blond version of myself in his new uniform, twirls in front of me, arms stretched as wide as the grin on his face. Beside him, short, slight but identically attired is Benjamin Woodrow, a pensive David in the shadow of an ebullient Goliath.

The sight of Hooper's chin with its gingery thatch and his tricorn hat perched precariously on his mass of curls reminds me that we are all in need of the services of a barber. There are several around the edge of the large square where we are all assembled, all with long queues of newly red-coated figures.

My two new companions accept my suggestion that we shall all be a damned sight finer fellows following a haircut and a shave and we make our way through the milling throng to await our turn.

As we wait, I ask Hooper how he came to know my name.

'Back in Ramsgate 'twas,' he informs me – (I have no recollection of ever being in Ramsgate) – 'when the two coves handed you over to the sergeant-at-arms just prior to embarkation. Hauled you up the gangplank like you wor a sack o' turmits. "Jack Weaver," they said all triumphant-like, "reportin' fer dooty. 'E's all yours now, our dooty's done." An' they 'ot-footed it down the gangplank a-leavin' you on the deck. Sergeant sees me a lookin' and orders me to move you aside. Which is wot I done.' He digs me in the ribs. 'Drunk as a wheelbarrow you was. Some night you must have had. Mind you, the two of us was flashing the hash over the side most o'next day, an' me not 'ad a drop.'

I learn that both Hooper and Woodrow arrived at Ramsgate by a more conventional route, making their way on foot, together with other recruits.

Unlike myself, they both have volunteered for service. Hooper from his home in Dorset, the third of three sons on a small farm about to be reclaimed by the land owner who intended to enclose his lands. 'No future there for me no more, 'cept as menial labourer. So I decided I'd see the world and took the King's Shilling.' He fingers the unfamiliar red-coat with a grimace of almost puzzled pride. 'And 'ere I be, a new-minted Jack Lobster!'

Woodrow has come from London. Although the only son of a relatively well-off merchant, he had not the means on leaving university to set himself up as a lawyer on his own account. Nor, due to his facial disfigurement, was any established lawyer willing to take him on. 'However, an uncomely visage, it seems, is no bar to being shot at,' he says ruefully, 'and mayhap my education may help me advance beyond the lot of common soldier.'

A few minutes later, sitting in the barber's chair as he crops my hair and razors my chin, I have liberty to look about me at what I now know to be the port of Ostend in Flanders.

From where we are in a large cobbled square next to the dockside I can see the furled sails of the barque that brought us rising and falling against the blue winter sky. On the opposite side from the sea there is only a stretch of high, battlemented walls and a glimpse of domes and towers beyond. Ostend may be small but it seems a heavily fortified town.

Not that I am about to discover much more about it, for within the hour, as a dying winter sun burns red on the horizon, we are all mustered into a makeshift column and ordered to follow the officer on horseback at our head.

With a great deal of jocular banter to hide our misgiving at what may await us, we shamble - as yet with scant notion of marching although one or two swaggerers attempt a vaguely military pace - towards the unknown.

Drill

We do not go far. A couple of miles perhaps beyond the town.

With dusk thickening around us, we arrive at a cluster of buildings which have the appearance of once being a farm. No sign of livestock, but only fields set to grass, neglected thatched barns and cattle sheds. At a short distance a light burns in the window of the only cared-for building, what must once have been the farmhouse, almost a small mansion, gabled in the Dutch style.

Here, the one or two officers are to be billeted and, as the door opens, a waft of baking meat is carried out into the cold evening air.

But there is no such luxury for us. We recruits must make shift in the decrepit outbuildings with no bedding but rancid straw and no supper to stave off our hunger.

The jesting of the journey hither quickly fritters away, replaced by dismayed grumbles and squabbles over sleeping places.

Hooper, being from farming stock, quickly shepherds Woodrow and me away from the large barn towards the uninviting cattle sheds.

'Leave them ass-heads to fight over their five foot of

ground,' says he, knowingly. 'There be no sweeter resting place than a byre.'

And so it proves, for within the low stone-built shed are partitions of wood still standing between the former stalls, providing half a dozen cozy nooks free from draughts, each capable of accommodating up to five persons.

Fifteen or twenty other young men have had the same idea as us, but there is plenty of room and, by the time disgruntled refugees from the overcrowded barn start drifting in, having failed to secure an adequate billet, we are all settled in relative comfort.

Despite the hardness of the earth floor and the hollowness in my belly, I soon fall asleep and am only woken next morning by the sergeant rattling his cane against the wooden barriers.

'Rouse about, you insanitary frequenters of the casual ward! The sun's burnin' holes in your blankets. Up, you gutter rats!'

Bleary eyed, dusting flakes of straw from our clothes in which we have slept, we stagger out into the cold morning light.

'Insanitary be damned,' mutters Woodrow beside me. 'It's all right for him up at the house. He should try sleeping on straw with only the corner to piss in!'

'Aye,' I agree with a sour smile, 'and 'twould be nice to

have a blanket for the sun to burn holes in. Or,' I add, looking up at a sky grey with drizzle and low hanging clouds, 'to have a sun at all!'

At least we have food, or what passes for it. Two large metal cauldrons stand on a wood fire at a short distance from the barn and a couple of soldiers are ladling grey-looking oatmeal porridge into tin platters as sleep-tousled, heavy-eyed recruits file by and take them up.

The dusty figures in now creased red coats bear little resemblance to the strutting, sea-rinsed peacocks of yesterday. We stand around on the damp grass wolfing the sticky mess with jealous concentration as if it were manna from heaven.

At length, we are all called together and marshalled into lines. There are sixty of us and we are put into three lines of twenty facing the sergeant.

And here I learn, through much shouting and foul language, that these abandoned farm buildings are to be our home for the next week or two, these rough fields our parade ground while we learn to be soldiers in His Majesty's army.

Units similar in size to our own are being trained elsewhere in Flanders and in England and, when the call for duty comes and we march into battle, we will form part of a company of ten such units. And that company will, in turn, be one tenth of a regiment.

But, before we can aspire to any of that, we must be drilled interminably and incessantly, so the rest of the morning is spent forming up into ranks, learning how to march to the beat of a drum, how to turn, how to stand. Our bodies pounded by constant movement, our ears assaulted by the incessant drumming and oaths of the sergeant until, by the time a weak sun peers from behind the clouds at midday, we bear slightly more resemblance to greenhorn infantrymen than to mere raggle-taggle volunteers.

At noon we are allowed a temporary break. But not all are lucky. The sergeant singles out half a dozen men who have proved inept or ungainly in our morning's endeavours and, equipped with spades, they are ordered to one side of the field and set to dig a trench which will serve as latrines for the duration of our stay.

Woodrow, unfortunately, is one of their number and, as he plods wearily off, I catch sight of the fellow who was tormenting him yesterday jeering and pointing him out to his colleagues.

Meantime, the sergeant addresses the rest of us to inform us that tomorrow's breakfast will be the last that is provided for us. Our first week's pay will be distributed this evening and from now on, we will be responsible for finding our own food. There is, he tells us, a daily market in Ostend and the owner of the farm has a limited amount of supplies which we may purchase. Any who think to save their money and pilfer from neighbouring farms, however, will only earn themselves a flogging. The discipline and the reputation of the British army, he says with grim smugness, must be upheld.

An hour later Woodrow returns, mud-stained and with blistered hands and we tell him what the sergeant has told us. 'Aye,' says he with a dispirited sigh, 'and when are we supposed to make the journey to Ostend to buy provisions if every hour of the day is spent marching up and down this bloody field?'

And, as if to underline his point, the sergeant is even now calling us back to line up for the resumption of drill.

I hope there will, despite Woodrow's reservations, be time to get into town – and with it, perhaps, an opportunity for me somehow to get word to my friends at home of what has befallen me.

A Flogging

I almost lose count of the days we spend hammering the turf with our boots on dry days or squelching through mire when wet.

Our *peleton*, or platoon as our officers prefer to call it, *peleton* being a French word and the French being our enemies, is commanded by First Lieutenant Bancroft, though we see little enough of him. He makes brief appearances to supervise progress as Platoon Sergeant Latham puts us through our paces, offers one or two words of advice and with a clipped, 'Carry on Latham,' retreats to the comfort of the mansion.

Scarcely older than myself, he is either a gentleman with the natural air of disdain that betokens privilege or, as I suspect is more likely, a junior officer newly promoted who is ill at ease with the authority thrust upon him.

Probably he, like the rest of us, is equally ignorant of what lies in store, and I doubt he has seen any real action beyond being a junior *aide-de-camp* to some peacetime officer.

Sergeant Latham, by contrast, is an experienced soldier, his senior by half a dozen years. He shows all necessary respect but I detect subtleties of expression that suggest he does not hold his superior in high regard.

And then there is Brogan - the lout Hooper and myself had occasion to restrain in his treatment of Woodrow on our first day.

The more I've seen of him these last few days, the less he has endeared himself to me. He has the swagger of the bully and, with his perpetual sneer, never a good word to say about anyone. Deprived of his prey on that first encounter, he has since lost no opportunity to denigrate and provoke Woodrow, or to disparage Hooper and myself as his protectors.

The worst of it is that he has his followers. Some of the fellows who sloped off when challenged that day have since slunk back into his orbit. They laugh when he imitates our platoon commander's clipped, upper-class tones. He does not, I note, mock Sergeant Latham. But I have no doubt that, sooner or later, he will make mischief for Woodrow, Hooper and me. Men such as he cannot bear to be bested and I see in his sidelong glances that his desire for revenge burns slow but tenacious.

In the meantime, though, our every waking moment seems to be taken up with drill. Perfecting the length of our stride, the distance between us, the regularity of our pace.

Once we are competent in marching in a straight line, four or five abreast, we are taught to wheel.

'Move in column, fight in line' is the slogan which comes to dominate our manoeuvres as we learn the art of this complicated manoeuvre where the inner flank must march on the spot whilst the outer flank puts its best foot forward in double time.

It is an art which takes some time to master and results in many a wrong turn and stumble. At first our clumsiness provokes much mirth within the ranks, but all laughter quickly dies when repeat offenders are singled out to be flogged.

The first of these is a clownish youth with limbs and features so ill-assorted that he seems to have been constructed almost at random. Throughout all our practice, he has maintained a grimace of concentration, but his legs and arms seem incapable of acting together, with the result that he has stumbled more than most.

Lumbering, amiable, with a puzzled half smile he seems not to realize what is happening as he is led into the hollow square formed by the rest of the platoon who have been ordered to witness his punishment.

In the centre stand three pikes, their points tied together to form a pyramid. Marched up to this, he is ordered to halt while the charge is read out.

'For persistently failing to comply with regimental commands and thereby bringing disrepute upon your comrades and upon the King's army, you are sentenced to twenty lashes. Strip, sir!'

Fumbling yet more as the reality of his situation dawns, the poor fellow becomes all fingers and thumbs. Impatiently, Sergeant Latham orders a man to rip the shirt from his back. Then, naked to the waist, his wrists are tied to the apex of the pyramid while his legs are pulled roughly apart and his ankles fastened to two of the pikes.

Stripped as he is, a reason for his ungainliness becomes apparent. He has a withered right arm. Thinner than the left and slightly misshapen, its lack of flexibility as it is wrenched up to be pinioned twists his whole upper body painfully askew.

I remember learning from Susan, the kitchenmaid back in Bow Street, how such deformities can stem from a difficult birth. A friend of hers had borne such a child. 'Arm twisted right round its neck, poor mite, and so blue 'twas given up for dead before the goodwife saw it stir. Then so much slapping and pummelling to make the blood flow that the arm was damaged yet more.'

My heart goes out to poor fellow. A body blighted from birth and now about to be subjected to further harshness. And with little hope of amelioration for, this being deemed only a minor punishment of twenty lashes, there is no army surgeon standing ready, only a bucket of salt water to hand.

Sergeant Latham looks to First Lieutenant Bancroft and, receiving the nod, gives the order 'Proceed'.

It is only now that I see which of our number has been recruited to dole out the punishment.

It is Brogan who is handed the short whip with several knotted tails and he glances back at his cronies with an evil grimace of satisfaction as he steps up to do his duty.

The first blow causes the poor wretch to jerk and utter a cry, half yelp, half sob at the sudden shock of pain. As the half dozen tails of the whip fall away and Brogan lifts his arm for the second strike, I see the raised weals and the gouts of bloody flesh where the knots have torn the skin.

Around me, I hear indrawn breaths and sense the revulsion. For most of us, this is our first experience of such brutality.

The object of our horrified attention sags against the pikes, trembling in anticipation of the next impact. But he has drawn courage from somewhere and as the whip snags his bleeding flesh once again, he lets out barely a whimper, though the spasm which racks his body is ample evidence of his agony.

Eight more times the whip connects with his back, Brogan making sure the first three strokes have covered the whole area from shoulder to waist. Then he does his best to land the following blows directly upon the first wounds so that he opens them further. By now, the poor fellow's back is a mess of blood and tattered skin.

I, and those lined up around me have winced with each successive blow, hardly able to imagine what agonies he must be enduring. I have heard a couple of people vomiting and another, away to my right has fainted, whilst others have set their faces, staring ahead in an effort not to see.

Now Brogan turns to the the sergeant and displays the whip to him. Pieces of flesh are clogging the knotted cords and Brogan is asking for a new cat-o'nine-tails to continue his work with maximum effect.

But, though the punishment is not yet half administered, Bancroft steps forward.

Immediately there is an expectant silence.

'I believe …,' he begins, but his voice is husky. He clears his throat and starts again with greater strength. 'I believe this man to be a willing soldier and am very sorry to see him brought to this pass. Is there any man here who will speak for him?'

There is a pause which lengthens into an embarrassed silence. Then, unexpectedly, from my side, Woodrow speaks up.

'I will, sir. It is not through lack of application or contrariness that he is here, but through maladroitness resulting from an innate deformity. He wishes, I am sure, to be a good soldier and a credit to His Majesty. And with your permission, I will pledge to assist him in achieving that end.'

'Well said, soldier.' Bancroft turns with evident relief to Latham. 'Sergeant, untie the man and have his wounds attended to. You may dismiss the men.'

Latham, stone-faced, signals to two men to take the reprieved man down, but I see him exchange a glance with Brogan who has a thwarted look on his face.

The glance is only momentary, but it is enough. An opinion has been shared, a possible alliance made.

An alliance against our commanding officer, on the one hand and, on the other, against Woodrow, the champion of the reprieved man.

Town

In the intervals between stints of training there is, despite Woodrow's initial pessimism, occasionally time to make the twenty minute walk from our temporary camp into the town of Ostend to buy provisions.

It is the natural order of things that large gatherings of strangers thrown together in circumstances such as ours will separate into smaller bands formed from friendship, common interests or geographical kinship. And so it is with us. Before we have been stationed here a week, the platoon has organised itself into a dozen or so disparate groups.

That consisting of Hooper, Woodrow and myself is augmented, following the flogging, by the victim of that act of barbarism, Josh Barley.

Hardly more than a simpleton, he is nevertheless a good-hearted soul whose open, trusting nature unfortunately makes him the butt of ridicule to would-be wags and a prey to bullies such as Brogan. However ungainly his body may have proved, his constitution proves sound and, with careful tending, his injuries are within a few days showing signs of healthy healing.

For the two days following his ordeal, he is allocated a bare, stone-flagged room in the farmhouse where Woodrow is allowed to visit him.

Brogan's reaction is typical of his foul nature. 'A bracket-faced shuffler playin' nursemaid to a cow-handed cripple. What use is either of 'em?'

Uneasy lest insult manifests itself in action, either Hooper or myself accompany Ben whenever he goes to change Barley's dressings or take him bowls of broth cooked with what we purchase from the shops and market stalls in town.

Our trips to town usually take place at midday or late in the afternoon and the three of us go together, frequently keeping company with others on the way.

After the first few visits it is clear the townsfolk look suspiciously upon large groups of English soldiers. So, whilst many of us keep company on the road, as soon as we near the town walls with its close-spaced towers we split into twos or threes and go our separate ways along the narrow cobbled streets.

Ostend is not a large town. Crammed within its walls is a maze of narrow streets winding their way into a succession of open *pleinen* or squares. Chief amongst these is the *Stadsplein* surrounded by impressive three or four storey buildings with stepped or rounded gables and grand porticos behind which I guess the burghers of the town sit in council and conduct their business.

The other squares we discover are neither so spacious nor so grand, some being little more than sizeable courtyards hemmed in by gloomy looking, flat-fronted houses whose regimented windows look blindly out onto the silent enclosed space.

Our destination, though, is the *Marktplaats* where stalls are a permanent feature, laden with all sorts of goods and produce during the day, but cleared or shuttered at night-time.

Here we buy turnips, parsnips and potatoes for our stew and haggle for scrag ends of meat to impart a little flavour. Some stall-holders are friendly, others less so, keeping a wary eye upon us as if afeard we may steal what we cannot buy. And I have no doubt there are plenty of my fellows who might well do exactly that or offer to overtip a stall if they do not get their own way.

Indeed on one occasion we see two of Brogan's confederates in a heated argument that culminates in their sweeping a pile of swedes off a stall and kicking them as they bounce and roll over the cobbles.

Fortunately Hooper, Woodrow and I are at the other side of the marketplace and do not get caught up in the chase as they take to their heels pursued by a half-dozen burly stall-holders. Nevertheless, we discreetly retreat into one of the narrow lanes leading off the square.

Nor are we the only ones to have taken such refuge from the affray. A few yards further along the shadowy lane I catch sight of Brogan himself. He is in close conference with another man who has his back to us and it is clear from the way Brogan darts surreptitious glances about him, that their business is not to do with buying supper provisions.

I stay my two companions with a nod in Brogan's direction and we turn into a side alley to avoid encountering him. However, such is the nature of these labyrinthine narrow lanes that we find this side alley curving back towards the street we have just left at a point beyond where Brogan and the stranger are in such earnest conversation.

But, just as we emerge, I almost run into Brogan's companion coming the other way and am obliged to press myself against the wall to let him pass.

Although the afternoon is well-advanced, with the growing dusk even denser here under the overhanging eaves of the crowded houses, and he is muffled up with his hat pulled down over his eyes, there is something in the brief glimpse I get of him that seems familiar.

Where or when I have seen him before I cannot recall, but I am sure that he, too, gives a start of recognition before hurrying on his way.

A glance at my two companions shows that they have noticed nothing. Hooper is too busy scanning the lane for any sight of Brogan, whilst Woodrow has retreated into the shadow of the wall as soon as the stranger appeared.

Tom assuring us that the way is clear, we continue on our way.

But Brogan's absence is not uppermost in my mind. As I puzzle over the stranger's identity on the way back to camp, memories begin to fall into place.

Yet they make no sense.

If this ghost from my past is really who I think he is, what is he doing here in Ostend? And what dealings can he possibly have with the likes of Brogan?

By supper time, I have all but decided that I am mistaken. Yet try as I might to dismiss it, a hard knot of foreboding has begun to tighten in my gut.

Whilst reluctantly resigned to maintaining my imposture as Jack Weaver for the present, I am more resolved than ever to expedite my plan to regain my freedom and my true identity as soon as can be managed

Next day, while Hooper and Woodrow go to visit Josh Barley, I hurry off to town by myself.

Orders are that we must wear uniform whenever we go to Ostend, but I have under my arm a bundle which contains the clothes I was wearing when I was abducted in London.

All of us retained the clothes we wore on the sea-journey

hither and those of us who have not discarded them as worthless rags, sold them for a few shillings or bartered them for other goods have washed and stowed them in the canvas knapsacks we were issued with on our second day. Strapped upon our backs when the time comes for us to move from our present quarters, these knapsacks will contain all our worldly goods and possessions.

At this very moment, mine - minus the items I have tucked under my arm - is leaning against the wall of the byre which serves as our sleeping place.

On one of the previous journeys into town I have noted a deserted, roof-fallen stone hut in the shade of a small copse and it is here, some minutes later, that I exchange my uniform coat and britches for the apparel of my former life.

Today I walk into Ostend not as a soldier but as an ordinary gentleman. My destination is the dockside which, as it is just past midday, is busy with porters wheeling barrows, merchants haggling over goods and a whole variety of fellows engaged in maritime tasks, boatmen hauling skiffs up onto the narrow beach, fisherman mending nets or stacking wicker creels.

But these are not the people I seek. My quarry is like to be found in one of the taverns near where a three-master rides at anchor, its sails furled, the piles of crates upon the quay showing that it has just been unloaded. The flag which flaps limp about the topmast bears the red cross of St George.

My hand goes involuntarily to my pocket in which nestles a folded piece of paper. It is the flyleaf of a book I found on one of our visits to Josh Barley at the farmhouse.

The same occasion afforded me a quill and ink and the opportunity to write the short note which my fingers now briefly caress as a desperate hope of salvation.

A pair of drunken sailors erupt from the doorway of a tavern as I approach and stagger a few steps to the corner of an alley where a runnel trickles down to a hole in the harbour wall. Here they unlace and, with arms about each others shoulders to keep them upright, employ their other hands to direct hot streams of urine into the narrow channel.

I wait until they have finished and are re-lacing themselves before I draw near.

'Good morrow, gentlemen. You are English by your voices, I think?'

'Aye, that we are,' replies one fixing me with a suspicious look as best he can with eyes that are having difficulty in focusing. 'What of it?'

'From London?'

'Nay, from Bristol, me. And Jem 'ere,' he says with an expansive gesture that so nearly topples him that he has to cling onto his companion, 'Jem's a Devon man.'

The pair of them find this piece of wisdom so amusing that they burst into roars of laughter, thumping each other upon the chest with merriment.

I wait patiently for them to subside, plastering a grin upon my face to suggest I share their amusement, then ask, with a nod in the direction of the anchored barque, 'You sail tonight?'

'In the morning. At first light. Straight up the Thames and in to the Pool of London. And a fleeter voyage 'twill be without that lot on board.' With an exaggerated wink towards the stacks of crates, he draws me close and whispers in an overpowering stink of spirits, 'Supplies for His Majesty's war. 'Tis imm – immin – nimmim - 'twill take place any day, they say. There's troops already over here, y'know?'

'So I've heard,' I reply. 'So you sail into the heart of London tomorrow? And are there any Londoners among your crew?'

He turns to his mate, Jem, who so far has remained silent apart from the occasional belch of assent.

There follows some discussion as to who may or may not hail from the capital. At length he says, 'There's none o' the hands to my knowledge, Kentish men the most on'em. But I believe Midshipman Bolton to be a Londoner.'

'Where may I find him?'

'Sure, 'e don't mix wi' the likes o'us. 'E'll be in the *Koning Johannes* if he's anywhere.'

He points out a larger, more reputable looking building towards the end of the quay.

I thank him, wishing him and Jem calm sea and fair weather for the morrow and bend my steps to the *Koning Johannes.*

It proves to be more a Coffee House than a tavern, reminding me with a sudden pang of homesickness of the Bedford in London where Mr Garrick may even now be taking coffee and reading the daily news-sheet.

I have no difficulty in recognising the Midshipman in his blue, long-skirted coat. He is a fresh-faced youth, barely eighteen I would guess, and I'm relieved to see he is sitting alone reading a book, with a dish of coffee at his elbow.

'Do I have the honour of addressing Midshipman Bolton?'

He starts at my interruption, having been immersed in his book and a blush suffuses his clean-shaven cheeks.

'I – er – I'm sorry...?' he stutters, half rising in confusion.

I sit opposite him, motioning him to resume his seat. 'My apologies for startling you, sir, but I was told by some members of your crew that I might find you here.' I extend my hand. 'My name is Will Archer and I wonder if I may ask a favour of you?'

It is odd how unfamiliar my own name sounds upon my tongue after all these days of being someone else. Some of my hesitation must impart itself to him for it takes a moment for him to accept my proffered hand. Clearly he is still uneasy at being accosted by a total stranger.

'A favour, Mr Archer? I don't know...'

'I would not normally impose upon your good will thus, Master Bolton. But the circumstances in which I find myself leave me little option.'

Now that he has had chance to study me and to hear my voice, his initial reservations seem to have eased, and I see that I have aroused his curiosity.

A glance at the book he was so engrossed in shows that it is not some tome of maritime law but a copy of Mr Henry Fielding's new novel, *The History and Adventures of Mr Joseph Andrews*. Mr Midshipman Bolton is, it seems, of a romantic turn of mind.

I therefore give my imagination free rein.

'You see before you, Master Bolton, a foolish fellow who, believing I was aiding a lady in distress, travelled hither with her and her maid under what I fondly imagined was my protection. Imagine my chagrin, then, to discover 'twas all a sham. In rescuing her, as I supposed, from a tyrannical father and an enforced betrothal to a loathed suitor, and delivering her to a sympathetic Aunt in Bruges, I was in fact assisting her to meet up with and elope with her secret lover. Not only did she dupe me totally, but she also made off with what little money I had, leaving me destitute in a foreign country.'

I can see I have him enthralled. His eyes glitter with anticipation and his mouth hangs open in wonder.

But I do not wish to strain his credulousness too far.

'The favour I would ask of you, Master Bolton, and I shall quite understand if you refuse, for you are under no obligation....'

A see a momentary doubt cloud his eyes. *Is this stranger about to ask me for money – or smuggle him aboard as a stowaway?*

'Could you deliver a letter for me upon your return to London?'

His relief is almost palpable. 'A letter? Is that all? Most certainly, Mr Archer.'

I take the note from my pocket. 'Forgive the nature of this missive, Master Bolton, but I had to use whatever material came to hand.'

He nods understandingly and peers at the superscription.

'Mr David Garrick? Why, is not he the famous actor?'

'To be sure,' I say quickly, 'but also, and more importantly, a friend to me and my family. He will, I know, do whatever is in his power to assist me in my present pecuniary plight.'

Apparently satisfied with my credentials, Bolton is now scrabbling in his pocket. 'Pray, Mister Archer, will you not accept...?'

I hold up my hand. 'Indeed not, Master Bolton. I appreciate your generosity, but pray pocket up your purse. To deliver the letter will be service enough and I shall be eternally in your debt.'

Our business thus concluded, we shake hands and I take my leave.

Brown Bess

We are near two weeks into our marching and drilling when, one morning, Sergeant Latham lines up the platoon and holds up a musket. It is the first firearm we've seen in our time here.

'From now on, this will be your closest companion. She's a flinty-lipped jade, but you'll need to treat 'er better'n than your favourite harlot, for she's a rare bite on 'er.'

His vulgar innuendo elicits coarse sniggering from several of the men.

'Wot's 'er name, sergeant?' calls out one bold wag.

'It's said 'is Majesty calls 'er 'brawn buss' – which them 'as 'as more brains than me say is German for 'strong gun'. But to us commoners, she's Brown Bess.' Another round of crude laughter, for all but the most innocent among us know 'tis a nickname for a prostitute open to entry by the back way. 'And she'll need careful handling, like what I'm about to show yer. Stow yer laughter and make sure yer eyes is proper peeled, for you'll be doin' this yerselves anon.'

So saying, he demonstrates how to load and fire it. With the weapon at half-cock, he bites off and spits out the paper twist of a cartridge. Then he dribbles a modicum of black powder into the weapon's flashpan and draws the steel backwards to close it off.

Sloping the weapon against his left leg, he empties the rest of the powder and the ball from the cartridge into the mouth of the barrel, followed by the screwed-up paper casing as wadding. Deftly sliding out an iron rod from its mounting under the barrel, he rams it all down firmly.

Finally, bringing the musket to full cock and with the wooden stock firmly against his right shoulder, he averts his face and presses the trigger.

One or two start at the muffled boom of the explosion with its accompanying puff of smoke and sparks. And, as the noise dies away, there is a tentative ripple of applause soon crushed by an angry look from Latham.

He orders two men from the front rank to unload and distribute the muskets.

As mine is handed to me I experience a sick feeling in my stomach. This object of varnished wood and oiled metal, near on five foot from stock to muzzle and weighing, I would guess, about ten pounds, inspires awe, but also great unease.

Feelings which only increase as the day goes on. Firearm drill proves as tedious – but considerably more dangerous – than marching drill. By the end of the afternoon there are several with burned cheeks from the powder flashing in the pan, one unfortunate half-blinded, and nearly all of us have blackening bruises from the savage kick-back against our shoulders.

And we have not yet practised firing in line upon which, Sergeant Latham informs us, both our lives and success in battle will depend.

That comes next day when, lined up in three ranks confronting our imaginary enemy, we are enjoined to follow our drill to the letter. The front row discharge their volley, then kneel to reload as the second row fire. As they kneel in their turn, the third row shoots, by which time the front row must be ready to stand and shoot again. And so our whole day goes - shoot, kneel, reload, stand, shoot again. Hesitate, fumble or stumble and you risk getting your head blown off not by the enemy but by the fellow behind you.

When evening comes and the different groups sit and lounge about the field cooking their supper the mood is sombre, all hilarity muted as, bruised and weary, we contemplate the reality of what lies ahead of us.

Barley, sufficiently recovered from the flogging to return to duty, now forms the fourth member of our little group though he speaks little to either Hooper or myself. Since rescuing him from the torment of flogging, Woodrow has become the object of his devotion. Like a faithful hound, Barley now hardly ever leaves his side and, though Woodrow occasionally sighs with exasperation at such unremitting fidelity, I sense that he is highly gratified by it.

In saving Barley out of abhorrence for the cruelty being inflicted on him, and perhaps also out of fellow feeling for another marked by cruel chance, Ben Woodrow has only increased the ire of his enemies. But now this ungainly man-boy is proving a useful bodyguard. Josh Barley may be a simple, gentle soul but his bulk and strength is like to make any would-be adversary think twice before tackling either him or the altogether slighter, weaker man who has become his adopted master.

Now, as the twilight thickens with drifting woodsmoke, our heads are full of the day's training and forthcoming conflict.

Hooper says, in between mouthfuls of our habitual stew, 'Third rankers, Josh and me, for sure. We got the height, y'see, and Josh 'ere needs room to wield 'is gammy arm to pull the trigger. And Ben, you'd better be in the forefront. Us don't want little runts like 'ee wielding a musket behind us, we're a'most as tall kneeling down as you be standing!'

'What makes you think I'd want you two behind me?' scoffs Ben, good-humouredly. 'Why, we've been at it all day and you still don't know one end of a musket from t'other. Far better you're in front as a barrier to draw the Frenchies' fire!'

It is times like this that help to remind me that we are all still individuals even if, as Jack Weaver, I have been deprived of my true identity. The whole of the last few weeks with its constant drill and privations has, as I see it, been designed to strip us of any uniqueness and make us mere teeth upon a big cog-wheel. A wheel which will soon turn with other identical ones to form one vast military machine.

It is while I am lost in such morbid reflection that Sergeant Latham appears in our midst. It is such an unprecedented event (Latham almost never mixes with the men) that we are slow to react. It takes several seconds for the four of us to spring to attention.

'Which of you is Weaver?'

'Me, sergeant,' I reply.

He looks me up and down as if seeing me for the first time. 'You're wanted. Follow me.'

I follow in silence. Latham offers no explanation of where we are going or of who wants me. As we stride through the gathering darkness, lit only by the flickering of cooking fires about the field, upturned fire-lit faces briefly turn in our direction. Only to be quickly averted with a premonition of misfortune as they see who is leading me.

Soon, the lights of the mansion are ahead of us and within minutes I am being led into the presence of the platoon commander, First Lieutenant Bancroft.

He looks up from the desk where he is sitting. 'Private Weaver?'

I salute, 'Sir.'

'Thank you, Sergeant Latham,' says Bancroft. It is a dismissal.

Latham hesitates. I sense he is about to protest but then with a curt 'Sir,' he leaves the room.

Bancroft rises and pointedly closes the door which Latham has left ajar, then returns to his desk where he surveys me in silence. From the mantel to my left, I hear the steady tick of a clock.

After almost a minute, he reaches into a drawer and, taking something out, holds it up between his fingers.

It is the letter I entrusted to Midshipman Bolton.

'Would you care to explain this, Private Weaver?'

Has Bolton betrayed me? I cannot think so, he seemed so convinced and ready to help. More likely a senior officer, aware of military preparations in the area, has discovered the matter and, being of a less romantic turn of mind than the ingenuous young Midshipman, has taken a more cynical view of the supposedly lovelorn but now penniless champion of a maiden in distress that I represented myself to be.

Still holding the letter aloft, Bancroft does not wait for my reply. 'Did you write this?'

'Yes, sir.'

'And who is this *Will*? One of your fellow soldiers?'

It is clear to me that Bancroft is unskilled in the art of interrogation. After his initial silence he is proving too fond of the sound of his own voice. Sir William Hervey, His Majesty's chief spymaster and my occasional employer, knows that, when wishing to elicit the truth from a suspect, silence is a more effective ploy than direct questions.

Now Bancroft is reading the letter out loud.

' *"Dear Mr Garrick, I pen this brief note to put your mind at rest. I am enlisted as a soldier through loyalty to His Majesty. I crave forgiveness for not writing sooner. Pray do not reprehend me. I hope all are well at Bow Street. Give my regards to Charlie and his black beetle. Yours, Will."* You write a fine hand, Private Weaver.'

'Thank you, sir.'

'I ask you again, is this fellow, Will, a soldier in this platoon?'

His lack of questioning skill has given me time to think and I sense from his tone that he would regard it as an inconvenience if I answered in the affirmative. I decide that as romantic fabrication landed me in this scrape, so it might get me out.

'No, sir. I met him on the passage from England, sir. As you see from what he says, sir, he was worried what those at home would think of his importunate departure. Being illiterate, and seeing me with a book, he asked me to pen a letter for him. Which I did upon the flyleaf of the book I was reading, being the only paper to hand. Alas, upon reaching Ostend, he contracted a fever and was among those taken to the hospital. I know not if he be still alive, sir, but I felt honour bound to see his letter was delivered at the first opportunity.'

'Very commendable of you, Weaver.' He peruses the letter one more time, then lets it fall to the desk. 'Well, I see no point in pursuing the matter further. I see nothing treasonable in this communication, merely a boy writing home to reassure his loved ones.'

'Yes, sir, I agree,' say I, then decide to chance my arm. 'May I have your permission to find another courier, Mr Bancroft? I would like to think his family might have their minds put at rest. '

All this time, I have stood rigidly to attention, keeping my eyes to the front. But a glance at the First Lieutenant's face reveals a dawning half-smile. 'You are bold, Private Weaver.'

'I'm sorry, sir.'

'Do not apologise. It is an admirable quality in a man. As is your concern for, and loyalty to the wishes of Master Archer, wherever he may now be.'

He rises from his chair and comes to stand beside me. 'I like you, Private Weaver, and believe I could use a man such as you. Considerate, determined, with a good turn of phrase and a fair, round hand. I should like you to be my *aide-de-camp* if you are willing. What say you?'

For a moment I am at a loss for words. I have come here expecting to be reprimanded, possibly even to be punished, but find myself being offered promotion!

Gathering my wits, I reply, 'I should deem it an honour, sir.'

'Good,' he claps me upon the shoulder, 'that is settled, then. You will be promoted to Corporal with immediate effect and shall move into quarters here first thing in the morning. Dismissed.'

New Quarters

It soon becomes clear that my new role is, in effect, to be a general factotum to First Lieutenant Bancroft. To act as scribe, secretary, drafter and dispatcher of communications. To be informant, guardian and occasional valet.

And (as becomes increasingly apparent) friend.

From the very first time I saw him, I sensed that Bancroft was ill at ease in his new command, isolated by experience, class and breeding from those over whom he has been put in charge but amongst whom he is forced to live. It seems that in me, though obviously he knows nothing of my circumstances, some instinct within him has recognised a kindred spirit.

But in becoming friend and confidant of the Platoon Commander, I also make enemies.

Sergeant Latham for one. He is still my senior in rank, yet I am now effectively his equal in responsibility and status and he doesn't like it. I do my best to be civil and respectful to him but he makes it clear that he regards my promotion as undermining his authority and warns me off trespassing on his territory. 'You stick to your paperwork and running errands for 'is Lordship,' says he, getting me alone the day after Bancroft informs him of his decision, 'but the men is my responsibility. Just you remember that, sonny.'

My new role does not excuse me from training sessions in the use of weapons or conduct in action, but it does mean that I am not required to attend every parade-ground drill, and I no longer have to take my turn in the rota for the menial tasks about camp.

My duties and my NCO status may bring the benefit of freedom of movement and more comfortable quarters in the house, but the drawback is that I have less time in the company of my friends Hooper, Woodrow and Barley.

Nevertheless, I make what opportunities I can, contriving to spend at least half an hour a day with them. They alone seem genuinely pleased at my change of role, the rest of the platoon regarding me with renewed wariness, and some, such as the lout Brogan and his cronies with barely disguised derision and hostility.

An immediate effect of my unexpected elevation, however, is that my message to Mr Garrick can be sent more securely through official military channels.

An accompanying note containing Bancroft's official approval will ensure it reaches its destination, but it is still unusual enough to attract attention, so I make no alteration to its enigmatic contents, for I do not know who else may read it.

I hope that Mr Garrick will show it to Charlie, as he is mentioned therein and I'm confident that the boy will understand my cryptic reference to being enlisted '*through loyalty to His Majesty'* as code for being kidnapped in retribution for recently foiling the attempt on King George's life. I trust to Charlie's quick-wittedness that he will then seek out Nathaniel Grey, Sir William Hervey's man, whom he himself christened '*the black beetle'* and report my plight to him.

With my mind temporarily set at rest, I devote all my energies during the next few days to carrying out my duties as efficiently and as diplomatically as possible whilst, at the same time, settling into my new quarters at the main house.

I learn that the van Andels the owners of the mansion – o r *herenhuis* as I suppose it is called in Flemish – are a husband and wife from Rotterdam.

He is from a banking family, his businesses in Rotterdam, Amsterdam and Antwerp now being conducted by a three grown-up sons.

She, the daughter of the last owners of the farm, sold off most of the land upon her parents' death and treated the house as a country cottage to which they have now retired.

The van Andels occupy the west wing of the house whilst Bancroft, Sergeant Latham and I have rooms in the east wing. Elsewhere there is servant accommodation for a cook, a maidservant and a manservant whom we rarely see. The cook prepares meals which we and our hosts eat together each evening in the rather forbidding dining room, dark with oak-panelling and heavy, ornate furniture. The maid, a skinny, plain woman in her thirties occasionally serves on, but more usually it is Mevrouw van Andel herself.

Her husband is somewhat austere but she is a plump, smiling, bustling woman who treats us more like welcome guests than as strangers who have been foisted upon her. At every meal, it is she who keeps the conversation going with local gossip about events in Ostend, fond chatter about her absent sons and their families and coy interrogations about our own lives, interests and romantic liaisons.

Bancroft, as I would expect, converses suavely and graciously, glad of this oasis of civilisation in his rough martial world. Latham, however, is awkward and taciturn and often absents himself, pleading military business.

As for myself, having mixed with a wide variety of persons from servants to nobility, I manage to hold my own in these surroundings with comparative ease. I take care to remember that I am Jack Weaver, failed itinerant actor, and not Will Archer, erstwhile member of David Garrick's company, but the element of truth makes the lie easier to maintain.

It is during one of these evening meals with just the van Andels, Bancroft and myself, four days after my promotion, that we are interrupted by Sergeant Latham asking to have a private word.

I see, from the malicious gleam in his eye, that it is a matter he wants to exclude me from, which gives me cause to suspect it is one that either concerns me nearly, or which he hopes may bring discredit on me.

Left alone with our hosts, I finish my meal with little appetite and pay scant attention to Mevruow van Andel as she tries to engage me in conversation about a guest who is about to arrive tomorrow or the day after. All I gather is that it is the daughter of an old friend, now dead, who after having a planned marriage in England frustrated (the details pass me by as my mind dwells on what Sergeant Latham may be saying to Bancroft) and who is recently returned in reduced circumstances to her native land.

As soon as is compatible with good manners, I take my leave.

Bancroft summons me first thing next morning to the room he is using as his office.

'We have a problem, Weaver.'

'The matter Sergeant Latham consulted you about last night, sir?'

'Yes. It seems that we have a thief in our midst.'

'Is that so strange, sir?' I ask as judiciously as possible. 'Recruiting sergeants are not over-particular when enlisting men...'

'That's as may be,' he interrupts, 'but the man accused is no Newgate good-for-nothing. He is a man of intellect and good-standing.'

He looks me direct in the eye, his brow creased with worry.

Surely Latham would not have the effrontery to accuse me?

My heart lurches within my breast, but not with relief, at Bancroft's next words.

'You are acquainted with the lawyer fellow with the facial deformity? Woodrow, I believe is his name.'

So, Latham has not the temerity to aim at me directly, he must do it through my friends!

I keep my voice as steady as the beating of my heart will allow. 'What is the nature of the accusation, sir?'

'It is alleged that he was discovered yesterday evening rifling through another soldier's knapsack. The soldier maintains that a knife given him by his father has gone missing.'

'Was the knife found in Woodrow's possession?'

'No. They say he must have thrown it away into the

bushes on being apprehended.'

'It has been recovered, then?'

'Apparently not. A search yielded nothing.'

'What does Woodrow say to all this?'

'As yet, nothing. He was taken up at once and held under guard by Sergeant Latham. He is to be brought before me this morning to answer the charge.' He gives me a troubled look. 'Latham has particularly requested that you should not be present at the hearing.'

'Why so, sir?'

'It is a matter of military discipline – which, he took pains to remind me, is his responsibility,' he replies apologetically, 'and, as Woodrow's friend, he feels you may try to sway my opinion of the matter...'

'Is that your opinion also, sir?'

He puts a hand upon my arm. 'You have been my ADC for less than a week, Jack, and in that time I have never known you to be anything but fair and even-handed in your dealings with me or with others. But you see my dilemma? Tell me honestly, Jack, - as I know you will – would you seek to influence the decision in your friend's favour?'

'If he is guilty as charged, he must face the consequences, sir. I would not seek to stand in the way of just punishment. But justice requires him to be heard.'

'Quite right, Jack!' A look of relief and determination

lightens his face. 'And Latham may go hang, but I *will* have you hear all. Not in this actual room, maybe (I cannot flout him so openly), but in the adjoining chamber with the door ajar.'

Having thus agreed, I depart for the daily session of arms training.

Woodrow, of course, is absent, being in custody. One of the small outbuildings not used for sleeping quarters has, I notice, a soldier posted at its door.

Latham says nothing to me and does his best to avoid my eye. Whether he knows that Bancroft has told me, I cannot guess.

Tom Hooper, however, is far from reticent when the platoon disbands at the end of the session. He and Josh Barley accost me, hurrying me to the privacy of their sleeping quarters in the byre.

Hooper is in a state of high dudgeon. Barley, on the other hand, looks like a stricken bull-calf, his eyes wide with distress. He utters not a word as Hooper gives vent to his ire.

'It's that bastard Brogan,' he tells me angrily, 'and his lickspittle mates. Hauled Ben up in front of Latham last night, saying he'd filched some poxy knife.'

'And had he?'

He looks at me, astounded. 'Damn me, Jack, how can

you ask! This is Ben we're talking about – do *you* think he'd do such a thing?'

'He is no friend of Brogan,' say I, playing devil's advocate.

'Show me who is,' he replies heatedly, 'apart from those bastards who buzz round him like blowflies round shit. We've all seen 'im strutting like a turkey-cock – showin' that poxy knife round like it was the sword o' bloody Solomon, saying how 'e'll carve up Frenchies. All said and done 'tis naught but a cheap dagger with a fancy haft.'

'You've seen it?'

'Aye, me an' twenty or more besides. A six-inch blade and a handle o' carved wood inlaid wi' bits o' ivory. What would Ben want with aught like that?'

It is a question I cannot answer. I leave Hooper and hurry back to the *herenhuis* to be in time for the hearing.

A Dilemma

Taking up a position just inside the door of the adjoining chamber I am able to hear all that passes.

Sergeant Latham speaks first, telling how Private Brogan and two friends brought the accused before him the previous evening, saying they had found him...

Here Bancroft interrupts him. 'The man may speak for himself by and by, Sergeant. Restrict yourself, if you please, to saying what you did when they brought him to you.'

'Very well, sir,' continues Latham, clearly put out. 'In brief, I asked to know what they accused him of and then, deeming it a sufficiently serious charge, I set him under guard for the night and came immediately to inform you of the situation.'

Brogan is then called to give his testimony which he does in an uncouth and rambling manner, earning repeated rebukes from Bancroft for coarse language.

The substance of his tale is that he and his two friends here present were at their usual place in the field, eating the supper they had just cooked upon an open fire, when they were alerted by a scuffling sound from the area where they had piled their knapsacks. Turning and peering into the darkness, they saw Woodrow on his knees with the knapsacks strewn around him.

'Caught 'im in the act, we did, lookin' guilty as sin – far as yer can see any expression on that devil's face of his.'

'Mind your tongue, soldier,' snaps Bancroft. 'Say what happened next.'

'Well, 'e protests 'is innercence, like 'e would, but my two friends 'ere 'olds him while I searches mi belongings and finds mi knife gone.'

'You're sure the knife was in your knapsack up until that point?'

'It's where I keeps it, sir. 'Twouldn't be nowhere else. And it weren't there then.'

'I'm told you searched the accused. Did you find it on his person?'

'Not at that present time, no – but 'e'd been flailing about wi' 'is arms something rotten when we took 'im up, so 'e'd likely chucked it away into the undergrowth.'

'Which you also searched?'

'Yes, sir.'

'But did not find the knife?'

'Not as yet, sir, but it'll turn up – 'less one of 'is friends 'as already found it and 'idden it, as like they might.'

With this last nasty quip, Brogan earns his final reprimand and is told to stand down.

Bancroft then calls Woodrow to give his version of

events which he does in a measured, lawyerly manner.

'After eating my supper, I was on my way to the latrines when I stumbled in the dark over several knapsacks piled in the field. It caused me to fall and, whilst still on my knees, I was set upon by these gentlemen. They proceeded to accuse me of stealing things from their bags, which I naturally denied and waited while they searched them. Two pronounced themselves satisfied that their belongings were intact but, Private Brogan vociferously maintaining that a knife was missing, the three of them subjected me to a humiliating search. Finding nothing, they manhandled me to Sergeant Latham who, apparently giving credence to their false accusations, incarcerated me overnight. That, First Lieutenant Bancroft, is the truth of the matter.'

'Truth my arse, you lyin' jaw-me-dead! You stole my knife, you wine-stained fucker!' yells Brogan.

'Silence, man!' barks Bancroft. 'Sergeant, take him out. In fact, take them all out. I will consider this in private awhile.'

From my hiding place, I hear the room cleared, but then I hear footsteps returning and realise Latham has come back into the room.

'Sir,' I hear him say in a low voice. 'This matter cannot be fadged. 'Tis not my place to say this, but I offer this advice with all due respect. 'Tis one man's word against three and whatever the rights and wrongs of it, you have to make an example of this man, Woodrow. Otherwise, the men will see you as weak and that is bad for discipline. The fact is, a theft has occurred and whether Woodrow be guilty or not, there must be punishment if you want to avoid unrest in the platoon.'

'Thank you, Sergeant Latham,' says Bancroft coldly. 'As I said, I shall consider the matter and give my judgement in due course. You are dismissed.'

When I am sure that Latham has gone, I emerge from my listening post.

Bancroft sits at his desk, head in hands. 'What am I to do, Jack? I do not think Woodrow is guilty. But a theft has been committed and discipline must be maintained. Whatever I decide will be wrong.'

'Unlike Sergeant Latham, I would not presume to advise you, sir.'

'Dammit, man!' he says with a burst of frustration.'Is not that the very reason I appointed you? To help and advise me?'

'In that case, sir... I know Woodrow, and I cannot see him committing such an act. Brogan is his sworn enemy, especially since Private Barley's flogging and I would remind you of Woodrow's humanity on that occasion. But putting aside any friendship I may have for the unfortunate fellow, I see you have no option but to act for the good of the platoon.'

'Latham will insist on the statutory fifty lashes,' says he hopelessly.

'But you, as senior officer, may mitigate that.'

'Yes, and thereby appear weak, earning the scorn of the men. Brogan and his fellows will make the most of that! How can I hope to command in battle if even this barbarity appals me?'

There is such helplessness in his look that I almost feel our roles are reversed. Yet even as I see the distress in his eyes, a possible solution suggests itself to me. Suddenly I recall the meeting between Brogan and the stranger in Ostend the other day and I wonder if it may prove a way of discrediting Brogan.

'You are caught between two fires, sir, but I think I see a way...' say I hesitantly.

Hope lights in his eyes. 'What is it, Jack? Pray tell me, I shall be for ever in your debt.'

His eagerness betrays his youth and inexperience. I could almost think him a callow schoolboy from the avid look upon his face and I am not sure I am worthy of the weight of expectation in that gaze. Until I have more evidence of the stranger's identity, I cannot tell Bancroft what I suspect.

'It is only an idea half-formed as yet, sir, I shall need to give it further thought. The only certainty for the present is that you must accede to Sergeant Latham and order the punishment to go ahead.'

So saying, I request permission to return to my room to formulate the plan.

But any thoughts of Woodrow's plight are temporarily vanquished by my next encounter.

Another Ghost from the Past

Leaving Bancroft's office, I become aware of activity within the entrance hall. Mijnheer van Andel is standing, stiffly formal, at the foot of the staircase whilst his wife fusses about a new arrival, just alighted from a carriage, relieving her of her cape and directing the coachman where to deposit the traveller's portmanteau.

This must be the guest whose advent Mevrouw van Andel was telling me of last night, to which I was paying but scant attention.

Instructions given to the servants, our hostess, like a mother hen, begins ushering their new guest towards the parlour and I take the opportunity to unobtrusively cross the hall.

Up till now I have only seen the newcomer from the back or in half profile, but as I walk quietly past she removes her bonnet and I am afforded my first full view of her face.

I stop dead as our eyes meet and see the same look of shock mirrored in her face.

It is but a moment. Chattering gaily as she leads her visitor towards the parlour, Mevrouw van Andel has not noticed me, let alone the startled glance of recognition that has passed between the new arrival and myself. Nor has her husband who is dutifully strolling ahead.

I beat a hasty retreat, my heart pounding with consternation.

Agnes Mayer. The woman who would have had me arraigned for a murder I did not commit.

The last time I saw Agnes Mayer was over a year ago, galloping away from an overturned coach in which her would-be husband lay dead.

Sir William Hervey, Nathaniel Grey and I had been pursuing the fugitives on horseback when the accident occurred. A drover's cart, emerging from the morning mist, had met the careering coach head on. The coachman and Agnes's lover were killed. She and the blackmailing villain who was holding her captive had separately fled from the wreck. The man was later captured and tortured by Hervey's men, then killed before he could come to trial. She escaped to the Netherlands.

Before that fateful day, I had fancied myself in love with Agnes Mayer. A hopeless attachment, even disallowing her duplicity, for she, though penniless, was far above me in rank. Even when she tricked me and left me unconscious in the same room as a dead man, expecting that I would be accused of his murder, I still could not believe there had been nothing between us.

A belief which was partially vindicated by the letter I

received from her some weeks after her flight, in which she recognised my feelings for her and begged my forgiveness. And urged me also, for my own sake, to forget her.

I found no difficulty in forgiving, but have never been able to forget.

Now, by some cruel stroke of fate, here she is in the same house and if she is feeling as confused as I by this turn of events, she must be dumbfounded indeed!

For the next half hour I seek to divert myself with the mundane business of requisitions and dispatches but find I cannot concentrate.

My hand falters and the words dance before my eyes as I think of Agnes Mayer under the same roof as myself, of us coming face to face once more over the dinner table this evening as we surely must...

It is almost a relief as I hear hurried footsteps approaching and First Lieutenant Bancroft bursts in.

But any sense of relief is immediately shattered by the news he brings.

'Come quickly, Jack,' he gabbles breathlessly. 'Latham says there is murder done.'

I cast aside quill and paper and hurry after him, my mind churning with hideous forebodings.

Has Brogan taken justice into his own hands and

attacked Woodrow? Or – the thought hits me with a horror occasioned by the dominant theme of my brooding - *has anything befallen Agnes?*

This latter dread is appeased as we rush out of the door and I catch a glimpse of two female figures taking a leisurely turn about the garden at the side of the house.

Chiding myself for such foolishness, my thumping heart calms a little. We join Sergeant Latham who is waiting for us at the gate and he guides us swiftly and wordlessly towards the cluster of outlying farm buildings.

Contrary to my other foreboding about Ben Woodrow, we bypass the small hut where he is still being kept in custody, the guard still at the door. At a short distance, the ever-faithful Josh Barley sits at the corner of a wall keeping an even more vigilant watch. Our eyes meet momentarily but he quickly averts his gaze. Yet there has been such a moroseness in that brief look that I sense he blames me for Ben's misfortune.

Meanwhile, Latham is leading us straight towards the barn where most of the platoon live and sleep.

Groups of soldiers are scattered around the farmyard outside the barn, lounging against walls, chatting or cleaning their kit. But, for all this appearance of regular evening routine, I notice that all eyes turn in our direction as we make our way to the barn. They are trying not to appear watchful, but the weight of curiosity in the air is almost palpable.

The two men on guard are pale-faced and uneasy. Latham tells one to remain outside the door whilst the other accompanies us.

Inside the barn is deserted and it takes a moment for our eyes to adjust to the gloom.

The animal aroma of stale straw settles around us, overlaid with the lingering stink of sweat and unwashed bodies as we follow Latham, carefully wending our way amidst the piles of clothes and belongings with which individual soldiers have marked their makeshift territories. And as Latham leads us ever closer to the scene of the crime I begin to detect a sweeter, metallic smell – the smell of fresh spilt blood.

At last we come to a dark corner of the barn where the straw has been haphazardly pulled aside into disordered piles, and where, in a clearing upon the bare earth floor, lies a spreadeagled body.

'More light here!' calls Bancroft as he stops some two or three feet from the corpse, loth to approach closer for fear of stepping into the dark stain that surrounds the body, and from which the metallic smell arises.

The soldier who has come in with us hurries forward with a covered lantern. No open torches can be allowed here amongst all this combustible wood and straw.

By its light I see over Bancroft's shoulder the body of a man lying in a pool of his own blood which has seeped into the packed earth floor turning it into patches of mud and staining the scattered straw a rusty brown.

His clothes are saturated with it, clinging damp to his twisted limbs. Hands and face are smeared with crimson but it is the expression on his face that compels attention, the mouth agape with pained surprise, the stare of blank-eyed terror.

And below this hideous mask a gash like a second red mouth where the throat has been savagely slashed open. No wonder there is such abundance of blood surrounding the body. He must have bled out within minutes as the chalky pallor of the skin under the blotches of red testifies.

Bancroft swallows, steeling himself to the sight. 'Who found the body, Latham?'

'Bailey here,' says the sergeant, indicating our lantern bearer, 'and Reeves at the door. They have their billet just there, sir.'

He points to an area some two yards distant. 'The rest of the men were outside, or away to town, sir, but these two came in for something and discovered – this.'

He is more shaken than I have ever seen him. He swallows and goes on, 'Straightway they sought me out and when I came and saw what had happencd, I set them to guard the door and keep their mouths shut while I came to find you.'

'Who is it, Latham, do we know?'

The soldier holds the lantern closer and the sergeant bends to peer at the contorted face.

After a moment Latham clears his throat and says hesitantly, 'It's hard to tell under all that blood, sir, but I think 'tis one of the fellows who came with Brogan to report the theft of his knife.'

As Latham is examining the corpse, I cast a glance about the scene and my eye is caught by something near the body.

'What is that?' I ask, drawing Bancroft's horrified attention to a crumpled heap amidst the welter of blood.

'Lend me your pike, Private Bailey,' I say

The fellow shoots a brief, questioning look at Sergeant Latham, who nods grudging assent. Taking the stave from him, I step gingerly towards the crumpled heap and with the metal point hitch up the corner of what appears to be a sodden wool blanket.

Bancroft looks at it in bewilderment. 'The poor fellow was murdered in his sleep?' he asks.

'I think from the way this has been thrown down away from the body that it is more likely his assailant used this to prevent being stained with the evidence of his crime,' I reply. 'Face and hands might quickly be washed, but clothes are not so easily cleansed. Mayhap the attacker wrapped himself in this before committing the deed.'

Bancroft turns to me with an appalled look. 'He came prepared, you think, Jack? That implies this killing was premeditated?'

I sense Latham's frown at the use of my first name. But my attention is distracted by something else. As I lifted the blanket, I saw something fall to the ground.

I bend, squatting on tiptoe to avoid contact with the sea of gore around me and pick up the object delicately, holding it between my finger and thumb.

Latham takes a pace forward as I straighten up, pointing towards the thing I hold with a smirk of triumph. 'The stolen knife. We need look no further, sir. The mystery is solved.'

'How so, Sergeant Latham?' I ask.

' 'Tis clear, surely? Woodrow stole the knife. Woodrow must be the murderer.'

'But Woodrow has been under guard these last twelve hours and more,' I reply, 'unless you are accusing your guards of dereliction of duty, Sergeant Latham?'

He gives me look of angry outrage as I press my advantage home. 'And, unless I am mistaken, there is yet no positive proof that Woodrow stole the knife – or that the knife was stolen at all. We have only Brogan's word for it.'

'Corporal Weaver is right, sergeant,' agrees Bancroft, a little too eagerly. 'We cannot trust Brogan's word, for it would now seem he accused Woodrow of theft to draw attention away from some quarrel he had with the dead man. Brogan must have been in possession of the knife all the time and has now used it to settle the dispute in the belief that Woodrow would be blamed. I suggest Woodrow be released immediately and that you take Brogan into custody.'

To my mind, this explanation is as unconvincing as Latham's. Much as I dislike Brogan and am sympathetic towards Woodrow, I feel there is more behind this than meets the eye.

But I have no opportunity to demur as Bancroft is already striding away.

'Have all this cleaned up,' he orders Latham as he goes. 'See the body disposed of in a suitable manner. And quell any rumours, I want no unrest among the men. Arrest Brogan and bring him before me first thing in the morning.'

Allegiances

There is yet an hour until supper when, after Bancroft has dismissed me with orders that I attend Brogan's trial in the morning, I return to my room in the *herenhuis*.

I have only just shut the door when there comes a gentle tap upon it. I open it to see Agnes Mayer standing there.

With a swift glance both ways along the corridor, she brushes past me into the room and shuts the door behind her.

Her cheeks are flushed, her eyes glittering.

'Will Archer!' she says breathlessly. 'My eyes did not deceive me, it really *is* you! I cannot believe it.'

'Miss Mayer,' say I, masking my agitation under a tone of polite civility. 'A coincidence indeed.'

'Come, Will,' says she taking my hand and bidding me pull out a chair and sit opposite her, 'we have little time. Mistress van Andel is in conference with the cook, but will soon enough miss me. Tell me how you come to be here.'

I explain as briefly as I may how I was press-ganged off the London streets and carried hither half unconscious and against my will. How my identity has been stripped from me, but how my fortunes seem to be looking up with my promotion to *aide-de-camp* to Bancroft.

She listens with rapt attention and, as I conclude my brief history, says, 'So I must call you Master Weaver.' She nods as if committing it to memory. 'But at supper tonight we must pretend to be strangers until our hostess introduces us. Can you maintain the pose, d'you think?' She looks aside, embarrassed. 'You know, unfortunately to your cost, that I am adept in such matters.'

'Agnes...' I murmur, seeing the pain that the memory causes her.

She puts her finger to my lips, silencing me. 'Did you receive my letter?' she asks solemnly. 'Can you ever forgive the wrongs I did you?'

I gently remove her finger from my lips, clasping her hand between mine and looking directly into her troubled eyes. 'It is true, Agnes, that you used me cruelly. But I was nothing to you then. A convenient gull for your subterfuge, no more...'

She makes to protest, but I continue, 'Do not deny it. We both know it to be true. But that is past and, whilst I cannot forget the hurt you caused me, I forgave you long since. For,' I continue softly, ' I know that you, too, have suffered. You have lost the man you loved.'

'Aye,' she interrupts wretchedly, 'and fortune and reputation!' She stands up briskly releasing her hand from mine, but then with a brave smile, takes it again. 'I have much to tell you, Will – or *Jack* as I must now call you – but it will have to wait. Mistress van Andel will be fretting at my absence. Till supper, then.'

She turns with her hand upon the latch, 'I *am* pleased to see you, Will Archer,' she says, looking fondly into my eyes. 'I know I used you ill in the past and made you believe you meant nothing to me. But you are not nothing to me now, believe it.'

Then, without allowing me time to reply, she slips quickly out of the room and is gone, leaving me almost giddy with joy.

I have just time before the evening meal to pay a quick visit to my friends. The clandestine meeting with Agnes Mayer, though to my tremulous heart it seemed much longer, has lasted less than ten minutes.

Buoyant with happiness, I arrive at the accustomed eating place to find that Ben Woodrow, newly released, is once more part of the company.

'Jack,' he cries, hugging me gratefully, 'is it you I have to thank for my release?'

'Not I,' I reply, 'though god knows I would have compassed it if I could. No, 'tis fate you must thank.'

'The murder of Brogan's crony?' says Tom Hooper looking up from stirring the stew over the fire.

I am not surprised that the news has already spread.

'Is it true he is to be sentenced tomorrow?' he continues with eager relish. 'They say Bancroft will order he be shot or broken on the wheel. Come, Jack, you are in the know, are you not?'

'I know no more than you, Tom,' I reply reasonably. 'Justice demands that Brogan must have his say. Matters may not be as they appear.'

'Aye, don't I know it!' interjects Ben bitterly. 'I was like to be flogged upon that villain's word. Yet for all that, I would wish him to have a fair hearing.'

'There speaks a lawyer,' scoffs Hooper good-naturedly, doling out the stew.

'You're a good man, Ben,' say I. 'You suffered no ill-usage during your captivity, I hope?'

'No more than a soldier might expect,' replies Woodrow with a hint of bitterness. 'Sergeant Latham may dislike me, but he is too much a stickler for military discipline to let personal animosity influence his actions. I was treated as fairly as any other prisoner.' He makes an approving sound as he takes a mouthful of stew. 'Missed Tom's cooking, though. This is good.'

'They only treated you well 'cos they wanted you in good shape for the flogging,' mutters Barley grudgingly. ' 'Twould be no spectacle if you were to pass out after five strokes.'

'I'll wager Brogan would last the course. He's a tough bastard,' says Hooper waving his fork for emphasis. 'I hope Bancroft don't sentence 'im to be shot. Breakin' on the wheel's what he deserves. Let the bugger suffer.'

'Nay, Tom,' reproves Ben Woodrow. 'No man deserves that. 'Tis a hellish torture so I hear. I thank god I have never seen it done, nor ever want to.'

'I thought lawyers believed in justice?' says Tom Hooper.

'Aye, in swift, clean punishment for crimes committed. Not in inflicting agony for its own sake. That makes us no better than the criminal himself.'

I leave them to their stew and their philosophical discussion, expressing once more my satisfaction at Woodrow's reprieve, and return to the *herenhuis* hoping for some enjoyable discussion over my own supper.

'May I introduce Miss Agnes Mayer,' says Mevruow van Andel at supper. 'She is a dear friend of the family who is visiting for a few days.'

She then presents us one at a time. 'First Lieutenant Henry Bancroft – he is the *peleton commandant*, my dear. And this is his *aide-de-camp* Corporal Jack Weaver.' We both bow as she delicately places her hand in ours smiles politely, and I am rewarded with a barely perceptible squeeze of the fingers.

'Usually there would be a third gentleman, Sergeant Latham – I am sorry, he has never vouchsafed his forename, do you know it, Lieutenant?'

Bancroft looks flustered and a slight redness suffuses his cheeks. He laughs nervously as if guilty of a social indiscretion, 'I regret not, Mevruow. We military men, y'know – rank and all that – I only know him, refer to him as Latham – and I think he would be discomfited to be addressed any other way...'

'Ha, you English and your *formaliteit*! Come, please take your places. I have taken the liberty, Agnes, of placing you between these two gentlemen. I hope you will not find it disagreeable?' simpers Mevruow van Andel with a mischievous twinkle.

'Not at all,' replies Agnes with a gracious smile to the pair of us. 'I am sure we shall get on famously.'

The maidservant having been drafted in to serve this evening, Mevruow van Andel leads the conversation, her husband, with his limited command of English, being his usual taciturn self.

'Poor Agnes has had a tragic life, gentlemen,' she says by way of preamble once the soup has been served.

'Pray Elsje,' protests Agnes, 'let us not talk of that, it is all in the past and can be of no possible interest to these gentlemen. We must be merry this evening. Tell me,

Corporal Weaver, what did you do before you joined the army?'

'I was an actor, ma'am. Not, I regret to say, a very successful one. Hence my presence here.'

'An actor?' she exclaims in delight. 'Why, then, that must be why you carry your uniform so well. And are you adept at playing characters other than your own?'

I see by the mischievous twitch of her eyebrow that she is teasing me.

I return her smile. 'I do my best ma'am, but sometimes, as I said, with limited success.'

'I have never really seen the point of acting,' interrupts Bancroft. 'Pretending to be someone else – what possible use can it be in real life?' It seems he is piqued at not being included in the conversation and determined to have his share of our charming guest.

I am quite happy to accommodate him and, as the soup gives way to a second course of grilled turbot and a main course of suckling pig and bottled peas, Bancroft does a decent job of discovering as much of Agnes's history as she is prepared to tell him.

Thus I learn that, following her 'misfortunes' in England, she returned to Amsterdam where the van Andels, friends of her late father and mother took her in. Through the good offices of Mijnheer van Andel and his banking associates, some small measure of her father's lost fortune was restored to her. Enough to live as a lady of modest means but not enough to attract a suitor of any note.

'Sure, ma'am, your beauty would be dowry enough,' says Bancroft with somewhat mannered gallantry. I get the impression from his gaucheness that he is not totally at ease in female company.

'You don't know Dutchmen, sir,' she replies prettily. 'We are a merchant race and a fine face is little consolation for lack of a full purse. But, having been once disappointed in love, I am in no hurry for a husband.'

'Then mankind is the loser by it,' says Bancroft politely.

Fortunately the arrival of a Florentine pudding stems the flow of strained flattery and talk turns to more mundane matters.

'Tell me, Lieutenant Bancroft, are you to be billeted here long?'

'I do not know, ma'am. Despatches tell that since the Treaty of Breslau which saw Frederick of Prussia retire from the war, the Austrian army is making headway against the French in Bohemia. So much so that the whole of the Franco-Flanders border is left vulnerable. I expect a despatch any day to mobilise the troops and join with other platoons in the Earl of Stair's regiment.'

'Exciting times, Lieutenant,' says Agnes. Then, with a

sympathetic wrinkling of her brow, 'Tell me, are you not just the tiniest bit afraid?'

'Soldiers are trained not to be afraid, ma'am. Fighting is our way of life, our sole purpose. To fight and, if necessary, to die,' replies he animatedly, considerably more at ease discussing martial matters than affairs of the heart.

'And Sergeant Latham,' says she as Bancroft promises to wax even more lyrical about a soldier's duty, 'why is he not with us tonight?'

Bancroft appears somewhat deflated by the sudden change of subject, so I answer for him. 'The Sergeant is engaged in a matter of camp discipline, Miss Mayer. A soldier met with – er - an accident earlier today, and he is attending to it.'

'An accident?' Her gaze is suddenly attentive. 'A *fatal* accident?'

'Unfortunately so,' I reply, feeling that she is attributing more significance to my remarks than I intended to give.

'Oh tut, tut, Corporal Weaver,' scolds Mevruow van Andel, 'this is no fit conversation for the dinner table. Come, my dear, now that we have finished eating, will you not delight us at the *fortepiano*? We have one in the parlour and it gets so little used with just me and Mijnheer...'

'Very well,' agrees Agnes charmingly, 'but on one condition – I shall only play for you if Corporal Weaver here will promise to escort me to see the troops performing their manoeuvres tomorrow.'

'It will be my pleasure, Miss Mayer.' Seeing Bancroft's warning look, I add. 'I have pressing business in the morning, though, so will an afternoon inspection be acceptable? I am sure Lieutenant Bancroft can arrange the matter with Sergeant Latham.'

Thus agreed, we all retire to the parlour and, after Agnes has played several pieces upon a small and rather out of tune instrument, Bancroft and I take our leave and return to our quarters in the east wing.

On the way, once we are alone, I make the request that has been gnawing in my head since seeing the corpse in the barn this afternoon.

'I would like, if possible, to examine the body, sir, if you would permit me.'

Bancroft looks startled. 'Examine? Whatever for?'

'I believe a corpse may provide information about the manner of death, and possibly clues as to the murderer, sir.'

Bancroft shakes his head in bewilderment. 'You never cease to surprise me, Jack. Clues to the murderer, indeed! Very well, if you must. I can't see that it will harm the poor fellow now.'

Then, as we part at his door, 'That Miss Mayer. What did you think of her? Are all young ladies so confident?'

Again, I sense his lack of experience. 'I cannot speak for all women, sir, but she is a remarkable lady, to be sure.'

Body

Just after dawn Sergeant Latham takes me to the small store-room where the body has been kept overnight. He has detailed two men to dig a grave in a remote corner of the farm estate for a private interment to take place as soon as possible. It has been given out that the man committed suicide, which explains why he is being buried in unconsecrated ground.

Latham is clearly unhappy about my request to view the body. He obeys Bancroft's order with a brusqueness just short of insubordination, and once we are alone he makes his feelings plain.

'You overstep the bloody mark, Weaver. Meddling with the dead, thinking you're so fucking clever. You may wriggle your way up the skipjack's arse but snivelling tongue-pads like you don't impress me. First wrong step, I'll 'ave you, chew you up and spit you out, understand? '

I remain silent under his threats and insults.

Reaching the store room, he unlocks the door. 'You've got five minutes,' he tells me as he places himself just inside the doorway.

The dead man has been stripped of his clothes and lies stark naked on a bare board. In response to my shock at such disrespect, Latham says, 'Body 'ad to be washed, din't it? 'Taint right to send 'im to his grave covered in blood and cow-shit.'

'And his clothes?'

'Decent duds. Be more use to the living. 'Sides, the A'mighty sent 'im naked into the world. 'E can't complain o' gettin' 'im back the same way.'

At least someone has had the decency to close the man's eyes, despite subjecting him to the other indignities.

In the faint morning light that seeps through the window, the corpse lies white as alabaster, the cold flesh almost translucent and largely unblemished save for the hideous gash at his neck.

I quickly scan the torso for any marks of struggle and, finding none, turn my attention to the head and shoulders.

The cut around the neck has severed all the blood vessels upon the right hand side with a clean, deep cut. The sliced ends project from the pulpy mass of yellowy fat and scarlet flesh like sinews in raw liver.

In the middle of the throat, the Adam's apple has been cleft horizontally in twain, revealing the ridged tube of the windpipe. Enough to immediately render the victim speechless, unable to scream or cry out.

The left side of the neck is less damaged, the cut less deep with only one vein severed as far as I can see.

Whilst it is the dreadful gash about the neck which draws the eye, I also notice several scratches about the area of the upper chest and collar bone. *The victim clawing at a restraining arm, perhaps?* Also the upper lip is split. *By a hand clamped tightly over the mouth?*

A small patch of raw skin at the hairline argues a missing clump of hair.

'Time's up,' growls Latham. 'Poked around enough to make you prick-proud, 'ave yer? Don't want to screw the bugger, too?'

'I've seen all I need, thank you, Sergeant,' say I, refusing to acknowledge his offensiveness . 'May I ask, do we have a name for him yet?'

'Brogan, who I took into custody last night, says 'e's called Scatchard, known as Ned to 'is mates.'

Well, Ned Scatchard, say I to myself as I leave Latham to lock the door, *at least you still have your name. That is one thing they have not robbed you of.*

Ten minutes later, I am reporting my findings to Bancroft.

'In my opinion, there is little doubt that Scatchard was murdered, sir. From my examination of his body, I reckon his assailant must have been a well-built man, strong and above average height. The evidence suggests that he seized him from behind, and Scatchard tried to claw his arm away, causing abrasions around the collar bone. In the scuffle, the assailant also seems to have grabbed his hair for there is a clump of it torn out, leaving a small patch of raw skin.

'I would guess that he then dragged the struggling victim – hence the scattered and disordered straw around the scene – to the deserted corner of the barn where we found him.

'Once there, he cut the poor fellow's throat with a single bold swipe from right to left. The depth of the cut, deeper upon one side, tells us not only the direction in which it was made, but also a very important fact about the murderer.'

Bancroft looks puzzled, 'I do not follow you.'

'I shall demonstrate, sir, if you will allow it.' Then add with some diffidence, 'It will require one of us to play the victim, sir, whilst the other plays the murderer.'

He enters into the pretence, even allowing me a grim smile. 'By all means be the murderer, Jack. You say the killer was a man of certain stature and you have an inch or two on me, therefore I shall play the part of the unfortunate victim.'

'If you would be so good, sir, as to turn your back to me...'

'Like this?' says he, turning about and holding his arms out wide. 'See, I am at your mercy.'

'By your leave, sir,' say I, pulling him towards me and placing my right hand across his mouth as respectfully as I may. Then I proceed to draw an imaginary knife from right to left across his throat with my other hand.

'There, sir,' I say, releasing him, 'do you see what it proves about the murderer?'

He shakes his head, puzzled. 'I confess myself at a loss still.' Then, with an eagerness that seems unbefitting the gravity of the demonstration, he once more presents himself to my murderous embrace. ' Show me again.'

Somewhat perturbed that he appears to be treating this more as a schoolboy game than as a serious investigation, I repeat the process, but this time with commentary. 'See, Lieutenant, I put my right hand across your mouth to muffle your cries – then drag you backwards with my other arm, which holds the knife.' I step backwards a pace. 'Then, having got you to the corner of the barn, I raise the knife and cut deep upon this side of your neck, drawing the blade across your throat with some consequent lessening of pressure as the blade travels from one side to the other.'

'Aha! I think I see what you mean,' says Bancroft, delightedly, seizing the arm holding the imaginary weapon, thus retaining my hold upon him. 'This is your left hand, so the murderer must have been left-handed.'

'Precisely, sir,' I say, releasing my arm respectfully from his grip, 'the nature of the cut, deeper upon the right, shallower upon the left, allows of no other explanation.'

'Hmmm,' says he, casting off his playful manner as if conscious of some embarrassing lapse of manners, 'our murderer, then, is a fellow of above average height – as Brogan is – and strong enough to drag his struggling victim – as Brogan is – which leaves only one more thing to be determined...'

He strides to the door and summons Sergeant Latham to bring the prisoner up.

'Now, Jack,' says he, rubbing his hands together in satisfaction, and allowing me no chance to demur or advise against too precipitate a conclusion, 'let us dispatch this matter with all convenient haste.'

Five minutes later, Brogan stands before us, a mutinous scowl on his face. Bancroft sits behind his desk, whilst I stand at his shoulder.

Besides Sergeant Latham, the only other in the room is the fellow who was with Scatchard as a witness at the previous hearing where Ben Woodrow was accused of theft. He gives his name as Seb Williams.

'Now, sirrah,' says Bancroft to Brogan. 'Tell us what you know of Ned Scatchard's death.'

'The answer's simple, yer honour – nothing.'

'When did you last see Scatchard?'

'Yesterday afternoon followin' on drill. Me and Seb 'ere,'

says he with a nod to Williams, 'we went into Ostend but 'e - Scatchard - says 'e 'ad kit to clean. An' that's the last we seen of 'im, ain't that right, Seb?'

His companion nods and mutters an affirmative, though I notice he keeps his head bowed and avoids all eye contact.

'Did anyone see you both in Ostend?' I ask.

'You accusin' us of lyin', *Corporal?*' snarls Brogan insultingly, giving me a vicious look.

'I accuse you of nothing, Private Brogan, I merely ask if anyone saw the pair of you – any other members of the platoon, anyone you spoke to or met.'

'Who says we met anyone?' he asks defensively.

'Mind your manners, Brogan,' snaps Bancroft. 'Corporal Weaver asked a simple question. Give a direct answer if you please.'

'No, we saw no-one we knew, nor spoke to no-one neither.'

I notice that his crony, Seb, is shifting uneasily from one foot to another.

I address him directly. 'Were you with Private Brogan the whole time, Private Williams?'

'Yeah, most on it – that's ter say, not *all* the while – we split up...'

It is fortunate that he keeps his eyes downcast and that he doesn't see the basilisk stare that Brogan gives him.

'Brogan?' invites Bancroft.

'Right, then – we split up and came back to camp separately, what of it?' he replies insolently. 'But 'twas gettin' on dusk by the time I got back and by that time Scatchard were dead, weren't he? Topped 'isself, I were told.'

Bancroft reaches into his desk drawer and pulls out the knife we found next to the body. 'Do you recognise this, Brogan?'

' 'Slife, that's my stolen blade. Wheer'd you get that?'

'It was next to Scatchard's body. It was the weapon used to slit his throat.'

'He used my knife?' says Brogan in outrage. 'The bastard!'

'The knife you swore was stolen by Private Woodrow.'

'Aye, well...,' grunts Brogan, reluctant to admit his fault. 'So Scatchard was the thief all along.Would you credit it, Seb?'

From the disbelief on his companion's face as he raises it for the first time to stare in horror at the weapon, he obviously can't.

'Can either of you think why Scatchard would take his own life?' asks Bancroft.

'Nay,' says Seb, provoked to speech, 'no more than he would steal that dagger. 'E were a god-fearin' man an suicide's a sin in the good book. 'E wouldn't risk 'is eternal soul, not Ned.'

'You realise what you're saying, Private Williams?'

Williams shakes his head uncomprehendingly, but Brogan is sharper.

'Seb's right, sir. Ned would never take his own life. Nor steal.' There is a note of triumph in his voice as he works towards the inevitable conclusion. 'You think 'e was murdered, don't yer? And you thought I done it. But I weren't even 'ere, so you've no business arrestin' me. I were right in the first place, that sneakin' Woodrow did steal the knife, and it's 'im what's done Ned in! What the 'ell are we wastin' time for? You need to string the fucker up.'

'Calm yourself, Brogan,' orders Bancroft. 'Woodrow was in custody at the time Scatchard met his death, so it cannot have been him. There is also other evidence. Corporal Weaver, would you care to present your findings?'

I step forward and explain how the evidence from the scene and from my examination of the body point to a struggle with a man both tall and strong – neither of which could be said of Woodrow.

'That's all bollocks!' yells Brogan. 'You're tryin' to pin this on me, but I were nowhere near. You fuckin' nobs, you all stick together!'

He is silenced by Sergeant Latham's fist in his belly,

causing him to buckle under the blow.

'Take him away, Sergeant!' shouts Bancroft angrily. 'His guilt is self evident.'

But even as Latham drags the half-stunned Brogan to his feet, I know he is not Scatchard's killer for, in instinctively putting up his arm to deflect Latham's blow, it was his right hand that he used to defend himself.

As his muffled protests die away into the distance, I turn to Williams who stands, head bowed, apparently cowed by the scene he has just witnessed. Not for the first time am I struck by how unlikely a follower he seems for a lout such as Brogan.

'Did Brogan meet anyone in Ostend, Williams? You had best be open with us, man, lest you share your colleague's fate,' I say sternly.

'I know not, sir,' he replies earnestly, 'and that be God's honest truth. All I know is that 'e tells me to get vittles for to take back to camp and not to wait for 'im as he 'as business to attend to in town. I didn't see 'im after that, nor know if he met anyone or not that day.'

I take him up on his last words, '*That day?* You mean he *had* met with someone on previous occasions?'

Williams shuffles uneasily. 'Aye, once or twice. Us saw 'im, Ned an' me – but us never 'eard ought that passed between 'em, for Brogan allus told us to get lost whenever the stranger appeared, like.'

'What did he look like, this stranger?'

'Us never got a good look at 'im. All muffled up, 'e wor, 'is 'ood over 'is face.'

Seeing that no more is to be got from Williams on this subject, Bancroft asks, 'And on the day of Scatchard's death, Brogan maintains he did not return until after the body was discovered. Is that true, Williams?'

'Sure I didn't *see* 'im afore then,' replies Williams warily, perhaps starting to sense which way the wind is blowing and chary of being caught in its blast. 'Me and some others were talkin' together as us often do, an' so caught up in what us were discussin' that 'e might a' come back wi'out me knowin', I couldn't say.'

'That must have been some discussion to have engaged you so?' I observe sceptically.

For the first time, he looks at me directly. 'The Lord's work is a topic fit to engage any man, Corporal Weaver.'

The candid rebuke in his gaze triggers an image in my brain: Woodrow thrashing about in the sea as Brogan held him under, his companions shrinking away, talk of "the mark of the devil" in reference to Woodrow's facial disfigurement. And suddenly the pieces fit together - Williams must be an evangelical Christian, the like of which I have seen preaching on street corners back in London.

'Was Ned Scatchard usually one of your debating group?' I ask.

'Aye. A true, god-fearin' man. To die like that – 'tis a bad business.'

That such men should consort with Brogan seems even more incongruous – yet just as I begin to puzzle out an explanation, Bancroft interrupts, clearly failing to see any relevance in my line of questioning.

'Thank you, Private Williams, that'll be all. You may go,' says he, 'but bear in mind "a still tongue makes a wise head." You will say nothing of what has transpired here. Understand?'

'Yes, sir. I give you my word,' replies Williams with feeling, 'my lips shall remain sealed.'

'Make sure they do,' says Bancroft. 'You may go.'

Once Williams has gone, Bancroft turns to me. 'What is all this about Brogan meeting someone in Ostend, Jack? Is it pertinent to the murder?'

I tell him of the time I saw Brogan in conference with the stranger whom I thought was familiar.

'It may be nothing, sir, but there was a furtiveness about them which struck me as suspicious.'

'We shall have him back and get to the truth of the matter,' says Bancroft determinedly getting up from his chair.

'By your leave, Lieutenant Bancroft,' I say, causing him to pause on his way to the door, 'I would advise against it for the present. Brogan believes he is to be punished for murder...'

'So he is!'

'A murder which, saving you presence, sir, he could not have committed.'

'What! Not commit? What mean you, Weaver, we have seen him as good as confess his guilt.'

'We have seen him lose his temper, yes. He is undoubtedly guilty of gross subordination. But he is not guilty of Scatchard's murder.'

'How so?'

'The murderer was left handed. Brogan is not. If you execute him, you will be executing an innocent man – innocent of this crime at least.'

I explain how Brogan's instinctive reaction to Sergeant Latham's punch is incontrovertible proof.

Bancroft sinks, disconsolate, back into his chair.

'Jack, Jack, what am I to do with you? Do you delight in putting me in a quandary thus? First you tell me I must make an example of Woodrow for a crime he did not commit. Now you say I must acquit this villain.'

'Not acquit him, sir. He must be punished for insubordination - which we may report as inciting a comrade to take his own life - but not for murder. However, he does not know that. He doubtless expects this day to be his last on this earth. Will you let me work on him? In offering him a commutation of his sentence, we may get to the truth of his clandestine meetings with the unknown stranger.'

'Very well, Jack. But let him stew a little longer. Wait till the day's end. It will do his belligerence good to ponder upon death for a while.'

A fellow agent

Shortly after noon I find Agnes waiting for me at the front door of the van Andels' house. Waiting for me to honour my promise to let her view the troops – though I have a suspicion that this was exacted merely a ploy for some other matter entirely.

As we walk at a leisurely pace towards the field where Latham is drilling the troops, she slips her arm through mine. An action which I gallantly accept, without letting her see the great pleasure it affords me.

'I fear the sight of the men marching up and down the field will not prove the engaging spectacle you expect,' I say.

She laughs prettily. 'I am sure it will serve its turn, Jack Weaver.' There is the barest hint of mockery in her tone. 'Tell me, how does your imposture suit you? Is it not a trial to remember all the time that you are not Will Archer any more?'

I consider a moment, preparing my answer. 'To tell truth, Miss Mayer, I have never, in my inner being, felt any other than Will Archer. If the pretence of being Jack Weaver had not been forced upon me, it might be different. But I have hopes that I will soon cast off the guise of Weaver, just as my master, Mr Garrick, sloughs off the character of Richard III or any of the roles he plays.'

'But in the meantime, you aim to play your role of Weaver as convincingly as Mr Garrick does his?'

'It is a matter of necessity. I am in so deep with so many people that there is, at the moment, no going back,' I say morosely. 'It is only the certainty that I *am* and will once again be Will Archer that keeps me going.'

We have arrived at the edge of the field. Latham has the men lined up in three ranks and practising, though without live ammunition today, the drill for firing at the enemy. To see each line in turn point their muskets, shout 'Bang!' and drop to their knees at first appears a comical sight, were it not for the thought that in a matter of weeks this pantomime will be performed in all too deadly earnest.

Agnes's eyes are on the platoon but her thoughts are elsewhere. 'You are well used to playing a double role though, are you not, Will?'

'What mean you, Agnes?'

'Mr Garrick is not the only master you serve, is he? There is a certain gentleman in Westminster.'

'There are many gentlemen in Westminster,' I say, guardedly.

She turns to me now, her face serious. 'Come, Will, do not prevaricate. We both know I mean Sir William Hervey, the Head of the King's Secret Service.'

We are far enough away from the racket of the drill and Sergeant Latham's bellowing for none to overhear our conversation, but I caution her to be discreet all the same.

'Nay, Will Archer,' she says with a sigh, 'I am all too well versed in matters of discretion. Sir William's tentacles spread wide. You know that his creature, Nathaniel Grey pursued me to Gravesend when I fled the scene of my ruin?'

'Aye, so I was told,' say I, keeping my eyes upon the manoeuvres but laying my hand gently upon hers where it lies in the crook of my arm.

'What you do not know is that a short while later Hervey found me out in Rotterdam, whereto I'd sought sanctuary and - to be brief, Will, I, like you, am now in his service.'

'Oh, Agnes,' I say, my voice heavy with sympathy. Further words elude me, for I know too well how Hervey recruits his spies through knowledge of their history and thereby exerts his hold upon their loyalty. In the case of Agnes and myself, it includes, amongst other things, a murder in which both of us were implicated.

'Up till a few weeks ago,' she continues, 'he has not called upon me. But now that England has entered openly into the war, he apparently needs my services. My coming to stay with my friends, the van Andels, whilst troops are stationed on their land is no mere coincidence – though finding you here is an unexpected, and,' here she gives me a look which quite melts my heart, 'a most agreeable surprise.'

As we stroll about the perimeter of the field, she informs me of the task Hervey has assigned her.

'The talk in London is that the King disapproves the battle plans of his commander in the field, Sir John Stair. His majesty has sent his youngest son, the Duke of Cumberland, to persuade the old soldier to his point of view, but is also determined to come over here and lead the army himself.'

'There have been hints of this in the despatches which, as Lieutenant Bancroft's ADC, I am privy to,' I tell her. 'Stair, it seems, regards the French as the enemy and would act decisively against them whilst the bulk of their forces are still engaged against the Prussians. He has plans to attack Dunkirk, defeat the French garrison there, and then march on Paris, thus putting an end to French ambitions. But orders from London say we are not officially at war with France. Ostensibly we are here only as allies of Austria...'

'Who *are* at war with France.'

'Exactly. The Austrian generals want King George to put pressure on some of Hanover's neighbouring German Principalities and Dukedoms to join with Austria against French aggression. It is thought that we shall receive orders any day to start marching eastwards to join up with the

Austrian army.'

'And have your despatches mentioned anything about King George leading the English army?'

'Only hints, as I said. It is to be supposed that His Majesty may come across to Europe in person to rally the support of his neighbouring Princes for the Austrian cause, but as to him leading a British regiment alongside the Austrians, I have seen nothing. Nor would I expect to. Ours is only a small platoon a long way down the chain of command.'

'One in which you have recently had a sudden unexplained death – can you tell me about it?' She sees my hesitation. 'Not as the shockable young lady Mevruow van Andel thinks me, but as a fellow agent.'

There is nothing in my remembrance of Agnes Mayer that leads me to view her as a 'shockable young lady'. She is as used to violent death and subterfuge as I have become over the last two years. I have no qualms in relating all the ghastly details of Scatchard's death.

'This Brogan sounds a nasty piece of work,' she says. 'Yet his alibi holds up?'

'For the murder, yes.'

And I proceed to tell her of his covert assignations.

Her eyes light up at mention of the mysterious stranger and the familiarity I sensed upon my brief glimpse of him.

'You thought you recognised him, and he you?'

'It was but a fleeting glance. I may have been mistaken.'

'Nay, Will Archer, I know you better than that,' says she with a teasing smile. 'But, very well, I shall humour you. You cannot be certain – but who did you *think* it was?'

'A man whose plot I helped to foil in Ireland when Mr Garrick was engaged to play a season at Dublin's Smock Alley Theatre.'

I tell her of how Mr Frederick Handel's first performance of *The Messiah* was very nearly blown up by a pair of malcontent Irish brothers who escaped Hervey's clutches, and who were thought to have fled abroad.

Even as I recount the story to her, I am back in that dark cellar with the smell of gunpowder in my nostrils. And I remember Sir William Hervey's words some days later: *"They are probably aboard ship to Europe to fight in King George's War."*

And Nathaniel Grey's enigmatic, murmured rejoinder: *"For which side I wonder."*

Now, as Agnes and I turn back towards the *herenhuis*, the smiling face, the firm handclasp of a red-haired Irishman come into my mind and I tell her the name of the man I thought I saw.

'Finn Kelly,' I say and add, though I can't explain why, 'He was a talented violin player.'

Brogan

Brogan is being held in the same makeshift cell where Woodrow was held. But whereas Ben Woodrow had only one soldier posted outside, Sergeant Latham has taken the precaution of assigning two guards at the door.

It is a small outbuilding at a distance from those occupied by the men,. Through a tiny slit high up in the stonework the setting sun paints the rough stone walls a ochreous red. The cramped space smells of mouldy earth and Brogan's sour fear.

He is sitting in the corner on the bare earth floor – there is no scrap of furniture in the place – his arms clasped around his knees.

A short-lived look of hope as one of the guards scrapes open the door to let me in is replaced at once with a scowl as he sees who it is.

'Come to crow, 'ave you? Well you can just fuck off.'

If the guard wasn't standing just behind me in the open doorway, I have no doubt the violence in his words would be extended to my person.

All the same, I signal to the guard to retreat outside and push the door partially closed.

Brogan lowers his head again, deliberately ignoring my

presence.

I stand, silent, waiting.

It is a trick I have seen Sir William Hervey use in interrogations – a stillness that makes the prisoner so uneasy he cannot help but speak. And so it is with Brogan.

'Gonna stand there like a bastard mute all day are yer? For fuck's sake say what you've come to say, then get the bloody hell out of 'ere, you fucking arsehole.'

'I don't like you, Brogan...,' I begin.

'The feelin's mutual, mate,' he spits back.

'…but you deserve justice the same as any other man. You're a bully and a liar – but you're not a murderer.'

He gives a contemptuous laugh. 'Ha! Not 'ere to crow – just to bloody preach!'

'No, Brogan – to save your miserable life if you'll let me.'

'And how'll you do that?' he retorts scornfully. 'Promise to suck pretty-boy Bancroft's cock to let the nasty rough man off?'

'You've a foul mouth, Brogan,' say I with a weary disdainful sigh. 'I pity you.'

'Shove your pity up your fucking arse, I don't want it!'

'Very well,' I reply harshly, 'I'll remember that when they break you on the wheel tomorrow. When you're strapped to a cross and your hands are cut off and when Sergeant Latham takes an iron crow and smashes all your bones to splinters. I'll remember it when they loosen the ropes and you wreathe to the ground like the sack of rubbish you are and as you lie in agony, begging them to finish you off. Do you know how long a man can continue alive – a man like you, hale and strong in life – with every bone in his body broken, every nerve shrieking in agony, Brogan? Hours? Days? Will you ask for pity then? Beg them to end it all by striking your screaming head from your miserable body?'

I see that my description of the hideous punishment has had its effect. Brogan is still defiant, but now his voice is unsteady betraying his fear. 'You seek to frighten me, you bastard?'

'No, Brogan,' say I urgently, squatting on one knee beside him, 'I seek to save you from all this. I know you did not murder Ned Scatchard and have proof incontrovertible that I can lay before your accusers. I cannot save you from being punished for indiscipline and insubordination, but I can save you from a horrible death for a crime you did not commit.'

I pause briefly to let this sink in, then say, 'But I require something from you in return.'

'Ha! I knew it!' he sneers. 'There always a fucking price to pay.'

'At least you'll be alive to pay it, man. And 'twill be easier than the torment of having your limbs shattered piece by piece.'

'Depends,' says he with a crooked grimace. 'Sometimes death may be the better option. Well, say your piece. What do you want of me?'

'The name of the man you meet in Ostend and the nature of your business with him.'

I expect truculence, prevarication. But his reaction takes me by surprise.

First he laughs, then disbelief clouds his face. 'Is that all? And for this you will save me from death?'

'You have my word. But no holding back, Brogan, I require the whole truth if I am to plead for mitigation.'

'Very well, 'tis no great matter. 'Twas five weeks ago, just after we'd arrived 'ere, when this chap approached me. Wanted to know if I was one of the soldiers up at the farm.'

'Did that not put you on your guard? A stranger asking questions about English troops.'

' 'Course it bloody did! I was all for tellin' 'im to sling 'is 'ook. But then 'e said, "Look, you and I, we're fellow Irishmen, all I'm after is news of a pal o' mine what's gone missin'. And I'm willin' to pay for news of 'im." Well, I didn't see no 'arm in that.'

'Did he describe this friend of his?'

'Aye, but to be sure it could've been any of a dozen or more of the fellows here. So 'e asks me when I'm in town to point out any groups from the camp and to let 'im know if there's any arguments or such like in the camp, as his friend is of a quarrelsome nature. And that's the long and short of it. All 'e wanted was gossip, no more.' He gives me a gloating leer. 'Well, your lordship, that's God's 'onest truth. Now you'd better bloody well keep your side of the bargain.'

'I will, but there's one more thing - I also asked you for his name, Brogan.'

'The name 'e give me was Kelly. Finn Kelly.' He pulls himself to his feet and, bunching my lapel in his fist, brings his face so close to mine I feel his spittle on my cheeks and am all but overwhelmed by his stinking breath. 'Now that's us done, Corporal bloody Weaver, so get the hell out of here and crawl up that sapskull Bancroft's arse or whatever you have to do to get me out of this stinkin' rat-hole.'

He releases his hold, thrusting me away as he hawks a foul gob of phlegm which just misses my face and clings, glutinous, on my jacket.

Orders

Next morning, Bancroft has Latham assemble the platoon and announces the punishment that Brogan is to suffer.

'There can be no successful combat or engagement with the enemy without discipline,' he announces, 'and that discipline must apply to all ranks and areas of the militia, at all times and in all places.

'A soldier who flouts orders or by his behaviour brings disrepute upon his unit, or spreads unrest amongst his fellows must expect to be punished with the full force of military discipline.'

Standing at his side, I can see apprehension on many of the faces ranged before us. On others there is a grim look of agreement. None, I think, have failed to hear the rumours that have circulated during the last few days. Accounts of Scatchard's death and the manner in which he died have been told, retold and embellished with ever more ghastly detail.

Now, in silence, they await the official version.

'One of your fellows, Private Brogan, has been guilty of insubordination to both Sergeant Latham and myself. In addition, his words and actions caused such distress to a fellow soldier as to induce him to take his own life – a sin before man and God. That soldier was Ned Scatchard.

'In sentencing Private Brogan to the punishment of Running the Gauntlet, I trust that each and every one of you will demonstrate by your actions the abhorrence that any right-minded man must feel for a wretch who for his own wicked pleasure was prepared to damn the immortal soul of one who accounted him a friend.'

As soon as Bancroft steps down, Latham orders those who have a belt about their person to remove it, and to those who haven't he sets about distributing switches, canes and crops.

Then, when all the men are issued with instruments of punishment, he forms them into two parallel lines facing each other at about four foot distance.

Brogan, stripped to the waist, is then led out and a sergeant's halberd is strapped to his chest. With the five foot shaft impeding his legs and the razor-sharp blade so close to his face, there can be no question of his moving quickly between the serried lines of his assailants.

Latham reads out the sentence, his voice coolly dispassionate, too much the stickler for discipline to let his opinion show.

Brogan is to do two 'runs', the first for insubordination, the second for his part in compassing Scatchard's suicide.

As Latham reads, Brogan glares defiantly around him,

attempting to catch the eye of his fellow soldiers.

But if he looks for sympathy, he is disappointed. Seb Williams and the others who were his former confederates now apprized of his crimes return his gaze with steadfast zeal. Amongst all his sins, that of damning another's soul to perdition is the most heinous. Little as they relish the forthcoming punishment, they believe it to be just.

Meanwhile, those who have at one time or another borne the brunt of his ire flex their scourges with jaws set and the fire of revenge in their eyes.

I run my eye along the rows until I find my friends. Tom Hooper is one of those already doubling up his sturdy leather belt. Beside him, Josh Barley looks more apprehensive – perhaps he is recalling the sting of the whip on his own shoulders not so long ago. And, two or three places down, Ben Woodrow displays, as far as the wine-stain birthmark livid on his pale face allows me to judge, an expression of apparently profound sadness.

Considering what he has suffered from the man, I find this perplexing, but then I can only imagine how I would feel were I in one of those lines about to inflict such pain upon a fellow human being, even one as odious as Brogan.

As it is, I must stand beside First Lieutenant Bancroft and Sergeant Latham and witness the punishment and whilst all eyes may not actually be on me, I feel as if they are and endeavour to keep my face blank of all emotion.

At a signal from Latham, a soldier propels Brogan into the narrow human corridor and the cruel ritual begins. Forced to walk at a steady pace, restricted by the weapon tied to his chest, Brogan must bear the stroke, and sometimes two or three, of every whip he passes. Nor are his tormentors holding back. Jeering and yelling, they lay on with vigour, some from righteous anger at his crime, some remembering how he relished flogging Josh Barley, and others merely in the belief that, if they are seen not to exert themselves, it could well be them in his position next time.

Whatever else may be said of Brogan, he is tough. Not a sound escapes his lips as he walks doggedly through the flailing wood and leather. By the time he emerges, limping only slightly, his flesh is torn ragged and he is soaked in his own blood, but his face is set like stone, only his staring, pain-filled eyes giving any clue to the agony he is suffering.

The first run over, he is doused with buckets of salt water to cleanse the wounds. His body spasms momentarily with the cold shock of water and sting of salt but then, without waiting for the order, he turns back to face the return passage.

His silent fortitude, it seems, has made its mark upon the men, for as he enters once more between the two rows, the jeering is less harsh and the blows less fierce. Nevertheless, by the time he is half way along, he staggers and nearly falls. Only the halberd holds him upright and I notice his fingers curl themselves around its shaft for support and see how he leans his cheek against the flat of the blade almost as if it were a lover. Thus he hobbles, increasingly slowly and haltingly towards the end of the line, now almost in total silence from his persecutors and under strokes which are at best half-hearted.

His steps falter as he reaches the end of the line and, once out in the open, he comes to a halt, swaying, almost unable to stay upright. Sergeant Latham steps briskly forward, uses a bayonet to slice away the cords that tie him to the halberd and signals two men to catch him before he collapses and to bear him to the makeshift medical room in the *herenhuis* – the same room where Barley was taken after his flogging.

As they pass Bancroft and myself, I glance down at the gruesome burden hanging heavy as a corpse between the two panting bearers. In truth Brogan seems barely half alive, his body bruised and gouged, his skin hanging in strips and dripping with blood.

But, as he is borne past, his swollen eyes, half shut, sense our presence and his head jerks back. A guttural groan escapes his lips.

'What says he?' asks Bancroft.

'I did not hear,' I lie.

In truth, I heard well enough. 'Fuck you, Weaver,' he'd moaned. 'Fuck you all.'

A despatch rider arrives from Command Headquarters in Bruges shortly after noon. It is the news we have been expecting, the order to prepare for departure as soon as practicable.

'Practicable' – a simple word were it not for the fact that we have not yet received supplies necessary for such an undertaking. To be sure, we have uniforms and weapons, but they will hardly suffice for a journey on foot of four or five hundred miles through open, unknown country.

Weeks ago, we were promised more blankets and tents but none have yet appeared. We have been lucky in our accommodation so far, but how many barns can we count on during such an odyssey? Or how many householders as amenable as the van Andels?

As Sergeant Latham, the most seasoned campaigner amongst us, points out, a sizeable town such as Ostend may tolerate us but no village will welcome a battalion of troops descending upon it.

'They are too bloody small and poor to feed strangers without destroying themselves in the process,' he warns. 'Inns are no better, and I've known plenty! Back in England,

The Angel treats soldiers like devils and *The Rising Sun* refuses 'em a light to go to bed by,' he jests grimly, 'and I can't see it bein' no different 'ere. No, Mr Bancroft sir, 'twould be folly to set out before supplies arrive. Men will die, sir, especially in this weather.'

I see his point, for the despatch rider isn't the only thing to have arrived today.

Even as the men dispersed from Brogan's punishment, handing in the bloodied birch switches and buckling on belts hastily wiped on the grass, big flakes of snow began to swirl from a leaden sky.

There is now a four inch layer of white blanketing fields and roofs and lying heavy on groaning branches. And the noonday sky, dark as night, is pregnant with more to come.

Not that this will be of any concern to the number counters back in the Treasury at London who are responsible for military supplies. They will be counting the costs in pounds, not in men's lives. The requisite forms, properly signed, will have more priority than lives lost from cold and starvation.

The problem is that they are not used to supplying military operations on so large a scale. In keeping England out of European wars for over thirty years, Prime Minister Walpole left the country sadly unprepared for conflict.

My afternoon, therefore, is spent penning urgent requests

for information about supplies, and letters explaining the extenuating circumstances for our delayed departure.

At the same time I must oversee preparations for the imminence of that departure, searching out local muleteers and carters who may be prevailed upon to transport all the expected equipment.

Sergeant Latham cancels afternoon drill and sets the men to work with brooms and shovels to clear pathways through the snow, a Sisyphean task as the heavens continue to discharge their whirling, billowing burden.

With ill grace he releases Hooper, Barley and Woodrow from snow-clearing to accompany me into Ostend in search of carriers.

'Enjoy your petty power while you may, Weaver, givin' your orders,' he growls. 'You think you're one o' them now, but you ain't. Come the day, they'll be sittin' astride their 'orses on an 'illtop surveyin' the battle while you an' me an' all the other poor fuckers get torn to shreds with blades and bullets.'

I give him cool thanks for his advice and, collecting my friends, together we battle our way through the snowstorm.

It takes us twice the normal time and, though the snow is abating somewhat by the time we reach the gates of the town, the flakes now smaller and less dense, falling straight rather than billowing like clouds of goose down, our boots and greatcoats are already wet through.

Brushing wet strands of hair from my forehead, I issue instructions to my friends.

Hooper and Barley I send off to enquire out any owners of beasts of burden who are willing either to sell or to lend. Better still, I instruct my friends, if the owners can be persuaded to accompany us as drovers and take charge of the animals on our journey.

Meanwhile, Ben Woodrow and myself go in search of carters whose vehicles we may call upon.

Before going our separate ways, we agree to meet back at the city gate when the clocks chime five.

The snow storm has driven many of the citizens off the streets but the traders, hoping perhaps for some alleviation in the weather, have not yet shut up shop and have time to give us the information we require.

Our quest yields some success. By the end of the afternoon Ben and I have definite offers of two ox-carts and the promise, if terms be right, of four more.

Not that I have played much part in the bargaining. After my first inadequate attempts, Woodrow persuades me to let him try and he proves a canny negotiator, being able to haggle in both Flemish and French as well as English. I bow to his lingual superiority and leave him to do the business.

It is while he is brokering one such agreement, closely inspecting an ancient wooden cart, pointing out its deficiencies as the owner equally volubly attempts to extol its merits, that I, standing at the gate of the yard in which it is housed, become aware of a muffled-up figure beside me.

'Your friend speaks good French, Will Archer. Uncommon – and perhaps dangerous - in these troubled times. Let him have a care – and you, too.'

I hardly have time to turn round before he is gone, striding away with surprising speed through the trodden snow. I make to pursue him but, in turning, slip upon a patch of impacted snow and fall heavily against the gatepost, jarring my shoulder. By the time I have recovered enough to run to the end of the lane there is no sign of him.

Returning to the yard, I find Woodrow concluding the transaction and curious as to the cause of my sudden flight.

'Someone I thought I recognised,' I tell him, 'but I was mistaken. It was a stranger.'

But a stranger who spoke my name. And one who recognised me as surely as I recognised him by his soft Dublin lilt.

But what meaning am I to ascribe to his words?

Has Finn Kelly just given me a warning – and if so, as a friend or an enemy?

Contact Established

It is three days before I have chance to speak in private to Agnes again. Days which I am obliged to spend in writing innumerable letters, checking despatches, calculating the cost of hiring the necessary transport where we might not have it for free.

And calming Bancroft's irritability, caught as he is between demands from on high and concern for the welfare of his men.

Vexatious as the days may be, the evenings are yet more exasperating for though at dinner I enjoy many a conversation with Agnes, I am unable to converse to any real purpose.

She talks gaily of sleigh rides with the van Andels, of the prettiness of the snow and of skating, fur clad, with townsfolk upon the frozen pond. She condoles with us about how cold the men must be in their draughty barn and hatches plans with Mevruouy van Andel to provide them with hot soup.

Every evening, upon retiring from the dining-table, I hope she will vouchsafe me some private word. But no, our ever present hostess unwittingly denies all opportunity.

Every night I spend in anticipation of a soft knock upon

my door. But every night I go thwarted to my bed, and after much fruitless tossing and turning, resort occasionally to summoning up her vision in my mind whilst seeking my own hand's intimate embrace.

But then, one morning, she is suddenly there in person as I leave the house on my way to see how my friends, whom I have sorely neglected during the past few days, are faring.

She is warmly wrapped in furs, the hood framing her beautiful face, rosy-cheeked in the cold morning air.

Without any hesitation she extracts a gloved hand from her fur muff, puts her arm through mine and replacing her hand in the muff, leads me briskly away from the house.

'Walk with me, Will. I have much to tell.'

Once out of hearing of anyone in the house, she begins, 'I sent word to Sir William the day after our last conversation and had his reply only yesterday afternoon. Mevruouw would have us go to a music recital in town and during the interval I was passed an envelope containing a note addressed to you. I have it here.'

She gives a quick look over her shoulder, then extracts a paper from her muff and hands it to me.

'Nay, do not read it now. Put it up lest anyone be watching. Fie, what kind of spy are you!'

Quickly I conceal it in my waistcoat pocket. 'It is from

Sir William?'

'Of course it is, and he commends me for acquainting him with your whereabouts.'

'Is he going to rescue me?' I say with a surge of hope.

'Rescue you? Why, what a thought!' she laughs. 'Do you not know Sir William better than that? You think he will be satisfied with my poor efforts now he has someone in the thick of it?'

'The thick of what?'

'He has not told me all. Only that he is concerned at the news that King George is on his way here. His Majesty has always been of a martial turn of mind and apparently no amount of talk from his ministers about his advanced years or the simmering Jacobite threat at home has been able to dissuade him from so rash a course. Sir William fears it will be an opportunity for England's enemies to work some harm upon the King.'

I raise a cynical eyebrow. 'More harm than being shot at, blown up or stabbed with a bayonet? Does he not know that men are in constant danger on a battlefield? Not that His Majesty is like to be too near the heart of the battle.'

'You are incorrigible, Will Archer!' she giggles. 'No, it is not the overt threat that concerns him so much as the viper in the bosom.'

'He suspects a traitor in the camp?'

'Aye, and he is very interested in this Brogan fellow and the Irishman he secretly meets – what was his name, Finn Kelly?'

'Aye. But as for Brogan, I think we need not worry overmuch about him at present.'

I explain how he will be no threat for another week at least until he has recovered from his punishment. I also impart what he has told me of his dealings with Kelly.

'You believe him?'

'Yes. He is a loathsome fellow, but I do not think him overly intelligent. He had not the cunning to disguise his satisfaction at believing he'd tricked me into keeping my part of the bargain despite having so little to tell me. And I must admit to some satisfaction of my own that the lesser punishment did not prove as easy as he thought.'

'And all he told you was that Kelly was seeking to contact a 'friend' within the platoon?'

'Yes. I doubt Kelly gave him more information than that and, whilst Brogan may have suspected something underhand, the smell of money would blunt his curiosity.'

'So the 'friend' Kelly is so eager to find might be the traitor Sir William suspects?'

'It may be. Or, on the other hand, Finn Kelly may be the traitor and the 'friend' someone he sees as an enemy to his own plans.'

And I tell her of his mysterious remark at the carter's yard in Ostend.

'He revealed himself to you directly?' she exclaims in surprise. 'That is bold behaviour. And he said that it was dangerous to speak French in these troubled times and warned you to take care? What did he mean by that?'

'I have no idea. Perhaps he was alerting me to a French spy in our ranks – but whether he was advising me to find him out or to leave well alone, I do not know.'

I see her mouth pout with worry. 'Do you not think that is something you must find out – and with some urgency? Kelly's warning implies some danger to yourself and I would be loth to lose you so soon after finding you again, Will Archer.'

'Agnes...' I begin, but cannot express the emotion that wells up inside me at her words. Instead I say, 'I fear fate may disappoint us both in that respect. The platoon is under orders to prepare for departure as soon as supplies arrive – and I expect to receive notice this morning that the ship which docked yesterday contains those very supplies. I anticipate that we will be striking camp first thing tomorrow.'

She glances up at me, her eyes bright with dismay. 'So soon? In that case, we must make the most of what time is left.'

I find my friends playing at cards in the comparative warmth of the byre. They are pleased to see me but that doesn't stop them jesting about my neglecting them.

'Too common are we for you, now you're one o' the nobs?' laughs Tom Hooper. 'Up in that warm house, supping wine I'll lay and livin' off the fat of the land while we poor cods heads freeze our arses off down 'ere.'

'Supping wine? I wish,' I reply. 'But we may none of us be here much longer. A day at most. Then, begod, we'll all know what cold is!'

'We're heading east, then?' asks Ben Woodrow. 'Are we to meet up with the regiment?'

'Aye, so it seems, though where is still uncertain. The Austrians are said to be advancing on the River Danube where they hope to engage with the French. But most of the French troops are still encamped around the River Moselle. '

'These are but names,' moans Josh Barley. 'Be these places east or west? Far away or near?'

'In truth, I have only the vaguest idea myself,' I tell him. 'It is only from studying the map that I can tell you our direction is like to lie east and perhaps somewhat to the south. A good forty days' march, I reckon, even in good weather.'

'Aye,' says Tom Hooper scornfully, 'and you may be sure

the generals won't be trudging, footsore through the snow, like us sapskulls. They'll be travelling in coaches with furs round their shoulders and pans of hot coals at their feet.'

'Fie, Tom, have a care what you say,' chides Ben Woodrow in mock disapproval.' You'll be taken up as an anarchist for sentiments like that. 'Tis lucky you're among friends.'

Then Woodrow turns to me. 'Tell me, Jack, is't true what they say, that General Stair is not allowed to make his own decisions but must defer to the Austrians? That King George is but the Empress Maria Theresa's puppet?'

'As to that, I cannot tell,' I reply. 'But, in confidence, friends, 'tis said King George himself will come to take command of his army.'

'Tell us something we don't know, Jack! Already 'tis the talk all about the camp.'

'Is that so?' I ask with interest. 'And who may be the instigator of such talk? He had better not let Sergeant Latham catch him.'

'Nay, I know not whence the rumour comes,' says Woodrow with wry grimace, 'merely that everyone has heard it. And, it has to be said, the prospect does not inspire confidence. Our German Majesty is about as well liked here as he is back in England.'

'Nay, Ben,' I laugh, 'now 'tis *my* turn to chide you as you just now chid Tom, this is revolutionary talk!'

'In that case, Jack,' says Hooper, slapping me heartily upon the back, 'you'd best not tarry to hear more. 'Tis almost time our fire was lit and vegetables put in the pot for supper. And unless you want to share our meagre fare – 'twill cost you tuppence, mind, now you're one o' the nobs! - you'd best get back to your arse-licking duties.'

With a not altogether polite rejoinder in the same vein, I take jocular leave of my friends and head back to the *herenhuis* where a cart already stands outside the door. I have not gone twenty paces before two more carts rumble into sight.

The supplies have arrived.

That evening we sup late, having spent several hours unloading, checking, counting and listing all that has arrived. The tents, groundsheets, blankets, extra boots and greatcoats and all the countless items necessary to an army on the move.

Then more time is spent distributing the portable items among the men and reloading the heavy items upon the carts and mules we have commandeered.

The two carters and three muleteers who have agreed to accompany us are given a meal in the kitchen but decline the offer of straw mattresses indoors, preferring to bed down with their animals in the stable.

Having issued the order that we will strike camp and be ready to march at first light, Bancroft and I come late to dinner.

Mijnheer and Mevruouw van Andel have delayed the evening meal for us and seem genuinely sorry to see us go.

'Why, sirs, you have kept us mightily entertained all these weeks,' says our hostess. 'Mijnheer and I shall be quite bereft, left by ourselves in this rambling place with only each other to grumble at.'

'Fie,' laughs Agnes, 'you shall still have me, for a few days more at least.'

'Of course we shall, my dear,' replies Mevruouw van Andel, patting her hand fondly. 'And you are delightful company. But it is always comforting to have men about the house, do you not think so, my dear?' says she with a twinkle in her eye.

Agnes concedes graciously but quells any further amatory raillery by asking about our preparations for the morrow's departure.

Having been immersed in such arrangements all afternoon I cannot help but think the topic dull, but Agnes and the van Andels express a lively interest in every detail.

'And where are you headed tomorrow?' ask Agnes after a while.

'East to Bruges....,' I begin but am interrupted sharply by Bancroft.

'We are ordered to meet up with other platoons such as ours. Initially at Bruges, but thereafter our destination is not certain. Even if it were, Miss Mayer, we would not be at liberty to disclose it. A time of war, you understand...'

'Indeed, sir, forgive me. I am but a silly woman, I know, but secrets are not the sole province of you men,' she teases, 'we ladies are often very adept at keeping them.'

The conversation moves on to the less contentious subject of the weather and how long this cold spell may be expected to last.

At length we adjourn from the dining room to the parlour where Mevruouw van Andel insists that both Bancroft and I shall severally accompany Agnes in duets around the piano. Bancroft exhibits a passable if rather hesitant tenor, but with my, albeit limited, dramatic experience I feel I carry the evening with my greater confidence, if not the quality of my voice.

As Bancroft and I are likely to be up early tomorrow morning before the van Andels are about, we say our goodbyes now before retiring to our beds.

Once back in my room, I take out the letter from Sir William Hervey which Agnes gave me earlier today. With all the preparations for departure I have had no opportunity till now to read it.

"*My dear Archer, or Weaver as I believe I must now call you, I am gratified to learn that you are safe, though dismayed to learn, via the admirable young Master Stubbs, that you come by your present plight from loyal service to His Majesty.*"

So, Charlie must have delivered my original letter, and Hervey realises its import, that my abduction is a direct result of foiling the assassination attempt at Kensington Palace.

"*I confess myself puzzled by your mention of a 'black beetle' however, and Master Stubbs declined to elucidate the matter. Could it, by any chance, be an allusion to a mutual acquaintance's sartorial taste?*"

I can almost hear Hervey's gentle mockery and see his quizzically raised eyebrow. He recognises Nathaniel Grey as well as I in the nomenclature.

"*Your present straits, though regrettably a source of annoyance to you, are in fact most opportune and though you will doubtless wish to return to your old life at the earliest opportunity, you may prove of infinitely more use to me in your present location than back here in London.*

The situation is thus:

The King is resolved, against all sage counsel, to lead

his army into battle alongside his younger son, the Duke of Cumberland. Apart from any personal risk to His Majesty, this parlous stratagem may also put the country in jeopardy on two fronts.

First, the Prince of Wales, who is, of course, well-pleased with this turn of events, may seek, during His Majesty's absence, to sway the populace towards himself and away from his father. And, second, the forces of Jacobitism are, as you are aware, never far from the surface."

I pause in my reading. I am indeed aware, for it is those very forces which have pitched me into my present situation. In helping save His Majesty's life at Kensington Palace, I incurred the displeasure of someone in the Prince of Wales's Leicester House circle who may well be a Jacobite sympathiser. The only clue I have to his identity is the scent of rosewater which he obviously favours as a perfume. I smelt it both during an attempt on my life and when I was abducted by the press-gang.

I turn back to Hervey's letter.

"As you are also aware, the Pretender is in exile in France and has the ear of King Louis. Though France is not officially our enemy, King George's alliance with Empress Maria Theresa makes it impossible that we shall avoid conflict, for to be Austria's ally is per se *to be France's*

enemy.

King Louis presently does not have troops at his disposal to support a Jacobite invasion of England during the King's absence. But he may go to work by covert means. Which is why I need your eyes and ears on the ground, my boy

I have my finger on the situation here, and General Stair will have regard for the King's safety on the battlefield. But a plot against either the King or the Duke of Cumberland hatched in the ranks of the army is a different matter entirely.

This is where I must rely on you, my boy, upon your instincts and your tenacity. You have already inadvertently discovered much that may pertinent as regards the Brogan fellow and his secret rendezvous with the Irishman, and all I ask is that you continue to watch and observe. I shall, in due course, take steps to see you safely delivered from your involuntary exile, but in the meantime, I would ask you to keep your eyes and ears open and to report to Miss Mayer anything you think may be relevant.

Yrs, WH.

PS You will need no reminder to destroy this note once you have digested its contents."

I re-read the letter and then hold its corner to the candle flame – as usual, I think as I watch the paper char and curl, Hervey has left me to my own devices, with no definite instruction. And how am I to report anything to Agnes when I am in the middle of an unknown country, marching towards an unknown destination?

I start preparing for bed, thinking how this will be the last time I shall sleep in this room. Regretfully, I bid farewell to its comforts, just as I have said my last farewells to all else at the van Andel's house.

But I am mistaken, for there is one goodbye still to be vouchsafed.

A little before midnight, when all the rest of the household are asleep, there comes a quiet knock upon my door.

Agnes, true to her word, is loth to let me leave without some token of her true feelings.

Half an hour later, as she slips from my chamber with one last parting kiss, I have learnt two things.

First that Hervey has given her orders to follow us on our journey eastwards.

And second that making love to Agnes Mayer transcends all other encounters I have ever had with the female sex.

Morning Departure

At sunrise next morning, Sergeant Latham musters the troops on the drill field.

It is a cold, crisp morning but the eastern horizon where thick clouds are massing is suffused with crimson, threatening – if the old adage about 'red sky in morning' be true - more snow to come.

The men, muffled in blankets and greatcoats, laden packs on their shoulders and with heads shrouded in woollen scarves, shuffle under the unaccustomed weight, stamping their feet on the packed snow, their breath misting in the morning air.

Many of them glance back at the barn which has been their home for the past weeks, perhaps regretting their grumbles and complaints about draughts and discomfort. Its now empty stalls and scattered mounds of hay represent a lost comfort and familiarity in face of the unknown territory that lies ahead.

Outside the barn, the Flemish muleteers, half a dozen of them, are checking the girths on their pack animals and the carters are leading out the oxen from the byre to harness them to the heavy wooden carts laden with supplies and equipment piled under tarpaulins.

First Lieutenant Bancroft is already a-horseback, trotting between the hired drovers and the assembled troops, checking that all is in order. He, Sergeant Latham and I are the only ones who will be riding rather than making the journey on foot, our mounts acquired through Mijnheer van Andel's influence with a local horse-dealer.

Only one other of our number will not be on foot. Brogan cannot be left behind but is not deemed recovered sufficiently to march with pack on back with the rest of the men. For one or two days at most, Bancroft has agreed that he and his pack may be trundled on a handcart at the rear of our procession if two or three men may be found who are willing to take turns to push it.

Seb Williams, the reluctant witness at Brogan's hearing, volunteers to be one and another three of his friends agree to join him. Not, I suspect, out of any love for their passenger, but more from a sense of Christian duty. Since discovering Williams's evangelical sentiments at Brogan's interrogation, I have often noted him and his group of friends – which seems to gradually increase in number as the days go by – engaged in earnest discussion or what looks like silent prayer. In the enterprise of impending peril on which we are embarked, it is, I suppose, understandable that some should look to the Almighty for reassurance. In a way, I envy them their certitude – but I confess to a certain unease at their air of righteousness.

Having marshalled the men into a column, Latham rides up and down its length issuing orders - to stay in formation, no breaking ranks, no lagging behind. To help keep up the rhythm of marching, a piper and drummer are found and the men are told they may sing if they choose, but not songs of scurrilous or ribald nature.

Despite all this activity on their doorstep, none of the household is yet astir. Nevertheless, as I mount my horse, I glance back at the empty windows, gleaming ruddy in the dawn, and breathe a silent farewell to Agnes.

In her room beneath those stepped gables, I know her to be still abed but I picture her starting up at the bark of Latham's commands and the tread of marching feet and imagine her running to the window with nightgown clasped about her and the warm glow of sleep still upon her, to press her delicate hand against the misted pane. I sense – or wish to sense - her longing gaze upon our retreating backs.

Then, at a nod from Sergeant Latham, Bancroft gives the order to depart, the muleteers gee-up their beasts, the carts lurch into motion and, with the crunch of packed snow under our wheels, hooves and feet, we are on our way.

We leave Ostend and the van Andels' *herenhuis* behind us and head into a strange and alien countryside where hedge and bush are mere swellings under a thick, concealing mantle of snow and where drifts blunt the sharp outlines of solitary buildings.

The track is distinguishable from fields only as a discoloured, slushy band meandering through an expanse of white.

At times, even this muddy thread disappears and we find ourselves trudging ankle deep through what could be meadow or rutted fields, or even on occasion plunging waist deep into some treacherous hidden ditch or dyke. At first such accidents provoke bursts of laughter and good-natured jeering, but this soon stops as the reality of having to march in sodden and continuously wet clothing begins to hit home.

Fortunately I discover that my mount has a cannier instinct than my fellow humans for what lies beneath the cold blanket. She proceeds slowly, probing the ground with delicate hoofs before entrusting her weight. A caution for which I am profoundly grateful. It is trial enough having to ride a horse again without suffering the additional indignity of being pitched headlong from the saddle.

It is a welcome relief whenever the faint, muddied trail reappears or when trees help define the course of the path. It is at these times that our piper and drummer strike up their liveliest tunes. Tunes to which we can march rather than merely stumble, even if overhanging branches frequently shed their icy burden around our unsuspecting shoulders.

In general, however, it is slow going, our pace set more often by the constant creak of cartwheels than by the skirl and beat of pipe and tabor.

By noon, the sky has become a solid sheet of lead. We have, at a guess, progressed not much above five miles. But as we emerge from a wood through which we have been trudging for the past half-hour, there comes a ray of respite in the form of a small hamlet.

If we nurtured hope of succour, however, we are cruelly disappointed. The buildings, no more than half a dozen, are poor, shapeless affairs, thrown together from unhewn lumps of rock, with roofs consisting of stone tiles piled one upon another. The whole structure seems in imminent risk of collapse.

The inhabitants are equally ancient and inhospitable, offering us neither food nor shelter which is hardly surprising for, as Sergeant Latham predicted, they themselves are starving in their meagre, cramped hovels.

One ancient crone disputes awhile with one of our muleteers informing him that there is nothing for us here. The young men have long since left to seek their fortunes elsewhere leaving the old folk to scratch a living from the soil – a soil which for weeks has been unworkable and yielded nothing.

She does, however, give directions to a clearing some

mile or so further on in the forest that may provide a kind of refuge, in return for which Bancroft leaves a portion of salt dried pork and a few handfuls of oatmeal.

'You were under no obligation to do that, sir,' grumbles Latham as we continue on our way. 'We have little enough as it is, and the chance of forage in the days ahead is uncertain.'

'They were starving, Sergeant, it was our Christian duty.'

'That's as may be, but with respect, Mr Bancroft sir, I'd recommend our main dooty is to our own from now on.' He wheels his horse about and returns to his position riding alongside the column of men.

For a further hour, we plod onwards until we arrive at the forest clearing.

Though only two in the afternoon, it is already dark as evening and Latham gives immediate orders for tents to be unpacked and branches to be hacked down to build fires.

Before a dozen tents have been erected, large flakes of snow start whirling about our ears as if some malicious being in the sky has ripped open a vast feather pillow.

There is a scramble to erect another half dozen tents and Latham orders that tarpaulins be strung from branches to provide extra protection.

After a great deal of cursing amongst the men charged with lighting a fire, a spark takes and a flame, albeit smoky and acrid, is coaxed from the damp wood.

Soon enough, the one fire has become several, dotted about the clearing. Cooking pots are filled with fresh snow and rations are distributed. Strips of dried meat and boiled oatmeal may be unappetising fare, but as we sit, huddled under blankets in a world of silently falling snow at the end of our first day's march, it seems like very manna from heaven.

Bruges

Three days later we arrive outside the walls of Bruges.

Three days of relentless ploughing through snowdrifts, of bone-numbing cold, of clothes that are never dry. Lips crack and hands are raw with cold. Perpetually wet feet begin to rot inside boots.

The lusty singing of the first day is now but a listless dirge as life is reduced to remorseless, dogged plodding through the snow during daylight hours and wrestling with sodden canvas to set up camp when evening overtakes us.

The one consolation is that, after the first night's storm which prevented us resuming our march till nigh on noon the next day, we have had no more snow.

Yet, for all the hardship, the men remain in tolerably good humour. When tents are pitched for the night and our evening meal of dried meat and gruel finished, the low murmur of voices is still punctuated with voices raised in song and bursts of ribald laughter.

Even the Flemish muleteers and carters join in with games of dice and songs of their own.

Bancroft, Latham and I form an uneasy group in our own tent in consequence of which, Latham finds much to do amongst the men and I, once my duty as ADC is done, seek out the company of my friends, leaving Bancroft to his books of which he has brought half a dozen.

My valeting duties as his *aide-de-camp* have afforded me intimate access to his possessions over the past few weeks and I soon discovered that his taste in reading is somewhat eclectic. As well as treatises on warfare by classical authors in the original Latin, which I would expect in one of his education, he also has the very same new novel by Mr Fielding that I found Midshipman Bolton reading back in Ostend. Also a copy of Mr Daniel Defoe's *Moll Flanders.* Though I made no comment at the time, he reddened a little upon realising that I had seen this and, since getting to know him better, I have sometimes wondered if that saucy whore's history forms as much a part of his self-education as the Latin classics.

Tonight, however, he is reading Caesar's *Commentaries.* He is to attend a meeting with other platoon commanders at the *Stadhuis* tomorrow, and perhaps hopes to prepare himself by getting in a suitably military frame of mind.

I leave him to it and make my way to my friends' tent.

I find Tom Hooper and Josh Barley playing at dice. Ben Woodrow, like First Lieutenant Bancroft whom I've just left, also has his nose in a book, peering at it with the aid of a stub of candle in the corner of the tent.

'Come, Jack,' calls Tom as soon as I put my head through

the flap of the tent, 'make a third with us. Ben is but a tweaguey squeeze-crab this evening and no company at all! Come, join us, and tell us how the war's going.'

'As for that,' I say, taking my seat between him and Josh, who gives me a doleful smile, 'I know no more than you or any man.'

I shake the dice and throw two ones.

'Ha, deuce!' laughs Tom. 'That's retribution from on high for being less than honest, you cunning shaver! 'Know no more that us' indeed! Come, you read all the letters, you must at least have some idea what's afoot.'

'All I know is that we are but one platoon among many assembled here at Bruges. Together, when all are arrived, we are to continue marching eastwards. But there have so far been no orders to say where exactly. At the moment it seems no one knows.'

'Or no one is prepared to tell,' comes a sour comment from Ben in the corner. 'We, after all, are of little importance. Our job is not to question. Our job's to die, haven't you realised that yet?'

Hooper heaves a huge sigh, 'God, just listen to him. He's been like this all day. A proper Job's comforter.'

'I, for one, shall do my best to avoid dying,' I jest and change the subject to something less morbid, 'What's that you're reading, Ben?'

'Coke's *Institutes*. 'Tis one of my law books.'

Tom Hooper raises his eyebrows and rolls his eyes at me. 'See what I mean, Jack? What sort of reading's that for when we're on our way to fight the Frenchies?'

'Ah, but are we?' puts in Woodrow. 'Officially we're not at war with France, are we? So,' he continues, wagging the book at us, 'if we find ourselves being lined up with the French army facing us, is it legal?'

'Faced with French canons and muskets, I don't think the legality of the situation would be uppermost in my mind,' I reply lightheartedly

'Too bloody true. Fight first, ask questions later,' agrees Hooper.

'Obey orders, do as we're told. It's all us can do,' agrees Josh Barley. An unusual burst of loquacity for him at the best of times, but even more so considering the sombre mood he's been in since poor Scatchard's death.

'Aye,' says Hooper, 'and the order this minute is, it's your throw, so get on with it.'

Woodrow clicks his tongue in resignation and returns to his book. The game proceeds for two more rounds before I say, 'Seriously, Ben, I should not puzzle my head about it if I were you. I cannot see there is aught we can do. There are no laws governing war that I'm aware of. Countries may justify themselves in going to war, generals decide on the best strategy and tactics, troop commanders enforce discipline - but no-one ever actually asks if it's *legal.'*

'No,' he replies passionately, 'but don't you think they *should?'*

'Aye, well I think we should leave that to better minds than ours,' says Hooper. 'As far as I'm concerned, if King George tells me to fight, I can't see as I've any option. Now, are you going to be a misery-arse all night? If so, you can bloody sleep out in the snow.'

He makes a pretence of offering to bundle Ben out of the tent and they wrestle awhile until Ben, laughed out of his grump, capitulates.

Thus, we spend the next hour quite companionably until I take my leave and return to my altogether less convivial quarters.

Sergeant Latham is wrapped in his blanket already snoring. How would he would react, I wonder, to the notion that his views on the plight of the common soldier are akin to those I have just been hearing from Ben Woodrow? But I'm unable to pursue this line of thought because First Lieutenant Bancroft is still up and clearly worried about tomorrow's meeting at the *Stadhuis*.

He has obviously been listening out for my return for as soon as I put my head inside the tent, he casts aside his book, pulls his greatcoat about his shoulders and beckons me to join him outside.

I leave my coat on and together we walk a little way from the tent.

It is a clear night, the sky a sheet of black velvet studded with stars and a sharp-edged crescent moon whose light, reflecting from the lying snow, suffuses the darkness with an eerie, ethereal glow. Like ruddy jewels, the dying embers of fires glimmer amongst the shadowed drifts, the only specks of colour in a silvered world.

The camp, for the most part, has fallen silent. Apart from a few muted murmurs of hushed conversation from a distant tent, only the shufflings and mutterings of sleepers disturb the universal quiet.

Although there is no wind, it is too cold to stand and talk, so Bancroft and I stroll slowly, collars round our ears and hands deep in pockets, along the boot-trodden paths between the tents, our feet emitting only the occasional squeak and wheeze from the compressed snow. Sounds which are unlikely to penetrate the deep slumber of weary men.

All the same, we tread as lightly as we can and keep our voices low.

'I am uneasy, Jack, about tomorrow's meeting. What if they should enquire about the state of the men?'

I do my best to reassure him. 'Why, sir, you have no cause for uneasiness. The men may be weary with the rigour of marching in such conditions but they are otherwise in good heart.'

'I fear you are too sanguine, Jack. Have you not heard them murmuring? They do not forget we have a man dead and I fear they do not accept the explanation of suicide. But you and I know the truth.' He sweeps his arm wide about the huddled, shadowed tents. 'And we know the culprit is somewhere out there laughing at our ineptitude. Preparing, for all we know, to strike again. I know not how many more days, or weeks, we may be required to march, and it is certain that death in battle awaits some of us at the end of it. But I would not have my men fearing that death also stalks us along the way, ready to attack in secret and by stealth.'

'Nor I, sir. But it may not come to pass. Mayhap with Scatchard's death the murderer has achieved his aim.'

Bancroft stops and regards me closely, his face pale in the moonlight. 'You do not believe that, Jack, any more than I. The false confidence in your voice, the uncertainty in your eyes, they betray you.' He extends his arm and grasps my shoulder and in his face I see that he looks to me for direction. 'You are my right-hand man, Jack. You are the one person I can trust implicitly. Advise me what is to be done.'

I avert my eyes to conceal my confusion. *Do I, with so many secrets -   my enforced guise as Jack Weaver and an agent in Sir William Hervey's service - really deserve his unmitigated faith in me?*

He takes it as bashfulness. 'Come, Jack,' he says with an admiring look, 'you cannot be ignorant of the esteem in which I hold you. You and I may be worlds apart in rank and education, but in wisdom you are more than my equal. I have come to rely on your good sense and sound judgement. Advise me now.'

Suddenly a bat swoops, flapping and squeaking about our ears. With a muffled oath, Bancroft ducks and brushes it away.

'God's wounds! I am beset on all sides, Jack,' he laughs nervously. 'You see how in need I am of your help.'

Fortunately the diversion has allowed me to collect my thoughts and as we resume our slow progress through the sleeping camp, I lay out the case as I see it.

'The most puzzling thing is, what can have been the motive for Scatchard's death? He was, by all accounts, a god-fearing man who did harm to none. His only fault, if fault it be, lies in his friendship with Brogan. I wonder if that may have been his undoing.'

'How so, Jack?'

'Let us suppose, first of all that Brogan was behind his

murder...'

'But, Jack, you yourself have proved he could not have murdered him.'

'Aye, he could not have done the actual deed. But he may have suborned another to do it. You have seen what a hold he seems to have on some of those about him.'

'That's true. Like the Devil, he seems to have followers who are in his thrall. Even these last few days, he has lorded it from that cart of his. But,' says he with a determined jut of his chin, 'that will stop tomorrow. The devil will march with the rest of the men, whether his pack chafe his scars or no. Yet, you were saying, Jack - why would he turn upon one of his friends?'

'Perhaps Scatchard, as a god-fearing, moral man, took exception to the way Brogan accused Ben Woodrow and remonstrated with him, refused to support his story – even, mayhap, threatened to speak against him.'

'I can see how that would enrage Brogan,' agrees Bancroft dubiously, 'but would that be sufficient reason for murder?'

'Maybe not,' I concede. 'Yet we also know Brogan regularly met with a stranger – whom he says was Finn Kelly, an Irish renegade. According to Brogan, all Kelly wanted was to trace an old friend. But what if it were more than that?'

'But Private Williams said that he heard nothing of what was said...'

'No, but Scatchard may have done. What if he overheard something that made him a danger to Brogan, a danger which had to be eliminated – something that might be accounted illegal – even treasonable?'

Bancroft looks at me in alarm. 'Treason?' he gasps, his face pale in the moonlight. 'Is it possible we harbour such malefactors in our midst? What we need is proof.'

'Of course,' say I quickly, guessing he is about to charge me directly with finding out the proof and attempting to deflect him, 'it may be that Scatchard was killed by someone else entirely – one of the many people Brogan had offended, who sought retribution but, lacking the courage to tackle Brogan himself, chose one of his friends instead.'

'Hmm, in which case your suggestion that Scatchard's death is likely to be the only one seems sound.' He is silent a moment, considering. Then he says musingly, 'Treason... I cannot... 'Tis a bit far-fetched, is it not, Jack? We have already put it out that Scatchard took his own life. Might it not be best, Jack, considering how we are now embarked upon our military tasks, to let the matter rest? Leave it to God to exact punishment – and trust the offender will meet his fate in the battle to come?'

'That would be the pragmatic solution, sir,' I reply

diplomatically.

At this moment, there comes a shriek from the neighbouring wood. A night owl pouncing upon its prey.

Bancroft takes it as an omen. 'There,' he says with a curt, startled laugh, 'the Almighty has spoken. "Retribution is mine, saith the Lord." That is the text we shall observe.' He gives a mighty yawn. 'Come, Jack, let us retire. 'Tis past midnight and we must be up betimes tomorrow.'

Next morning First Lieutenant Bancroft and I enter the west gate of Bruges and, walking along the cobbled street to the main square, are joined by two or three other platoon commanders and their adjutants.

Not all of us are in British uniform. Dispatches have indicated that we will be fighting alongside regiments from the Austrian army as well as soldiers and mercenaries from several of the small German states and principalities and here, in these unfamiliar grey and white uniforms, is the proof.

The buildings we walk between are for the most part old and have seen better days, the windows crazed and stonework crumbling. The few citizens we encounter pass by, sullen, heads down, ignoring as best they may this group of foreign soldiers.

Soon we reach the main square dominated along one side

by the *Stadhuis* itself. It is an impressive building with high pointed windows reminding me of the old Gothic style churches in London. But it is rather like a castle as well, with its turrets and crenellations.

It, like many of the town houses we have passed, has a sort of faded grandeur. Back in the 13th century when Bruges was a thriving centre of trade, its tiled floors and wall paintings of armoured knights and rich merchants must have shone bright, but now they are dusty and have lost their lustre.

They are paintings which I have ample opportunity to gaze at in the great hall in which we assemble and I can't help but marvel at how magnificent this place, now so sadly declined, must once have been.

There are about forty of us all told, representing about twenty units and we are here to receive directions upon our route for the next few weeks.

From a dais at one end of the chamber, a senior officer, a Major I guess by his uniform - (I am not yet familiar with all the significance of gold braid and epaulettes) - tells us we are to join up with other platoons to form marching squadrons of approximately 150 men apiece and set out at four hourly intervals, so as not to give the populace along the way the impression that we are an invading force.

Our route, as expected, lies eastwards, along the line of

the canal from Bruges to Ghent. Then overland to Bruxelles where we will be given further orders.

Numbly I write down names that mean nothing to me. Feeling like a helpless castaway upon a rudderless, wind-blown bark with no choice but to follow where the torrent takes me.

When the Major has finished, half a dozen Captains and Subalterns start calling out names and arranging the platoon commanders into groups.

Our platoon is to join forces with two others, one English, one Austrian. Bancroft will become second in command to Hauptmann Bauer who is the senior ranking officer, being the equivalent of an English Captain. Second Lieutenant Ward from the other English platoon will be third in command.

All formalities completed, we set off back to camp at just after noon, Bancroft's spirits noticeably lightened on being relieved of overall command.

But his lifted spirits are not destined to last, for a very unpleasant surprise awaits us upon our return. One which shatters any hope we may have of letting Scatchard's death rest without further remark.

The Hanged Man

As soon as we arrive back at the camp we are met by Sergeant Latham who has Private Seb Williams in tow.

'Looks like you was right, Lieutenant Bancroft, sir,' he says. 'I told Private Brogan first thing this morning that he'd be on foot from now on. He weren't best pleased. Whined that he weren't yet fit enough until I suggested another dose of the same might change 'is mind. Skulked off like a whipped cur. Then, half an hour since, Williams comes to find me. Tell Lieutenant Bancroft wot you told me, Private.'

Williams comes to attention. 'Sir, 'twas just gone nine when Brogan comes from seein' Sergeant Latham, face like thunder and swearing fit to shame a man. Savin' your presence, I'll not repeat what 'e said, but 'twas mostly directed at the Sergeant and your good selves.' Here he nods at both Bancroft and me. 'In partickler towards you, Corporal.'

'Me?' I exclaim.

'Aye, sir. I don't know what you done, but 'e were sore mad at you, swearing and blaspheming, the gist of which is 'e'd 'ave 'is revenge. 'E knew people as would cook your goose for you and sooner than you might think, those were 'is very words - the only ones I care to repeat - as God's my witness. Then 'e up and high-tailed it. When 'e didn't turn up for parade, Sergeant Latham asked where he was, an' I told 'im what I just told you now.'

'I 'ad a couple of men go round the camp, sir,' says Latham, 'but it looks like 'e's done a runner.'

'Deserted, you mean?' exclaims Bancroft. 'What time did you last see him, Williams?'

' 'Bout half past nine,sir. Then we went to Drill at ten.'

'That's not three hours,' says Bancroft. 'He can't have got far. Come, Sergeant - come, Jack. 'Tis clear to me that his flight proclaims his guilt. We have horses and he is on foot, we may catch him yet.'

Whilst Latham goes to order up our mounts, I question Williams.

'Did he give you any indication of where he was going?'

'None, sir. He just stormed off. Din't even put 'is coat on.'

'So he obviously didn't intend to go far?'

'I dunno, sir. All I know is he rifled a bit in his pack, tucked something in his pocket, then went.'

'Leaving his pack and his greatcoat behind?'

'Aye, sir.'

'Thank you, Private Williams.'

Bancroft dismisses him with a warning to say nothing to the other men.

'This does not sound like the actions of a deserter, Jack,'

says Bancroft, once he has gone.

'Indeed not, sir. To leave his belongings behind suggests he means to return. And from what Williams said, he seemed more intent upon revenge than upon flight.'

'And his ire was mainly directed against you, Jack? Does he blame you for his humiliation, do you suppose?'

'Plainly he does. Though it is not his threat of revenge but his reference to one who might help him accomplish it that intrigues me. I'd dearly like to know what he took from his pack and pocketed up before he left.'

The crunch of hooves in the hard snow announces the arrival of Latham with the horses.

Bancroft decides that the Sergeant shall take the road to Bruges and enquire around the town whilst he and I shall ride together in the other direction towards open country.

'You have the better mien to espy him by mingling with the crowd in town, Latham,' says he by way of explanation, 'Out in the open I'd wager he will have had to cut across country, for a lone traveller upon the road would be too conspicuous. Two pairs of eyes will prove better at discerning tracks in the snow.'

I have a feeling, however, that it is my company rather than my eyes that he has need of.

The afternoon is clear and bright as we set off from the camp, Latham direct to Bruges, along the road where the packed snow betrays no individual track, whilst Bancroft and I circumambulate our collection of tents before branching off in the most promising direction where a sheltering wood approaches within fifty yards of the camp boundary.

If Brogan wanted to avoid detection, this would be his most likely route.

Sure enough, just beyond the area trampled by many feet, two parallel channels mark where someone has trudged through the ankle deep snow.

After ten yards, it is clear that the tracks are heading direct to the edge of wood, which at its nearest point projects towards us in a kind of spur. To our left, it then fills out into a thick wall of trees. To the right, the spur recedes in an outward curving arc as far as the eye can see.

A few hundred yards along this curve I think I see a shadowy line upon the unblemished surface. I rein in my horse and shade my eyes against the dazzle of the snow.

'What is it, Jack?' enquires Bancroft.

'It looks like another set of tracks. It may be nothing, but I shall ride across just to be certain. If you continue to follow this track, I shall rejoin you at the edge of the wood, sir.'

Urging my steed into a trot, I head out across the snowy plain.

Sure enough, there is a scuffed track of hoof prints etched into the smooth surface. It comes from the direction of town and heads straight for the wood. A dozen or so yards beyond it is a similar track which on inspection suggests, by the depth of the hoof indentation and the profusion of the snow scatter, that the rider has made the return journey either in greater haste or with an added burden.

I follow the tracks to the point where they enter the trees which is about a quarter of a mile along the curve of the wood's edge from where Bancroft has arrived.

I canter along to join him and inform him of what I have found.

'So it was not flight, but an assignation?' asks Bancroft.

'It looks that way,' I reply. 'Though, as he has not returned to camp, it may be that he has continued his journey, either with the person he met, or alone. The horse's return tracks are deeper which might indicate a heavier load.'

'The rider entered the wood further along its perimeter, you say? Come, Jack, let's see if they met.'

The covering of snow on the ground under the trees being thinner and the footprints less distinct, we dismount and tether our horses, then continue to follow the trail on foot.

It is not many minutes before we have proof incontrovertible that Brogan has met with someone – but also that his journey ended here.

The first sign is an ominous creaking which, as we cautiously draw closer, we realise is coming from a large oak tree.

Suspended from the one of its mighty branches is a rope, and hanging at the end of the rope, swaying and rotating slowly in the breeze, is the body of Private Brogan.

'Dear God in Heaven,' mutters Bancroft despairingly, 'another dead man. What have I done to deserve this?'

I pity his distress. His first command, and already two violent deaths within his platoon! It is as if he sees his whole military career dissolving before his eyes.

Eyes which even now express desperation and helplessness. 'What do we do now, Jack?'

I know what I want to do, and I would prefer to do it without Bancroft's presence.

'Take courage, sir,' I say, taking him firmly by the shoulders. 'All is not lost. If you will fetch one of the horses hither, we may cut him down and carry him back to camp. This bears every mark of suicide, sir. It looks like he has taken his own life in a fit of remorse for Scatchard's death.'

'Brogan commit suicide?' He shakes his head in incomprehension. 'But what of his assignation with the horseman? The tracks you saw?'

'Probably just another traveller, sir, totally unconnected. It would appear the only assignation Brogan kept was with his Maker, sir. The knapsack and the greatcoat left behind – evidence, surely, that he knew he would not need them on the journey he intended to take?'

With a cry of relief, he clasps me tightly to him. 'Of course, that is how it must be! Oh, Jack, Jack! You see straight to the heart of the matter. What would I do without you!'

I submit self-consciously to his distraught embrace before gently pulling away. 'The horse - sir?' I remind him.

Flustered, he collects himself. 'Yes, yes – of course – we must carry him back to camp. Wait here, Jack, I shall make haste.'

Half running, he hurries away between the trees.

His departure gives me the opportunity I need to examine both the scene and the body.

Though I have done my best to persuade Bancroft that this is a suicide, I am far from convinced that a brute like Brogan knew the meaning of remorse, let alone would take his own life. And I do not think the unknown rider's tracks in the snow are mere coincidence.

Knowing I have not much time before Bancroft returns with the horse, I swiftly survey the tableau before me. The other end of the rope from which Brogan dangles is secured with two or three turns around the trunk of the tree and knotted just below a protrusion in the knobbly bark to prevent it slipping. It stretches taut up to a point on the overhead branch some three foot from the trunk, where it is twice looped about the branch.

Clambering up, I lean a little way along the trunk to see that the friction of the rope has scraped away the bark deep enough to reveal torn white wood beneath.

Greater damage than would be caused by a body, even of Brogan's bulk, just dropping and jerking. Scarring more consistent with a body being hauled up.

Regaining the ground, I examine the lower end of the rope. The loose end below the knot is cut cleanly and, on closer inspection I notice abrasions above and below the rope circling the trunk of the tree.

A brief exploration of the ground around the base of the tree confirms my suspicions.

This is no suicide, but a murder.

I have just taken out my knife to saw through the rope when Bancroft returns, leading one of the horses.

I direct him to take over the cutting whilst I take the strain of the rope. The body hangs too high for me to take its weight by clasping it. Nor would I wish to, as it is plain to see the britches are soiled with faeces. As it is, as soon as

Bancroft severs the last strand, the weight proves too much. I let go the rope and the body crumples with a thud to the ground.

Bending down, I start to ease the noose from around the neck. In doing so, I remark a peculiarity about the face I did not note before. The nose has in fact been cleanly sliced open, almost severed.

Bancroft, occupied in bringing the horse alongside has noticed nothing. In removing the noose, I drag it with deliberate clumsiness over the face. This has the effect of damaging the nose still further, thus obliterating the original mutilation. It is unlikely that anyone else will want to examine the corpse, but best to be on the safe side to avoid awkward questions.

As we manhandle the body onto the horse's back, I notice one more thing. There is a slit in the left side of Brogan's jacket just below his rib cage – just wide enough to have been caused by a dagger thrust to the heart.

None of this do I impart to First Lieutenant Bancroft. In the circumstances, it is convenient for both of us to maintain the fiction of suicide. I can see Bancroft has his doubts, not least in the way he looks assessingly at the distance Brogan's body has fallen and ponders how a suicide could hang himself so high. But he says nothing, either now or on the way back. I can understand why he chooses pragmatism over undue scrutiny. If Brogan has taken his own life, it provides a neat solution to a vexatious problem.

From my point of view, however, it is clear that Brogan has been murdered. The disturbed ground around the tree, the marks upon the trunk and the stab wound in his side – all are proof enough.

But the mutilation of the nose puzzles me. It seems designed to send a message.

I cannot conceive what that message may be, but I suspect it may be aimed at me, and I have a good idea who the messenger is.

Wharf

Next morning I accompany the carts and mules to the southern side of Bruges.

For the journey to Ghent, all the heavy supplies are to be transported by water on the canal that runs from Bruges to that city.

I noticed during our trip to the *Stadhuis* that there are numerous waterways within the town and as we circle the town walls, it is apparent that the whole city is like a vast castle surrounded not only by stone fortifications but by a huge moat of water as well.

The wharves lie outside the southern city gates and by the time the carters and muleteers from our platoon arrive, there is already a whole host of similar vehicles and beasts of burden from the ten other platoons being unloaded.

The Austrian army, it seems, is much more efficient at this sort of thing than we English and it is their adjutants who have taken command.

As our carts draw up, a brisk young man with waxed moustaches and a brusque manner demands my name and the name of my *Zugführer*. 'Ze commandant of your platoon,' he explains impatiently, seeing my look of incomprehension.

'First Lieutenant Bancroft,' I inform him.

He checks the name on a list. '*Ja, Oberleutnant Bencroft. Da drübe,*' he says curtly, directing me with a pointed finger where to take our supplies for transfer on to one of the countless barges lined up along the wharf.

The men heaving and hauling the bales and boxes with swift precision are all in Austrian uniform. Such tasks, it seems, are not to be entrusted to the tag and rag of vagabonds, felons and dabblers in military matters they take we English to be!

Realising my presence is superfluous in face of such daunting organisation, I stay only long enough to watch the first of our equipment loaded and note the name *Slanke Vos* upon the side of the barge allocated for our supplies before telling the carters and muleteers to make their own way back to camp once the loading is finished.

I set off on foot by the shorter route through the centre of town.

I know that, during my absence at the wharf, Bancroft will be assembling the men to tell them how Brogan, racked with remorse for his part in Scatchard's death and humiliated by his punishment, has taken his own life.

After conducting a short funeral service Bancroft intends to have the men watch him being interred in an unconsecrated grave – spades for latrines and hence for

Brogan's grave being among the basic essentials we carry with us for the next three days. He hopes thereby to deliver a salutary lesson and lay the matter as well as the offender to rest.

Having no great desire to witness any of this, I take my time wandering back through the streets of Bruges.

Busy with townsfolk going about their everyday business, the town takes on a different complexion from yesterday. Rather than seeming a sad reflection of its former glory, it strikes me as a town now at peace with itself, the peeling paint and cracked plaster as comfortable to its citizens as an old, familiar pair of slippers.

Away from the faded grandeur of the main square, the markets in the smaller squares are bustling. The piles of vegetables, stalls of meat and fish, the scolding huswifes and squealing children are so like those back home that I am almost overcome with a sudden longing for the well-known ways of London and my friends back at 6 Bow Street.

But, as I turn on to one of the wider highways where carts and horses rattle over the cobbles and the occasional coach and chair passes by, I am plucked from my reverie by a voice hailing me.

I look round to see a one-horse chaise draw to a halt. Holding the reins is Agnes Mayer.

Immediately, my melancholy mood evaporates.

'Ride with me, Master Archer,' she says as I step closer.

I scramble up to sit beside her and she flicks the reins to bid her horse trot on. The seat is so narrow that our bodies must needs be in contact from knee to shoulder. As we jog over the cobbles the swaying of the cart presses now her warm thigh, now her hip, now her arm against mine. We laugh in half apology at each soft, intimate collision.

'Sure, Miss Mayer, this meeting cannot be mere chance,' I say archly, 'have you been following me?'

'I have instructions from our joint master to follow the platoon and in following his orders, yes, it might be said I follow you,' she riddles teasingly. 'But as for this particular encounter, it is purely fortuitous.'

'A coincidence merely?' I say crestfallen.

'Let us say a *happy* coincidence,' she replies with a smile.

Turning into a quiet street, she brings the horse to a halt. Laying down the reins, she takes my hand in hers.

'How I wish, Will, that we might repeat our intimacy of five nights ago, but alas we must make do with brief encounters such as this. For the present we are hostages to fortune, to your enforced peregrinations and the whims of Sir William.'

I clasp her hand more tightly. 'The touch of our hands, Agnes, must act as a remembrance of that night – and a promise of what may be to come,' I say fervently. 'In the meantime our thoughts may enact what our bodies cannot.'

Were we not in an open carriage in a public street we might at this moment lean into a kiss, so intense is the feeling between us. But after a few heady seconds of gazing into each other's eyes, she breaks the spell by turning away.

I reciprocate by assuming a business-like air. 'I have news to report to Sir William.'

I recount in careful detail Brogan's disappearance and subsequent death whilst Agnes listens in concentration, using a small gold-tipped pencil to note the salient points in a little notebook.

'There is no doubt in my mind that he was murdered,' I tell her. 'Judging by the evidence at the scene, he met with someone who stabbed him, slit open his nose and hanged him. There was excessive damage to the branch from which he was suspended, marks around the trunk of the tree and surrounding earth, and the fastened end of the rope was freshly cut. I think the murderer flung the rope in a double loop over the branch, tied one end to his horse's pommel and, after securing the noose around Brogan's neck, hauled him up. Whether Brogan was dead by then, I don't know. My suspicion is that the knife thrust merely incapacitated him and that he was still alive when his face was cut – and when he was strung up.

'Once he was suspended, the murderer – judging by the

pattern of disturbance on the ground - led the horse two or three turns about the tree so that the trunk would bear the weight whilst he secured the rope. The abrasions around the trunk are what made me suspect Brogan was still alive at the time, for they were likely caused by his jerking about in his death throes. Once secured, the excess rope was severed and the murderer rode off.'

Pocketing up her notebook when I have concluded my account, she regards me solemnly. 'I see now why Sir William holds you in such high regard, Will Archer. You have a most observant eye and a questing mind.'

I give a diffident shrug. These are not necessarily the attributes I would have Agnes Mayer most admire about me. But for the moment her attention is upon the matter in hand. 'You think it was a pre-arranged meeting?' she asks.

'I know it,' I reply, 'for here is the proof.'

I take from my pocket a scrap of paper which I took from Brogan's pocket before surrendering the body to Latham on our return from the forest.

'His colleague, Williams, told us he left behind his pack and his greatcoat – but pocketed something from the pack before he went. '

Carefully, Agnes unfolds it and reads silently. 'This is directions when and where to meet, but it is not signed.'

'True, but I would hazard a guess that it is from Finn

Kelly, whom he met several times in Ostend. And,' I continue, 'from what Williams said of his foul mood when he left, I'd wager Brogan was going to ask Kelly to arrange an 'accident' for me. He thought to get his revenge, instead of which he met his own death.'

'You think Finn Kelly killed him because Brogan asked him to - kill you?' she asks with a sudden catch her voice as she realises the enormity of what she says.

'No,' I say gently, attempting to reassure her. 'I think Kelly came to the forest intending to kill Brogan. He had the rope and dagger with him. I believe Brogan – wittingly or not – had provided all the information Kelly wanted and had outlived his usefulness.' Then a sudden thought strikes me. 'But then, if Brogan talked of me – relating my part in his punishment and seeking to enlist Kelly's aid in punishing me - it maybe sealed his fate. In killing Brogan, Kelly found one last use for him....'

Agnes's brow furrows in puzzlement. 'One last use?'

As I articulate the thought, I begin to convince myself of its correctness. 'Finn Kelly would be reasonably sure that, even if I was not the one who actually found Brogan, I would ask to see his body. That's why he mutilated the nose – as warning to me.'

'A warning?'

'Aye, a most basic warning: keep your nose out!'

Canal

I arrive back to find the platoon already in marching order and as soon as final checks have been made, we set off to the Eastern gate of the town where we are to join forces with Hauptmann Bauer and Second Lieutenant Ward's platoons. The men march in column, five abreast, with Bancroft, Latham and myself riding in the vanguard whilst the carts, loaded much more lightly now with only our immediate provisions for the next three days, and the mules, enjoying a brief holiday from their burdens, bring up the rear.

At the request of the town burghers we do not march through the town, but around the perimeter of the walls.

Thus I am afforded no further glimpse of Agnes nor, if he still be here, Finn Kelly. Before we parted, Agnes questioned why Kelly should be tracking us.

'A curious watcher might ask the same of you,' I replied. 'We both know we answer to a master back in London. Perhaps Kelly, too, has a master to answer to, but who that master may be is a mystery we have yet to resolve.'

'The Irish insurgents who intend harm to King George?'

'Or mayhap he has allied himself with the Jacobite cause, or even the French.'

'And do you think, with Brogan's help, he has identified the traitor in your camp?'

'I think it likely, and I must work to find him out, too – whatever warnings Kelly may send me not to meddle!'

'I can do my part, too. Kelly does not know me. If you describe him to me, I shall keep watch for him on the road to Ghent and perhaps discover something of his business.'

Her suggestion makes me vastly uneasy. 'Do not approach him, Agnes, I beg you. He has great intelligence and charm, but he is a dangerous man. I counted him a friend once, yet he would have killed me and countless others without compunction for his cause.'

I took my leave of her, our fond endearments leavened with mutual exhortations to be cautious.

Now, as I trot towards the Eastern Gate of Bruges and see those who are to accompany us lined up, Bauer's platoon neat and orderly, Ward's, like our own, a little more tousled, I think of how Agnes and Finn Kelly will separately be shadowing our progress over the next days.

They will not need to follow in our footsteps alongside the canal as we keep pace with the transport barges. They will be able to travel along the road from Bruges to Ghent.

Whether they meet upon that road or not is a matter that is out of my control.

* * *

Precedence is established from the moment our three platoons rendezvous at the East Gate. Hauptmann Bauer takes command. His platoon will head the column, followed by ours, with Ward's bringing up the rear.

He, Bancroft and Bauer ride together at the front. All the baggage carts and mules follow on at the back. Latham and I continue to ride alongside our own platoon.

Inspecting the terrain as soon as we reach the canal, Hauptmann Bauer plans the best course of action.

The waterway, some fifteen feet wide, runs straight as an arrow into the far distance. It is bordered by a rough towpath of beaten earth inset with stones, along which a line of a dozen or so sturdy carthorses are already plodding, each towing a long, narrow barge laden with supplies.

Atop one or two of these, bargees loll, smoking long clay pipes or idly passing the time of day in a guttural sing-song accompanying the steady thud of hooves and the constant slap and plash of water.

Comprehending that we cannot share the towpath with these lumbering beasts, Bauer decides that we must march on the flat ground alongside it. Thus we may set our own pace.

It is clear that the contingent which set out earlier this morning has had the same idea. Trampled tussocks of grass stick raggedly above the remaining snow cover and a wide swathe of ground bears the imprint of innumerable boots.

Bauer orders us to reduce the length of our columns, and to proceed ten rather than five abreast to lessen further damage to the ground by spreading out the impact of our boots.

The recent snow has now all but gone, leaving a slippery surface on which we slither and lose our footing. Our boots churn up the mud and a persistent drizzling rain sets in mid-afternoon, compounding the problem.

By the time we encamp for the night, the men towards the rear of the column have been squelching through a quagmire of their comrades' making. We are muddied to our knees and above.

We pitch our tents in the lee of a copse of trees about twenty yards from the canal bank. The men from the different platoons have had little opportunity to mix during the day but during the business of unloading the carts, wrestling with damp canvas and scavenging for firewood a tentative fellowship develops. Coarse jests are exchanged, insults thrown and mutual acquaintance found between Ward's men and our own. The Austrians are more reticent and polite, but whilst most keep themselves to themselves, a dozen or more attempt friendly overtures.

By the time the smell of cooking and wood smoke begins to permeate the evening air there is the beginning of a feeling that we are all becoming part of one big troop rather than three separate units.

Bancroft, Bauer and Ward dine together, if the potage of dried meat and turnips accompanied by hunks of black bread that I and Bauer's adjutant, Fritz, prepare for them may be called dining.

After dinner, pipes and liquor are produced. Bancroft usually only takes a glass of port after his meal, but when Bauer produces a bottle of fierce colourless spirit which he calls *Jenever*, he and Second Lieutenant Ward politely accept the invitation.

Fritz and I leave them to it, retiring to finish off the remains of the stew and bread.

Fritz Dorn, blond haired and blue-eyed with frank, square-jawed features, is nineteen and he hails from a military family. His father fought the Spanish and the Ottomans back in the 1720's and his two older brothers were at Mollwitz and Chotusitz under Marshal Neipperg.

He is a pleasant enough young man and I look forward to his company in the days and weeks ahead. For the moment, though, I have existing friendships to nurture.

I find Tom Hooper, Josh Barley and Ben Woodrow in company with a couple of men from Second Lieutenant Ward's platoon and an Austrian soldier.

'Franz was at Mollwitz fighting against the Proosians,'

Tom tells me.

'Ve should have vun dat battle,' says Franz. 'Ve vere de stronger side. Our cavalry scattered de enemy. Even King Frederick himself ran avay. But Schwerin vould not admit defeat and it vos de Prussian muskets vich did for us. Many friends I lost dat day.'

'Lucky for us that the Prussians decided to come to terms with the Empress, then,' says Ben Woodrow. 'They are a formidable fighting force, 'tis said.'

'Ve Austrians, ve rely too much on de cavalry. Men on horses, dey are no match for de Prussian infantry and their musket fire.'

'And what about the French?' asks one of Ward's men. 'Are they good fighters?'

'Die Fransozen? Pah!' exclaims Franz in disgust. 'Dey may be good dancers, but dey are not soldiers.'

'That's all to the good, then,' laughs Tom Hooper. 'While they're tripping their allemande, we can mow 'em down wi' our muskets!'

'Say, Jack!' interrupts Ben Woodrow, turning to me. 'Has the King landed yet?'

'Nay, Ben,' I reply with a laugh, 'you know I cannot tell you that. But, between ourselves, 'tis rumoured that he is on his way to Hanover to meet with the Austrian commanders.'

'Naught new there, then,' scoffs Hooper. 'The King

spends more time in Hanover than he does in England!'

As the laughter subsides, Josh Barley asks, 'Is it true, Jack, that you were the one who found Brogan? Did he really hang himself?'

'Why do you ask? Do you not believe he is dead?' I say, making light of it.

'I'd sooner believe someone killed the bastard,' says Hooper. 'I'd've done it myself, given half a chance.'

'Well, you heard what Lieutenant Bancroft said. He took his own life in a fit of remorse for driving Scatchard to commit suicide.'

'Remorse, my arse!' retorts Hooper scornfully. 'No one swallows that, Jack. 'Tis common knowledge that he murdered Scatchard and then someone murdered him. Come clean, Jack, who was it? Whoever it was deserves a medal.'

'If I knew the truth of the matter, I'd give him a medal myself,' I laugh, 'but truly, I know no more than you, and until 'tis proved otherwise, we must accept the official version of his death.'

'Aha!' whoops Tom. 'So you admit you have your doubts?'

'Our platoon commander says it was suicide, and who are we to doubt him?' I say disingenuously.

'And you accuse me of lawyerly equivocation!' says Ben Woodrow wryly. 'It's clear that Bancroft wants the matter closed, and who can blame him? 'Twould only make the men restless to think we have a killer loose amongst us. But who's to say it's one of our platoon?'

'You're not accusing us?' protests one of Ward's men, scandalised. 'We never knew the man.'

'Nay,' laughs Ben, then turns to Tom and me. 'But do you two not remember that day in Ostend when we came upon Brogan hugger-mugger with that hooded stranger? Mayhap 'tis him?'

He says it in jest, but it is nearer the mark than I like.

I answer in the same teasing vein. 'For sure, Ben, I think you've hit it! Your lawyer's acumen perceives things that we don't. Well, friends,' I say, getting up to go, to avoid further questions, 'if some brigand be following us, 'tis best we all be on the *qui vive.* Who knows which one of us he will pick off next?'

'You may joke about it,' replies Woodrow, 'but it is a possibility, is it not?'

'If so,' I quip, assuming an air of mock authority, 'as your Corporal, I command you to report any suspicious behaviour to me immediately. Goodnight, my friends. Sleep well in your billets tonight and pray for more clement weather tomorrow.'

Whatever prayers may have been said, they go for naught as

far as the weather is concerned.

The next two days are a relentless trudge through mud and rain. Marching in damp clothes and sleeping between damp blankets, our bodies begin to fester and our bones ache with the penetrating cold.

A thick haze hangs over the waters of the canal, half obscuring the barges as they labour along, wallowing like misshapen leviathans. The lumbering beasts that pull them, heads down, flanks steaming, plod with unrelenting doggedness through a dripping, dun-coloured landscape.

They plough on regardless, but the progress of those of us on foot is more erratic, continually interrupted by the shouts of the carters from behind whenever a wheel sinks fast into the mud. I do not know whether, in commissioning the barges, those in command foresaw this state of affairs but it is fortunate that the bulk of our equipment and supplies is on water which is not subject to these frequent stoppages.

Such minor calamities, however, provide a welcome diversion from the interminable trudging. With jeering exuberance, the men break ranks and pile behind the cart, putting their shoulders to the boards, heaving with many an oath and ribaldry. Sometimes the great wooden wheels respond, squelching with a mighty sucking sound from their muddy prison. At others, stones and broken boughs must be found to provide purchase in the sludgy mire.

But as well as the ragged cheers that accompany each rescue from the ooze, there is the increasingly persistent sound of coughing as the cold and damp seep into lungs breeding phlegm and agues.

We have no medical aid. The invalids must shift for themselves, first limping, then hobbling, until by the end of the second day, there are half a dozen fellows lying on the carts among the mounds of damp canvas. Unable to march, either because their lungs are too congested to gulp in the dank air, or because of suppurating sores caused by skin peeling from foetid, clammy feet.

Meanwhile, we trudge on through the mud and mire in the hope that there will be rest – maybe even an army surgeon – when we finally arrive at Ghent.

Ghent

Our hopes are realised beyond all expectation. In Ghent for the first time we are housed in proper barracks.

It has taken us nigh on five days to cover a distance which would have taken barely two and a half in favourable conditions. As we tramp wearily towards the city walls, we fully expect our first task to be the unloading of our tents from the barges. We can hardly believe it when, instead, we receive orders to proceed to what looks like a castle situated on a spur of land almost surrounded by water on the south side of the city. After weeks sleeping in barns and byres or out in the open, the prospect of solid stone walls and indoor fires is like a vision of heaven.

The fortress stands upon the site of an old abbey, of which only a few buildings and ruined walls remain, near overpowered by forbidding rows of military barracks. Once home to a garrison of over two thousand troops in the time of the Holy Roman Emperor Charles V, it is now much depleted. The hundred or so Austrian troops permanently stationed here occupy only a small portion of the place, leaving more than enough for us.

This historical information is vouchsafed by the eager young soldier who directs us to the quarters which are to be ours for the next few nights.

With the efficiency I have come to expect of our Austrian allies, each contingent of the travelling army is allocated its own accommodation within the fortress. The platoons that started out ahead of us are already housed. Those that are following on are due to arrive tomorrow. Yet even with an influx of about 1000 men to add to the hundred permanent inhabitants, there is space enough and to spare.

Each platoon has a large dormitory complete with the luxury of straw pallets and blankets for the men. Bancroft, Bauer and Ward have rooms to themselves and I choose to share a room with Fritz Dorn, Hauptmann Bauer's ADC.

Sergeant Latham, with whom I might be expected to share, expresses himself well satisfied to share with the sergeant from Second Lieutenant Ward's platoon. It is, I think, despite military convention, an arrangement congenial to both of us.

In addition, all platoons are given use of a vast dining hall which may once have been the Abbey refectory, its wood panelling sadly defaced by successive generations of soldiers and the ravages of time. There are trestle tables and stoves and a selection of iron cooking pots, but the food and eating utensils we must provide for ourselves.

Within minutes of our arrival, our spirits are noticeably lifted. The injured and the ill from the journey have been housed in the infirmary. Provisions have been unpacked and the stoves lit and soon the savoury smell of boiling meat is filling the vast cavern of the dining hall, together with the sound of lively talk and laughter.

Taking a small area on one of the stoves to prepare our senior officers' meal, Dorn and I notice that in the general hubbub, it is no longer easy to distinguish the men of one platoon from another. The comradeship between our three platoons that has been established during the hardship of the last few days is now beginning to extend by means of shared reminiscence with the men from other platoons.

By the time we return to eat our supper in the dining hall, it is clear that friendships are growing and inhibitions being shed. Secret caches of liquor have appeared from packs and are being shared. Sodden clothes have been discarded and hang, steaming ripely, around the still warm stoves. Most of the men sit wrapped in blankets brought from the dormitory, but a few shameless fellows loll totally naked, laughing and chatting astride the wooden benches.

It does not worry me, I have seen enough naked bodies at Mother Ransom's Molly House and they do not embarrass me. I notice, however, that Fritz Dorn's lips are pursed in disapproval.

'Does their nudity offend you?' I ask.

'*Nein*, it is not *die nacktheit* – de nakedness. Dat is

natural. But de drinking I do not like. Ven men are *berauscht* – how you say, drunken? - they *der grobian* become.'

I guess his meaning. Fuelled by liquor, some coarse louts have become not only rowdy, but argumentative. The more contentious quarrels are quickly quelled by their more sober fellows, but in laughing off the pugnacity a certain amount of ribald horseplay is developing. Supposing my companion to have had a disciplined and civil upbringing, I can see such unrestrained, boorish behaviour must be distasteful to his sensibilities.

As soon as we have finished our repast, therefore, I suggest we retire to our room. I have to clean and prepare Bancroft's boots and linen ready for tomorrow and I presume Dorn has similar duties. While I draw a pail of water at the pump, put it to heat on a stove and rinse our plates, he returns to our room.

By the time I arrive with the hot water, I find he has lit a fire in the small hearth and has laid out our senior officers' attire ready for cleaning. To my surprise, he then strips off his own clothes and adds them to the collection bidding me do the same.

'*Sauberkeit ist das halbe Leben,*' he says with a serious smile. 'How you say in English, to be clean is to be...?'

'Cleanliness is next to godliness,' I say, pulling my shirt

over my head.

'*Ja das ist es,*' he beams, then wrinkles his nose in distaste. 'Faugh, Jack Weaver, *mein guter kerl, du stinkst!*'

And, to be sure, now the combined odour of sweat and sodden clothes and horse flesh from the last five days is released, he has a point. In fact I have not had a proper wash since leaving the van Andels' house in Ostend nigh on a fortnight ago. God alone knows what Agnes must have thought when we met at Bruges! No wonder she confined her endearments to just holding my hand!

'Come, before ve vash der clothes, we must vash ourselves. See,' he says, reaching into his pack, 'I have soap! I vill go first, I do not vant your smell upon me!'

Soaking a cloth in the warm water, he proceeds to wipe himself down. After a few moments, he hands the cloth to me. 'I cannot reach my back.'

Obediently I take it and wash his back. And, as I do so, I notice pale ridges on his skin, like the healed scars of a flogging. Feeling me lessen my pressure, he says, '*Mein vater,* he beat us, my brothers and me. Make us proper men, good soldiers.' It is almost a boast. 'Now, come,' says he, taking the cloth from me. 'I vash you.'

Rubbing the waxy lump of soap on the wet cloth, he proceeds to rub my chest and back with vigour. After a brief foray along my arms and down my legs, he rinses out the cloth, soaps it again and orders me to stand up straight with my arms above my head, before setting to work upon my armpits.

Professing himself satisfied, he douses the cloth in the pail and wrings it out then stands back to assess his handiwork, one unbidden result of which attracts his eye.

'Ha,' he observes, 'you think *deine liebste* – how you say, lady-friend – washes you, *dein Schwanz ist steif!* It, too, demands attention.' And, with brisk Teutonic efficiency, he wraps the wet cloth round his hand and applies himself to the relief of my erect little soldier. It takes but two minutes and is done in such a matter-of-fact, detached way, as if but a customary part of the general ablution, that there is no sense of embarrassment.

At the end, I feel it only polite to ask if he wants me to do the same for him. '*Nein, danke,* Jack. As you see, I have no need.'

So, turning our attention to the array of muddy boots, dusty coats and crumpled linen, we spend the next hour companionably enough polishing and scrubbing, oblivious of the fact that we are both sitting there completely naked.

When we eventually sink onto our straw pallets and fold our blankets around us, the boots are neatly lined up, gleaming, the coats hanging, well brushed, and the damp linen drying before the fire.

As I drift off to sleep, I think what a strange fellow my new room mate has turned out to be. Fastidious in manner, efficient in his duties and so idiosyncratical in his views upon violence and intimate contact that I find him difficult to fathom. Is it youth and inexperience that makes him so passionless, or is it simply his Teutonic temperament?

In the morning, he is gone before I wake up. It is not yet light, but his palliasse is shaken and his blanket folded.

All items of uniform belonging to him and Hauptmann Bauer are gone and, to my amazement, mine and First Lieutenant Bancroft's are neatly smoothed and folded. *A gesture of friendship – or just more Teutonic efficiency?*

I knuckle the sleep from my eyes and hastily don my uniform. It cannot be denied that both it and I smell and feel all the better for our last night's laundering.

I find Lieutenant Bancroft still asleep. Too intimate acquaintance with Hauptmann Bauer's bottle of *jenever* has made this a common occurrence of late, causing him to awaken tetchy and dark-eyed.

As he responds to my presence, the coverlet on his truckle bed slips off and he rolls over, still begunk with sleep, his under-drawers barely concealing the priapism common to most men on first waking.

Secretly smiling, I toy with the idea of emulating Fritz as

part of my ADC duties, but instantly dismiss it, suspecting that, whilst it may not be incompatible with his secret inclinations, it would offend his English reserve. Instead, I respectfully avert my eyes as he adjusts himself.

'Good morning, Jack,' says he as I hand him his shirt and britches, 'I trust you had a good night.'

'Yes, sir. And you?'

'Slept like a log. There is much to be said for stone walls and a decent bed.'

As I oil his face and shave him, he informs me that we shall be staying for three days here in Ghent.

'Our force is not yet all assembled. So we shall have time to recover our strength and prepare for the next stage. We are to receive further orders from the battalion commander, General Clayton, tomorrow or the day after. I shall address our men this morning to impress upon them the importance of comporting themselves well whilst we are here in Ghent.'

'Does that mean we are free to go into the town?'

'If you so wish, Jack.'

After fetching him his breakfast and completing such other tasks as he deems necessary, I take him at his word and set out to explore the town.

It is a fine, bright morning with a frisky breeze ruffling the surface of the water which surrounds the castle.

Arriving in dusk and drizzling rain yesterday, my only impression was of high, looming walls lost in mist. But this morning, I am able to see the full scale of the citadel.

Almost the size of a small town, its numerous buildings, including some which by their ancient pillars and arched windows I guess to be those preserved from the old abbey, are enclosed within high walls in the form of a vast square protected on all sides by a wide moat. As I cross a wooden bridge to the far bank I note that each corner of the castle is defended by projecting square built bastions.

In its heyday I imagine it would have been a well-nigh impregnable fortress but now it is in some disrepair. Sections of wall look to have been demolished and rebuilt and the foundations are in places being eroded by the water.

Walking on into the town itself, it is clear that Ghent is a prosperous place. The high gabled, five and six-storey, flat-fronted houses, their red brick walls and stone friezes glowing in the winter sunshine, speak of a merchant wealth long departed from its neighbour, Bruges.

Whereas the smaller town spoke of former glory, Ghent speaks of present day commerce. The cobbled streets are alive with richly dressed folk going about their everyday business, the market stalls piled high with fresh produce.

Unlike Bruges, where people slunk past trying to avoid the notice of fellows in uniform, here almost every second person smiles and wishes me good-day. It is not long before I am responding with a cheery *'Guten tag,'* as if I were a native of the place.

The main square is crowded with merchants discussing business, housewives gossiping over the best bargains whilst stallholders shout their wares. As in every prosperous town, there are also numerous beggars pleading for alms and street-hawkers eager to sell me laces or lavender for my lady-love. The language may be strange, but the meaning is clear.

I also notice one or two ragged children sidling amongst the crowd and immediately my thoughts fly back to London and to Charlie's pickpocket friends, the boys who live on the streets scratching a living on the fringes of the criminal underworld.

It is because I am thus distracted that I am caught unawares.

A stranger brushes closer than is normal and suddenly I feel something press against my side. The jab of a knife-point is unmistakable.

'Do not struggle,' mutters a guttural accented voice in my ear. *'Schreeuw niet uit* - do not shout out.'

Without removing the knife from my side, he takes a firm grip upon my elbow and compels me to walk alongside him. Turning to look at him, I see a grim, expressionless face, dark with stubble. For a brief moment, two gimlet-like eyes issue a further silent warning, then are fixed implacably ahead. Together we stroll out of the square for all the world like close friends – intimate, yet unspeaking.

But though no words are spoken, my thoughts race volubly. *Am I being kidnapped? Has my companion a grudge against foreign troops on his native soil?*

Or is this Finn Kelly's work?

Then, with a sinking feeling of dread, another thought crashes in on me. With all that has occurred during the last few weeks, I have all but forgotten that I am not only the hunter but also the hunted. My very presence here stems from that fact. *Could this swarthy fellow be an agent of my unknown enemy from Leicester House intent on silencing me for good?*

As we turn a corner, I berate myself for my lack of vigilance.

A coach waits, its blinds drawn. My unwanted escort propels me towards it.

Fearing that if I get in, I may never get out again, I try to stall. But his grip on my elbow is vice-like and he jabs me sharply with the knife. I feel the sharp point penetrate the cloth of my coat. Another deeper thrust under my ribs and I could be a dead man.

Arrived at the coach, he quickly releases my arm but

swings round behind me, putting me between him and the vehicle, using his body and the continued pressure of the knife to prevent my escape. He gives three sharp raps upon the door, which immediately swings open.

'In,' he orders.

I have little choice but to obey.

I climb into the dark interior and the stranger slams the door after me.

Secrecy

'My apologies for the overdramatic nature of our meeting, Master Archer, but secrecy is of the essence,' says the occupant of the carriage as I sink into the seat opposite him.

With a jerk the coach sets off, jolting over the cobbles, its rhythm gradually increasing as that of my pounding heart lessens.

'You look pale, Will. My messenger did you no injury, I hope? Gerard has, I'm afraid, a tendency to be over-zealous in the execution of orders. I have had to speak to him about it before.'

Sir William Hervey, England's feared spymaster-in-chief, sits facing me as wryly urbane as ever. He holds my life in thrall, yet I am unaccountably relieved to see him.

He, at least, is the devil I know.

'He has done me no physical hurt, Sir William,' I reply, 'though his manner of accosting me was, I admit, somewhat perturbing.'

'But necessary, I'm afraid,' says he, airily. 'It would not do for you and I to be seen together. To all intents and purposes *I* am not here. Also, I have your safety to consider.'

'My safety, sir?'

'Aye, Will. I fear we may be dealing with men who,

having a great quarry in their sights, will think no more of killing anyone who gets in their way than of crushing a bug beneath their heel.'

'And I am that bug?'

'I fear you may be.'

'It behoves me not to get in their way, then,' say I attempting to make light of it.

Sir William, however, is in no mood for levity. 'If what our mutual friend, Miss Mayer, tells me is correct, Will, I think it may already be too late. What she has relayed causes me some concern, but I would be grateful to have it from your own lips. Begin with this fellow Brogan, he is dead you say?'

'Yes, Sir William, it has been given out that he hanged himself in remorse for causing one of his cronies, one Ned Scatchard, to do away with himself.'

'But you think otherwise?'

'I believe both were murdered, sir.'

'Aye, very like. Tell me about the first man – what was his name?'

'Ned Scatchard. He was found stabbed with a knife that belonged to Brogan. A knife which Brogan said had been stolen from him.'

'Stolen by whom?'

'An honest fellow called Ben Woodrow. He has an

unsightly birthmark covering a large portion of his face, a disfigurement which caused Brogan to pick on him from the very first day. I and another colleague, Tom Hooper, rescued him on that occasion. Since when he has shown a humane and selfless disposition, first by speaking on behalf of a hapless fellow, Josh Barley, who was being flogged for mere clumsiness. Then by expressing no vindictiveness towards Brogan, even after suffering incarceration on the basis of the villain's ill-founded accusations. Indeed, he expressed a desire that Brogan would be treated justly, despite all the ill usage he had suffered at his hands.'

'This Woodrow sounds a veritable saint,' observes Hervey sardonically.

'He has suffered much through no fault of his own, Sir William. His facial deformity has made him prey not only to bully-ruffians, but also to learned men who should know better,' I say, somewhat needled by his sarcasm. 'He is trained as a lawyer, but briefs have been hard to come by.'

'Hmm,' says Sir William. 'Such treatment might do much to make a man bitter. You're sure your friendship is not blinding you to the fact that he might be the murderer?'

The suggestion offends me, but I reply with as much impartiality as I can, 'Certainly he came under suspicion, Sir William, but investigation proved he had not the opportunity for either murder. He was under guard when

Scatchard died and in the company of others when Brogan was killed. Besides, he has not the physical strength to overcome men so much more powerfully built than he.'

'Well, well, I accept your judgement,' says Hervey, unconvinced. 'So, if it wasn't this Woodrow fellow, who do you think it was?'

'As for Scatchard, I do not know. The weapon, Brogan's knife, would seem to implicate Brogan himself, but he cannot have done it. It was a left-handed blow and Brogan was right-handed.'

'Might he have induced another to commit the deed?'

'It is possible, but with his own death following so soon after, I persuaded my commanding officer it would be expedient to promulgate the theory of a double suicide.'

'A neat and effective solution - which I'm sure no-one believed - but which none would question for fear of possible reprisals. Military discipline is a wonderful thing!' says he sarcastically. 'Now tell me how and why you believe Brogan was killed.'

From the swaying of the coach I guess we have left the cobbled streets of the town and are upon the highroad outside the walls. I cannot think that we are headed for any destination in particular, only that Sir William has ordered the driver to keep moving in order not to attract attention.

I recount all the circumstances of Brogan's death and

how the evidence at the scene pointed to it being murder.

'And you think Finn Kelly was responsible for Brogan's death, but not for Scatchard's?' asks Hervey when I have finished. 'Tell me why.'

'Brogan met Kelly on several occasions while we were in Ostend. According to Brogan, Kelly had assigned him the task of finding a 'friend' whom he said may be in our platoon.'

'Might this 'friend' be an accomplice in some plot being hatched by Kelly?' ponders Hervey. 'Could he be Ned Scatchard's killer? He would have had the access that Kelly did not.'

'I am at a loss to know why Scatchard should have been killed,' I reply. 'He was by all accounts a god-fearing man who did harm to no-one. I can think of nothing that might connect him to Finn Kelly, let alone any reason Kelly might have to kill him. Besides, we do not know if Finn Kelly actually made contact with the 'friend' he was seeking.'

'In which case, it may be that this 'friend' is not an accomplice but rather an enemy whom Kelly seeks to eliminate. In either case, it is likely that if Kelly did, as you suggest, kill Brogan, it was because he knew too much.'

'I can only guess that was his motive, Sir William. But of one thing I am certain - after recognising me at a chance encounter in Ostend, Kelly has given me what I take to be two warnings not to meddle in his affairs.'

'And what do you suppose these 'affairs' to be, Master Archer?' inquires Sir William with a quizzical expression.

I recognise this look. He is testing me to see how much I understand or have deduced and expects me to speak plainly. Perception he will applaud, misconception he will remedy – but failure to theorize he will not forgive. Wrong or right, therefore, I plunge in headlong.

'The last time we encountered Kelly, he was planning an outrage against what he sees as English oppression in Ireland. On that occasion he failed.'

'Thanks in no small part to yourself,' interrupts Sir William, 'which gives him reason enough to be hostile towards you, and yet,' says he with an enigmatic smile, 'perhaps also to respect you.'

'Respect me, sir?' I exclaim, nonplussed.

'He could just as easily have slipped a knife between your ribs as whisper a warning in your ear when your friend in Ostend was haggling with the drover,' he says shrewdly. 'Perhaps we have misjudged him. Might his warning have been not so much a threat to a potential enemy as advice to someone he sees as a possible friend?'

'As to that, sir, I admit the same thought crossed my mind. Indeed, when we first met back in Dublin last year, he impressed me favourably. But any chance of friendship was surely destroyed by his subsequent actions.'

'He tried to kill you, yes. But then you *had* just foiled his plans...,' muses Sir William. 'So who knows? There is a saying, is there not, mine enemy's enemy is my friend? But continue, Will, to expatiate upon what you think him to be about.'

He has put me off my stride somewhat. However, I gather my thoughts and continue.

'I surmise that Kelly's antipathy towards the English encompasses the monarchy and all symbols of authority, of which the Army is one. It is possible he is plotting some act of violence against the troops, or a high-ranking officer. Even against His Majesty himself, if he is aware that he intends to lead the army into battle.'

'You think Kelly is working for himself, then? You don't think he is an agent for others who may wish His Majesty harm?'

'If you mean the French, Sir William, or the Jacobite sympathisers, I cannot see either of them serving his turn. From what I know of Kelly, Ireland is his main concern. To relieve his fellow countrymen from the yoke of English tyranny, personified by absentee landlords. There may, I suppose, be many connected with such personages among the commanding officers, one of whom Kelly may have in his sights.'

'I shall get Nathaniel to check the army lists.'

'As to your point of mine enemy's enemy being my friend, Sir William,' I add, 'whilst I admit to some sympathy with his views upon Irish oppression, I cannot see how, in view of our shared history, he would regard me as an ally.'

'Hmm,' he ponders with a sly twinkle, 'sympathy for the oppressed Irish, indeed! I shall pretend I did not hear those subversive views.'

He considers for a while in a silence broken only by the steady thud of the horses' hooves and the creaking of the coach. After a few moments he says, 'I am inclined to agree with you about Finn Kelly, Will. But the 'friend' is a different matter. I cannot think him an ally of Kelly, but nor can I see in what respects he is his enemy. But,' says he briskly, changing the subject, 'let that rest for the present. Miss Mayer has told you, I believe, that there are grave reservations at home about the King's determination to lead his troops into battle?'

'She has, sir.'

'He hopes, I think, to improve his standing with the people. But if anyone benefits in that respect, it is more like to be the Prince of Wales who will, I think, make much of his father's absence and would, I don't doubt, not grieve overmuch were his father to meet with some misfortune upon the battlefield.'

'Sure, Sir William, you do not suggest that Prince Frederick would conspire against His Majesty?' say I appalled. 'No son could be so unnatural as to contrive a father's death.'

'No ordinary son, no. But you know the hatred that exists between them.' He purses his lips in thought. 'However, you may be right. I would not put it past the King to harbour such sentiments – he has, indeed, expressed a desire to have his son dead before now – but Prince Frederick is of a different nature. I cannot see him actively plotting the King's death. No, there are more likely candidates.'

'The Jacobites, sir?'

He nods, 'Aye, Will, they are champing at the bit, but because their allies, the French, are engaged in European wars at present they cannot take open advantage. They need the French to help mount an invasion. The King's decision to lead his army into battle is a godsend to them...'

'Because King George may die on the battlefield?'

'Exactly! But they will not wish to leave such an opportunity to chance. I suspect they also have a second string to their bow. As you well know, they have already tried and failed at Kensington Palace.'

'Have you proof positive, Sir William, that the attempt on His Majesty's life which we foiled there was a Jacobite plot?'

'As positive as I need, Will. And I am certain that your abduction was a direct result of you frustrating their plan. I know now that it was someone from Leicester House who arranged your kidnapping, but I haven't yet discovered his name.'

'If it will help you in your search, Sir William, I can tell you he has a liking for rosewater perfume. I smelt it both at the attempt to drown me in the sewer and again when he set his ruffians to abduct me.'

'Is that so?' He nods with interest. 'Well that will help narrow the field. If only a little - for half the *beau monde* in London smell of the stuff!'

A change in the motion of the coach tells me that we are once again upon the cobbles of the town streets. My interview with Sir William must be near its end. He, too, seems struck with a new urgency.

'To return to this 'friend' whom Kelly is trying to track down,' he says, briskly. 'I do not believe he is an accomplice. Whatever Finn Kelly is plotting, we agree, from what we know of him, he plots it alone. The 'friend', therefore, is more likely someone whom Kelly fears will frustrate his plans.'

'If that is so, then surely the 'friend' must be on our side?'

'Ha, you are over trustful, Will. Being Kelly's enemy does not make him our friend. What if both aim at the same target, eh, but for different reasons? My informants tell me there is a spy – perhaps more than one – among our troops, whether working for the French or for the Jacobites, I do not know. But in truth, they may be considered one and the same for, just as King Louis espouses their cause, so they, in turn, solicit his help to accomplish their ends. This spy's task may be simply to collect and secretly convey intelligence, but I have reason to believe it is much more than that.'

I immediately see where he is leading. 'You think both he and Kelly plan to assassinate the King?'

'That is my fear, Will. If His Majesty is the 'great quarry' I mentioned at the start, I need you more than ever to be my eyes and ears. It will be dangerous work. As I said, they will not hesitate to destroy anyone they see as an obstacle in their path. If they should discover either you or Miss Mayer are working for me, your lives will not be worth a fig.'

My heart gives a great lurch as I recall what Agnes said when last we parted. *If she has, indeed, made contact with Finn Kelly, she may even now be in mortal danger.*

'I shall have a care both for Miss Mayer and for my own safety, sir,' I say determinedly. 'And I have the additional security that my real identity is not known. All who know me, know me only as Jack Weaver.'

'Aye, ' says Sir William solemnly, 'but that may not offer the security you hope. Kelly has already recognised you -

and remember who gave you that name in the first place.'

'Of course,' I say, realising the implications of what he has just said, 'the unknown Jacobite sympathiser from Leicester House! He gave that name to the ruffians who abducted me.'

'You must proceed with great circumspection, Will, for if the 'friend' and the suspected spy in the camp are one and the same, and if he has reason to pass your name on to his masters...'

I complete his thought, '...it may come to the notice of our unknown gentleman at Leicester House, who will undoubtedly give orders for me to be disposed of.'

Sir William Hervey leans forward and gives three sharp raps upon the roof of the coach.

As it draws to a halt, he tells me that Agnes Mayer is already arrived in Ghent and will contact me before our regiment leaves. He also tells me that he has assigned Gerard, the fearsome guide who brought me here, to be her coachman and guardian for the remainder of the route. News that I must admit affords me comfort and jealousy in equal measure.

Then, with a final exhortation to caution and, having ascertained the coast is clear, Sir William deposits me back into a side street in Ghent.

Discussion

Shortly after I've alighted from Sir William's coach I run into Fritz Dorn in the market, carrying parcels of meat and fresh vegetables for our senior officers' evening meal. We spend a pleasant hour together before returning to the *Spanjaardenkasteel - the Spaniards' Castle* - which he tells me is the name of the fortress in which we are billeted.

As more platoons have arrived, cooking meals for the troops is becoming a more organised affair, delegated to a handful of men with some culinary experience, but they have to work either with the dried supplies we carry with us, or scour the local market for produce affordable within the meagre budget they are allowed.

First Lieutenant Bancroft pays out of his own pocket for slightly better fare and I presume, judging by the quality of the produce purchased by Fritz, the same is true of Hauptmann Bauer and the other platoon commanders.

Just as I presume that other ADCs such as Fritz and myself who prepare their meals also claim our share of the pickings from their masters' tables.

How long I shall continue to enjoy this perquisite I cannot tell for, as our numbers grow, so my duties as Bancroft's adjutant will inevitably decrease. No longer will I personally have to dole out weekly wages, order in provisions, keep a record of ordnance or provide occasional medical help. The needs of the fifty-odd men in our original platoon are already being subsumed within the ever-growing regiment and will soon become the responsibility of commissaries in charge of pay, transport, supplies, medical care and all requirements of moving, quartering and supplying troops.

I shall be reduced to little more than Bancroft's personal cook and valet. Perhaps Sergeant Latham's sour predictions about the limits of my usefulness to my seniors will soon be realised?

Not that I complain, for it allows me more time with my friends who, upon my returning to the castle, I find engaged in a raucous card game of Sixty Six with two or three Austrians who insist on calling it *Schnapsen*.

They are playing in the open air on a trestle table set up just outside the dormitory block and have attracted a small crowd of onlookers. The afternoon sun, though sinking towards the horizon, is still warm and most are in shirtsleeves and britches. Other items of uniform are draped over walls and bushes.

'Been taking the opportunity to freshen 'em up in the moat,' says Hooper over his shoulder, his attention not shifting from the cards in his hand.

'Aye, I saw some men as I came over the bridge,' I reply, 'on the bank, scrubbing away. Lucky the water's clean.'

'The moat must be fed from the river,' says Ben Woodrow, 'for 'tis running, not stagnant, water. 'Twas our Austrian friends who led the way. They have a greater regard, it seems, for hygiene than most of our compatriots.'

'They shamed you into it, did they, Tom?' I ask jokingly.

But Hooper is not listening for with a whoop he signals that he has won the hand.

Josh Barley throws his cards disconsolately into the middle of the table. 'Nay, this game's too ticklish for me, I have not the wit. Can we not play something simpler?'

'Faugh!' exclaims Tom Hooper, 'Sit the next round out, then. Jack can supply your place.'

He beckons me to take Barley's place but I decline, holding up my hands in apology. 'Sorry, Tom,' I say, 'I have not the time. I must attend upon Lieutenant Bancroft shortly.'

'Why, you are as much use a castrated bull's pizzle!' he laughs good-humouredly, then looks round at the onlookers. 'Anyone care to join in?'

Ben Woodrow, seeing that there are more than a couple of volunteers, offers his place to one and gets up from the table.

'Shall we take the air awhile, Jack? I am in sore need of

intelligent conversation,' says he with a sideways look at Hooper who is busy dealing out the cards.

In response, Hooper merely holds up his middle finger in an obscene gesture, without either looking at us or missing a beat in his dealing.

Woodrow and I walk off, laughing.

But the laughter does not last for long, for Ben is in a pensive mood.

'What are we here for, Jack?' he says as soon as we are out of earshot.

I misunderstand him. 'You suggested we walk awhile,' I reply, puzzled.

'Yes, but why are we *here* in Flanders – about to fight and possibly die, and for what purpose?'

I look sidelong at him and see he is troubled. I do not know how to reply. But there is no need, for the question was clearly rhetorical.

'We fight against one tyrant in France in order to put another on the throne of Austria,' he continues. 'But do you think they spare a thought for commoners such as us, except as food for powder and shot? What have France or Austria to do with such as us, Jack? We are mere pawns in their political games.'

'Sure, Ben, you are in philosophical mood,' I say, 'and I hardly know how to answer. The doings of Kings and

Emperors are beyond my ken. All I know is that King George supports Empress Maria Theresa's claim as heir to the throne of Austria and therefore we fight against those who would deprive her of it.'

'Yet the chief of those, Frederick of Prussia, has already made peace with her, has he not? Now he has Silesia, he has retired from the game, and recognised her authority. Why have we not done the same?'

'Are not the French still our enemies?'

'Hers, not ours' he retorts animatedly. 'But the Austrians have force enough to push them back, now that Frederick of Prussia is out of the picture. So why must we remain involved?'

'The French still have territorial ambitions in Europe, do they not?

'Aye, they threaten Hanover. It is a case, I fear, of King George once more putting the interests of his German Principality ahead of his duty to England. And, like all monarchs, he is prepared to sacrifice we common folk to his whims. Is it not time we made a stand?'

'This is dangerous talk, Ben,' I caution him.

'Nay, it is rational talk, Jack. A monarch is nothing without his people and should rule by consent, not by tyranny. '

'You surely don't think His Majesty, King George, a

tyrant?'

'No,' he concedes, somewhat reluctantly, 'but that is only because we have a Parliament that prevents him from being so. Thank the Lord for the Whigs,' he says with bitter humour. 'God knows what straits we'd be in were the Tories in power – back under the Stuart yoke, I don't doubt.'

'You are no Jacobite, then?'

'In no way. The House of Hanover has many faults, but is a model of moderation in comparison with what has gone before.'

I sense a way to turn the argument my way. 'Why, then, there is the answer to your question. We are here to fight against the forces of tyranny in order to uphold our hard-won rights.'

'However few those rights may be!' he scoffs. 'But, yes, you have a point, Jack. We must preserve what we have in order that we may build upon it. And, believe me, we have hardly cleared the foundations. But there is hope. There are those about the Prince of Wales – William Pitt for one – who believe in the supremacy of the law.'

'Aha! I knew the lawyer in you would come to the fore!'

He shrugs, conceding, 'You have found me out, Jack. But 'tis an acknowledged truth, 'where law ends, tyranny begins.' 'Twas John Locke said that when James II lost his throne. It is a bitter lesson to gall every succeeding English monarch.'

'But we are agreed King George is no tyrant.'

I have all on to stop myself telling him how, having seen His Majesty at close quarters, I know him to be irascible and unmannerly, despotic in a domestic setting, but hardly the stuff of which tyrants are made.

Woodrow, however, does not seem so convinced. 'I think his foolish escapade of leading us into battle is a sign he hankers for the power his European neighbours seem to enjoy.'

'Then let us thank God for Parliament,' I reply, 'for unlike France or Prussia, it has shown that in Great Britain the monarch is the servant of the people and not the other way about.'

Our discussion has become somewhat animated and it is only now that I become aware of a figure shambling up behind us. Josh Barley must have been following us all the time but has kept his distance until now.

'Is all well with you, Master Woodrow?' he growls, throwing me a suspicious look.

'Aye, Josh,' says Ben kindly, 'Master Weaver and I were debating, that's all, and we became a little heated. We are friends, have no fear. You may let us alone to continue our discussion.'

He speaks with affectionate exasperation, almost as if to a simpleton, but Barley seemingly takes no offence. With a last glance over his shoulder, he plods back in the direction of camp.

In reply to my interrogative glance, Woodrow apologises with a wry smile. 'Josh Barley is a good fellow, but occasionally over-mindful of my welfare, I'm afraid. Since the Brogan business, he counts it his duty to follow me about like a guard-dog. It can be irksome sometimes, but his solicitousness is well-intentioned and I have not the heart to reprimand him.'

'It must be gratifying to inspire such devotion,' I say with unintended satire.

'For me it is unprecedented,' he replies wistfully. Then, with a wide smile, 'I had better make the most of it while I may, do you not think, Jack? For who knows where I, or any of us, will be in a month's time, eh?'

So saying, we continue our stroll as the coolness of evening settles about us.

Our remaining talk is of mundane matters, yet by the time we part I am uneasy in my mind. It is with an uncomfortable sense of disloyalty that, Woodrow's views following so hard on the heels of my conversation with Sir William Hervey, I recognise a small seed of suspicion beginning to grow in my mind.

Unexpected Guest

As soon as I set foot on the wooden bridge that crosses the moat around the fortress, I recognise the figure leaning across the balustrade at the far end, idly tossing sticks into the water below.

It is mid morning. I have seen to First Lieutenant Bancroft's needs and he is now in a meeting with all other platoon commanders in the Officers' Mess where General Clayton is to give details of the forthcoming campaign.

My morning duties over, and today promising to be my last free day in Ghent, I have decided to walk into town to see the sights which I missed yesterday.

Most of the men have already gone into town so I find myself crossing the bridge alone.

As I draw near, Gerard gives no sign that he has noticed me, continuing to gaze indolently into the placid water. But, as I walk behind him, he mutters, 'We are watched. Turn and pretend to ask me directions.'

I can see no watcher, but I comply with his instruction, strolling only a few steps further before stopping short as if caught by a sudden thought. Turning back, I bid him good-day and make a show of looking in a puzzled manner towards town.

He acknowledges me with a fine display of surly reluctance and raises an arm to gesture towards one of the streets into town.

'Take that lane, but turn right directly. Go left where the next lane crosses and then second right. There is a jeweller's shop. I will meet you there in ten minutes.'

Needless to say, his gestures in no way match the verbal directions he is giving me. Rather the opposite, for whenever he says right, he indicates either straight on or left. Then he resumes his position leaning upon the side of the bridge whilst I go on my way.

I stroll unhurriedly towards the road end indicated and, taking the first turning right, follow his directions to the letter.

Within seven minutes at most I arrive at the jeweller's shop and feign a keen interest in the baubles and trinkets on show, covertly observing in the window's reflection for any sign of a watcher in the street behind me.

But Gerard comes upon me so silently that I start with surprise. His sardonic smile does little to improve his saturnine features.

'Lost him, for the moment,' he murmurs. Surreptitiously he slips a note into my hand and, without once looking directly at me, says, 'Fifth door, name of Dekker. Third floor.' Then he is gone.

Slowly I walk on, affecting great interest in the shop windows and the architecture of the houses. Turning the first corner, I rapidly scan the piece of paper which he has thrust into my hand. It is a crudely drawn map with the jeweller's shop as its starting point.

For the next quarter of an hour I proceed by fits and starts, alternately ambling nonchalantly and ducking into doorways or round corners to check the course of the map.

At length I come out onto a bridge over one of the numerous waterways which thread the city. Along one side runs a walk-way lined with trees, behind which cluster the facades of town houses. Upon the other, there is but a narrow path and the tall, flat fronts of what seem to be warehouses, for several have wide wooden doors upon the second storey above which thick wooden beams hung with chains and pulleys project over the water.

At a couple of buildings, the upper storey doors are open and workmen are hauling sacks affixed to the chains up and down to waiting barges on the water below.

I descend the half dozen steps onto the narrow path and walk along to the fifth door, treading carefully, for the cobbles are uneven and wet with spray from the fast-flowing water. This is no placid canal, but a channel flowing directly from the river.

Sure enough, a tarnished brass plaque beside the door

announces: *Abraham Dekker, Graanhandelaar.*

I am at a loss to think what business I might have with a grain merchant, but this is without doubt the place Gerard has directed me to. I try the door and find it open.

I step into a cool, flagged hallway with dark wood doors along each side, all closed. In front of me is a wide stone staircase with a wrought-iron balustrade. From the landing at the turn of the stairs, a large square window filters the morning light through dust-covered panes.

The sound of my boots echoes in the heavy silence as I climb. Past the first floor which seems, from the metal and wooden nameplates upon the closed doors, to consist mainly of offices. Up through open, pillared warehouse spaces piled with sacks and boxes on the second and third floors. And so to the top floor where a carpet covering the wooden boards announces what are obviously living quarters.

There is a short landing with a panelled double door of polished mahogany upon which I tentatively knock.

It is opened by a maidservant, dressed in plain black. Taking one look at my soldier's uniform, she gasps, hides a giggle behind her hand and scuttles back inside. A moment or two later, Agnes Mayer appears and with a smile dancing upon her lips, offers me her hand to kiss.

'Come in, Will. Mijnheer Dekker is one of the van Andels' clients and has allowed me use of his home whilst I am in Ghent. He is away on business at the moment. Come, there is someone I think you should meet.'

She ushers me into a spacious parlour which is flooded with light from a large casement window. After the gloom of the hallway, I am for a moment blinded and see the figure who rises from an armchair only as a dark shadow against the light.

I extend my hand in greeting to the stranger, but when my eyes adjust to the brightness and I see who it is, my arm drops and I stand as if thunderstruck.

'Sure, I can understand that you'd not be for shakin' hands with me, considerin' the circumstances in which we last met,' says Finn Kelly. 'The business end of a pistol is not the most obvious declaration of good intentions, to be sure.'

The fresh, open face is the same, if a little more weather-beaten and careworn. The lips always seeming on the point of smiling, yet the eyes still glittering with the spark of fanaticism which I once mistook for the love of his musical art. And the shock of red, curly hair – a little more tamed now – like a halo in the morning sun.

I look in panic at Agnes.

She betrayed me once – has she done so again, despite all that has recently passed between us?

She regards me sorrowfully. 'Poor Will, I see the

consternation in your eyes. But believe me, all is well.'

Gently she leads me to a chair and bids me sit. My limbs feel nerveless and out of my control.

I sink, speechless, onto the seat, willing myself to suppress the trembling which threatens to overcome me.

A glass is put into my hand. The fiery liquor burns my throat and makes me cough.

But at length I summon up the power of speech.

'What means this?' I ask. 'God forbid you have led us into a trap?'

'I know how this must look,' she says gently, laying her hand upon my shoulder, 'but it is not as it seems. Do but hear him out and you will see that I have acted for the best. '

Kelly has silently observed this solicitous little scene with a wry smile. 'The lady is right,' says he. 'Sure, 'tis nothin' short of a miracle that I and your master, Sir William Hervey, should agree on anything but it is so in this instance.'

'Agree?' say I, totally bewildered. 'How so? On what?'

'Aha, succinct questions, Master Archer. Would I could answer so concisely!'

'Perhaps we might start by telling Will how we came to meet?' suggests Agnes.

There is an archness in her tone which tells me she has fallen under the spell of his undoubted charm. It is something I can understand for I felt it myself at one time and, despite all that since transpired, there are remnants of it still. I have plenty of reason to feel hostile towards Finn Kelly for what he did, but I also know him to be so convinced of the justice of his cause that he will not equivocate. I believe that he is, in his own way, a man of honour and principle.

All the same, I cannot deny the spark of jealousy I feel at the present easiness between him and Agnes.

My mind is but little set at rest on that score as Agnes begins her story.

'You recall that, when we parted at Bruges, Will, I told you I would, if possible, contrive a way to fall in with Finn' – (the use of his first name sends a pang through my heart) – 'on the journey hither?'

'Yes, and I recall warning you against it,' I reply truculently.

'As it happened, Fate decided the matter for us by causing my carriage to become mired in consequence of bad weather.'

'In which misfortune, I rode, bold as Cuchulainn, to the lady's rescue,' chuckles Finn Kelly, 'and, with the help of my trusty steed, released her and her swain from the mud. Then, as a true gentleman, 'twas only right I see her to her destination – a paltry ale-house in the next village where we sought refuge for the night, she in the one half-decent bed, whilst her driver and I bedded down before the parlour fire.'

'The weather continuing bad...' continues Agnes.

'…and the road a dangerous place for a lady travelling alone...' adds Kelly.

'...Finn insisted on accompanying us all the way to Ghent where we have been this last week, awaiting your arrival.'

'During which time your lady and I have been playing a delicate game of cat and mouse, Master Archer, each trying to find out what the other knows without revealing ought of our own intentions. A game in which Miss Mayer, thanks to you, started with the advantage, knowing far more about me than I of her.'

Their easy amiability with its shared looks and taking up of each other's sentences is beginning to irk me. I feel jealous and excluded.

'Sorry to interrupt your new found cordiality, but are you going to tell me what is this matter that you say we arc all agreed upon but of which I am yet ignorant?' I demand, somewhat too brusquely.

Agnes frowns at my tone. 'Now, Will, don't be petulant. All in good time.'

Finn Kelly regards me perceptively. 'Is it the green glint o' jealousy I see in your eye, Will Archer? I assure you, there's no cause,' he says gravely. 'We are dealing here with weightier matters.'

'Perhaps, then, you will enlighten me as to their nature,' say I, a little less fractiously, though piqued that he is able to see my emotions so clearly. Although only two years my senior, he makes me feel like a callow boy.

He gives me a look which, in other circumstances, I might interpret as penitent.

'First, there is the matter of Brogan's death to clear up,' he says with a wry grimace. 'Yes, I freely admit that was my doing. The fellow was becoming greedy and threatening to tell what he knew – or rather what he *thought* he knew – which made him a danger. I had to silence him.'

'And you slit open his nose as a warning to me not to pry,' I interrupt.

Finn's look of puzzlement creases into a laugh. 'Fie, Will, what an opinion you have of yourself! Warning to *you*, indeed! Sure, 'twas but an accident. We argued, he came at me with a knife and succeeded only in injuring himself. If I'd had my way, that would have been the end of it. But no, he came at me again and in the struggle he fell and broke his neck upon the tree bole, saving me the trouble of killing him. Rather than have his body found as a presumed murder victim, I strung him up.'

Cowed by his mockery, I ask, 'What business had you with him, anyway?'

'I want to find the man who intends to kill the King.'

The enormity of the remark seems to swell, filling the room. From outside come the distant shouts of workmen two floors down in the neighbouring warehouses, loading bales onto the barges. The creak of pulleys on the crane beams and the rattle of chains seem incongruous in the heavy silence which follows.

After a moment I ask, tentatively, 'Is this man you seek a French spy?'

'Nay,' he replies forcefully, 'the French do not seek to assassinate King George.'

'You seem very sure of that.'

'I am certain, Master Archer – for I have many a close contact among the French.' Seeing my look of astonishment, he continues, 'Be not so aghast. The Irish and the French have long been been allies. Lord Mountcashel's men fought many a time alongside French troops in foreign wars in return for France's help in the Williamite War in Ireland. You will find few Irishmen in the English army, save a few renegade Protestants like our late, unlamented friend, Brogan. The majority of loyal Catholic Irishmen fight for the return of the true King.'

'The Pretender, you mean.'

'We will not quibble about the name, Will, but we both know who we mean.'

'How then can you say we both seek the same thing? I have been tasked with keeping King George alive, but you would have him dead and put James Stuart on the throne. Is this why you seek the man you say wants to assassinate him?'

'No, Will, killing King George would not restore the Stuart line for there are Hanoverian heirs enough for another fifty years or more.'

'What, then, is your purpose in finding the man who would assassinate him?'

'To stop him, of course. I do not deny that it would suit both France and Ireland to have King George fall in battle. His death would then appear to be the direct result of foolish pride, putting his homeland of Hanover before the security of England, thus provoking anti-Hanoverian unrest. On the other hand, if he were to die at the hands of a suspected assassin, he would die a martyr for his country and the House of Hanover be lauded as patriotic heroes. His heirs would be unassailable and our cause would be lost.'

'The same may be said if he were to be victorious over the French,' I suggest.

'That is hardly likely,' he scoffs. 'The art of war has moved on since Marlborough's day when England last engaged in a European conflict. The Earl of Stair, your Commander in Chief, is nigh on seventy years old and King

George has no experience on the battlefield.'

'You see, Will,' says Agnes who has remained silent all this time, apparently enjoying the sight of two stags locking horns, 'however different your ultimate objectives, both you and Finn have one immediate purpose. You both seek the man who would have the King dead, in order to prevent him achieving that aim.'

'There is but one problem,' says Finn. 'I do not know who it is. That fool, Brogan, provided no useful information before he died. Would you believe he thought that *you* were the one I sought? He jumped to the conclusion that you were a spy and was all for denouncing you and calling me for witness. Which is why he had to die.'

'That day at the carter's yard... Had he led you to me?'

'Aye and, to be sure, when I recognised you I knew that, as an agent of Sir William, you could not possibly wish harm to your King, so I merely passed the time of day with you rather than slip my knife between your ribs.'

Suddenly, there is the sound of scuffling and raised voices from the landing beyond the door.

Agnes makes to go towards it but, with one accord, both Finn and I stay her. Then we fling it open.

The landing is deserted, but the noise of a struggle comes from the stairwell.

Peering over the bannister, we see Gerard fighting with

another man on the staircase. They tumble, interlocked, down the steps to the floor below but by then both Finn and I are taking the stairs two at a time.

Arriving at the third floor, we see that the intruder has taken to his heels, darting in between the pillars of the upper storeroom, hotly pursued by Gerard.

Finn and I run after them. I see Gerard seize him once more and by the time we reach them, they are locked together, struggling furiously just in front of the wooden door above the crane-beam outside. Suddenly they fall violently against it, bursting the lock asunder with the force and both pitch outward into the void.

Desperately, both Finn and I leap forward. I claw at the material of a coat but the weight of the falling body rips it from my grasp. I am thrown to the floor, the upper half of my body hanging over empty space.

Beside me, I hear gasps and grunts as Finn succeeds in pulling Gerard back from the brink of the precipice.

But my eyes are riveted on the sight of the man I failed to save as he thuds onto the projecting beam. I hear the crack of ribs, the harsh expulsion of breath as the air is forced from his lungs. I see him slide from the beam, tangling in the chains and pulley. Then he plummets, bouncing against the stone wall, his arm caught in loops of chain. There is a sudden jerk as the chain reaches its limit.

For one brief second he hangs suspended before his weight and the momentum of his fall rip the arm from its socket and, spouting fronds of blood, he plunges into the canal below. The jagged echoes of his agonised scream are swallowed by a mighty splash as he hits the water.

Strong hands pull at my legs, dragging me back onto the solid floor and then I am hurtling down the stairs to burst out into the open air where water from the backwash of his fall still swills across the narrow walkway.

I dive, unthinking, into the churning stream and strike out with ungainly strokes to where the body wallows feebly in the water.

Wrapping an arm around him, I heave him to the bank where willing hands haul us out on to the path.

Panting, I kneel beside him and confirm that it is indeed who I thought when I first glimpsed him through the pillars of the upper floor.

Josh Barley lies, half drowned, half dead from loss of blood and broken bones. His face is pale as lard and twisted in agony but his eyelids still flicker.

With his one remaining arm he reaches up to me. I bend to hear the muttered words forced painfully between his dying lips.

'I – make - peace - with - maker. Scatchard - 'twas me – God forgive...'

His voice fails as his eyes glaze and the grip of his one good, left arm on my coat loosens and falls limply to the ground.

Glancing upwards, I see the withered right arm that failed him at the last, still dripping blood, entangled in the metal chain.

Respectfully, I close the lids over his sightless eyes.

Explanations

Workmen have run from neighbouring houses and now crowd round in shocked curiosity.

Hardly have I covered Barley's face with my jacket than Gerard, followed closely by Finn Kelly, push their way through the knot of amazed onlookers. As soon as he sees the situation, Gerard turns and fires off a rapid volley of Flemish. I have no idea what he tells them but it does the trick. The workmen disperse, muttering animatedly amongst themselves.

Together, we carry to body indoors, laying it in the hallway on the ground floor.

Agnes hurries down the stairs, her face a picture of alarm. 'Poor fellow, is he dead? Who is he? What was he doing here?'

'He was following Master Archer,' says Gerard, dabbing at grazes on his face. Then, glowering at me from beneath his dark brows, 'Had you been less tardy, this may have been prevented.'

'Nay,' I protest, 'lay this not on me. I proceeded as circumspectly as I was able.'

'Gentlemen,' Agnes reprimands us with clear-voiced authority, 'pray do not quarrel. This is no time for recrimination.What's done is done and we must make the best of it. How shall we proceed from here?'

'I have told the men outside it was an accident, an argument between foolish English soldiers that got out of hand,' says Gerard, pointedly. 'And advised them that it will be in their best interests, should anyone come asking, to say they have seen nothing. Do not fear, they will not invite trouble if it can be avoided.'

'Nevertheless,' says Finn Kelly, 'I think it will be for the best if you and I depart forthwith, Miss Mayer. We will but draw attention if we remain.'

'Tarry a moment,' say I, annoyed, 'aren't we forgetting something? There is a dead man here, a man who was a friend of mine.'

This draws them up short.

'Your *friend?*' exclaims Kelly. 'Then why in heaven's name was he following you?' Suspicion clouds his visage. 'Did you ask him to do so?'

'No,' I reply indignantly, 'I did not. I know no better than yourselves why he should follow me. But what I do know is that he has more than paid the price for it and we are left with his body to deal with.'

'Do not trouble yourselves over that,' says Gerard callously. 'I shall dispose of him. He will not be the first drunken English soldier to fall in the canal and drown.'

'By no means,' I say. 'I will have him treated with dignity, at least. You must help me carry him to somewhere removed from here, whence I may enlist aid from my fellows to take him back for proper burial at the citadel. I shall make up some story of how he came to die. Much as it grieves me to traduce his memory, it is preferable to consigning him, nameless, to an unknown grave.'

And so it is agreed.

Taking care not to be observed, Gerard and I use Agnes's carriage to transport Barley's body, together with the severed arm which Gerard has rescued from the pulley chain, to a back street in a mean area of the city. Leaving it there, Gerard returns with the carriage in which Kelly and Agnes will depart before nightfall.

In the meantime, I return to camp, rehearsing in my head what story I shall tell of Josh Barley's death to my commanding officer and to my friends.

I arrive back at the *Spanjaardskasteel* to find First Lieutenant Bancroft just returned from the meeting of all the platoon commanders and eager to impart his news.

Fifty thousand French troops are reported to be gathered on the Moselle to bar any invasion through Lorraine, whilst all their forces in Flanders are presently stationed on the River Meuse ready either to join forces with their comrades to the West or to march to the River Neckar if the Allies should cross the River Rhine south of Cologne.

General Stair's first plan – for the English forces to close in upon the French from the west whilst the Austrians attack them upon the east – has been countermanded by King George himself. He remains adamant that, though the French are to be regarded as enemies, we are not officially at war with France. Such outright aggression would constitute an unacceptable declaration of hostilities.

Our orders, therefore, are to march on to Mainz and take up a position overlooking the junction where the River Main joins the Rhine, from which vantage point we may observe if the French intend to march south and act accordingly.

I listen with interest, but little understanding. Political prevarication is a mystery to me and the geography of Europe as alien as the surface of the moon. What I can grasp, however, is that tomorrow we are to march to Bruxelles and thence to Charleroi and then eastwards for two or three more weeks.

Having let Bancroft exhaust his enthusiasm for the coming campaign, I am eventually allowed to speak.

'I regret to inform you, sir, that there will be one fewer in our number. There has been an accident in Ghent which I had the misfortune to witness.'

'An accident?' It is as if I have physically struck him. All his eagerness has gone, replaced by a look of shocked anxiety. 'For god's sake, Jack, say this has naught to do with that damned Brogan business.'

'No, sir,' I reply with reasonable conviction. 'As I crossed a bridge over one of the numerous waterways of the town, I came upon an altercation involving one of our men. Two low ruffians were shoving him out of a building on the waterfront followed by a screeching female. I have no idea what they were yelling about, but from her attire I would say she was a common drab.'

Bancroft lets out an exasperated sigh. 'Did I not give the men specific orders, Jack? No drunken brawling, no whoring. Who is this fellow? I shall have him flogged forthwith.'

'It was Josh Barley, sir, but, god rest his soul, the poor fellow is beyond all mortal justice,' say I solemnly. Despite maligning poor Barley's character, I am secretly pleased that Bancroft is proving so easy to deceive. Mr Garrick would be proud of my developing thespian ability as I continue in suitably appalled tones, 'Poor Barley. What followed was horrible to behold, sir. Coming to the the edge of the water, still struggling with his assailants, he overbalanced and fell into the water where he fell foul of a swift moving skiff whose oar, cuffing him about the side of his head, rolled him into the path of a passing barge. Caught between the bow of the vessel and the wall of the canal, the unfortunate fellow's arm was wrenched from its socket.'

'Good God!' murmurs Bancroft in horror. 'Did his attackers do nothing to save him?'

'As soon as they saw what had happened, they took to their heels and the harlot with them. I would have given chase, sir, but Barley had the prior claim upon my attention. Unfortunately I could do nothing for him.'

'And where is he now?'

'I left him in a side-street, sir. I would have your permission to take a couple of men to retrieve his body.'

'Certainly, certainly, Jack. You are a good fellow. You acted nobly.' I acknowledge his praise with a single nod of guilty humility. 'Are the perpetrators to be found, think you? Can we bring them to justice?'

I shake my head sorrowfully. 'I got but a brief glimpse of them, sir. My attention was all on Barley. I do not know if I would recognise them again. Besides, it is a very mean area of town, sir, the stews of the city where such incidents are commonplace. I think we both know why he was there, sir, but any inquiry would, I'm afraid, be met with incomprehension or silence. In my opinion, it were best for Barley's sake that he be buried with what dignity we can afford him before our departure tomorrow and the circumstances of his demise be not talked of.'

Bancroft nods in acquiescence. 'Your opinion, as ever, Jack, demonstrates both your good sense and your humanity. Go about it at once. I will see the fortress commandant and arrange for the poor fellow's interment this very evening.'

Fritz Dorn insists on accompanying me. He does it with quiet courtesy but in a way that admits no argument.

'Soldiers bearing a body through de streets, dere vill be questions. I vith de language am more - vot is it, *vloeiend* – more flowing.'

'More fluent, yes,' I agree.

I enlist the aid of Tom Hooper and would take Ben Woodrow, too, but he has not returned from town. Dorn, therefore, brings one of his men and, with his customary efficiency, procures a small handcart which will serve as a bier.

I do not tell Hooper the purpose of our journey until we are on our way. He is predictably confounded by the news.

'Josh?' he exclaims in disbelief. 'Why, what was he doing at a nugging house?'

'What any man does with a moll, I imagine,' say I regretfully.

'Nay, not Josh, I don't believe it.'

'I, too, find it hard to credit – but then how much can we

really say we know of our fellows, even those we hold closest?' I reply, all too well aware of the irony of my own position during the last months.

'Aye,' admits Tom Hooper sadly. 'A simple soul, yet a man like the rest of us.'

We find the body where I concealed it in the secluded back street and load him onto the makeshift bier, covering him with a blanket which Dorn has also efficiently supplied.

'Dis injury,' he says, as I lay the severed arm on the dead man's chest before folding the blanket over him, 'how did he come by it?'

Carefully I recount my fiction of the passing barge trapping him against the canal side.

'Dat is very strange,' he says dubiously, 'I vould not have thought dat could happen.'

'I was not close at hand, and all happened so quickly that I cannot in all honesty say how it occurred,' say I truthfully.

I am not sure Dorn is wholly convinced, but he is content to let the matter rest.

As Hooper and his Austrian counterpart manhandle the cart across the cobbles, I engage Fritz Dorn in conversation about the forthcoming march east and thus, with only an occasional interruption to appease the curious looks of passers-by with a few friendly words, we arrive back at the *Spanjaardskasteel* without my having to further embroider my invented account of poor Josh Barley's death

That evening we lay Josh Barley to rest in a grave just outside the fortress.

As the last obsequies are read, it occurs to me that in my efforts to provide a explanation of his death, I have all but forgotten the reason that occasioned it.

Was he following me of his own accord   or was he ordered to follow me? Does someone know of my true identity and purpose?

And, as I ponder the answer to this, I also ponder the shock of his last words when he confessed to killing Ned Scatchard. *Why should he do such a thing?*

An answer is partially supplied by Ben Woodrow who, upon hearing of Barley's death, was wholly overcome by the news.

For several minutes he is unable to speak but eventually he succeeds in giving voice with broken words to his emotion.

'Oh God, forgive me, this is my fault. Oh, the poor fellow – so loyal...' He swallows back the tears. 'I spurned his devotion...'

I put an arm around his heaving shoulders. 'Come, Ben, you must not blame yourself. You were his friend, his saviour.'

'Do you not see,' he bursts out angrily, 'that is the very point? If I had not saved him from that iniquitous flogging, he would be alive today. It was his gratitude that killed him.'

'Calm yourself, Ben. Come, you are overwrought and speak words which make no sense.'

He shakes his head in mute despair, but at length he calms and, in a bitter tone, begins, 'Do you not understand? He killed Scatchard for me. To wreak revenge on Brogan who was his tormentor and would have been mine, too.'

'But why not kill Brogan himself?' asks Hooper, bewildered.

'Who knows how the poor fellow's mind worked? Perhaps he thought killing Brogan was too quick. I can only suppose he wanted Brogan to suffer, as he had made both Ned and me suffer.'

'With no disrespect to the dead,' say I, 'do you really think Josh was capable of such reasoning?'

'Not reasoning, Jack, but pure blind loyalty. You saw how he followed me about like a kind of faithful hound,' continues Ben, much calmer now as his lawyer's brain begins to sense a problem of logic. 'After Brogan accused me and had me incarcerated, Ned must have searched for and found the missing knife. His first thought might have been to hand it over to Bancroft to exonerate me. But that would have let Brogan off, too. Everything would have been dismissed as an unfortunate mistake.'

'But if the knife killed someone while you were locked up, then it stood to reason you couldn't be guilty,' says Tom Hooper. 'Aye, I can see Josh thinking that one out.'

'I agree,' say I, 'but the whole business of killing Scatchard to implicate Brogan...?'

'More like he mistook the one for the other,' says Tom. 'Brogan and Scatchard were of a size, and it was dark in that barn...'

'You may be right, Tom,' acquiesces Ben, disconsolately. 'But it does not alter the fact that he did it for me.'

Both Hooper and I do our best to console him and by the time I leave he is almost reconciled to the fact that, for whatever reason Barley did what he did, Ben should in no way blame himself.

As I return to the room that Dorn and I share, I find that our discussion has also partly answered the first question that was troubling me. It must have been Barley's jealous devotion to Woodrow that prompted him to follow me into Ghent, just as he followed Ben and myself yesterday evening.

Faithful hound, vigilant for his master's safety, he may have been, but if Ben had not assured him that all was well between us last night, I have no doubt I would have felt his teeth.

Ball

Next day is all a-bustle with preparations for departure. For days fresh platoons have been arriving and the force which eventually sets out from Ghent now numbers in excess of a thousand men, both British and Austrian, and we are but one contingent of the army which will eventually mass at our destination where the Rivers Main and Rhine meet. More Austrian troops, it is rumoured, are advancing from the West and it is confirmed that King George has a Hanoverian army of several thousand coming from the North, with a retinue of over 650 horses, 13 Berlin carriages, 35 wagons and 54 carts.

Being but the foot soldiers, the only horses we have seen so far have been officers' mounts and the big lumbering beasts that pull the supply and ordnance wagons or the dozen or so cannons which are now part of our ever increasing martial train.

Over the next few days and weeks, however, whenever we find ourselves upon a high road, we are with increasing frequency obliged to move aside by lines of Berlin coaches carrying high-ranking officers, officials and ministers of state on their way to the battlefront. Or by trotting ranks of cavalry, harness jingling, resplendent in their red and blue coats, plumed metal helmets shining in the sun. We look at them in awe as we tramp doggedly along, feeling like humble mortals in the presence of gods.

By the time we reach Bruxelles in mid-May, it is awash with soldiers who near out-number the residents of that city. It is fortunate that this inundation of military personnel brings its own supplies and tents with it, for none of the towns upon our route could hope to feed or house such a horde.

Reaction of the inhabitants is mixed. The surly distrust with which the rank and file is treated is very different to the welcome accorded to the officer class. Even I myself, though a very junior NCO, am treated as a cut above the common soldiery and, on the final night of our stay in the town, am included along with Bancroft and Ward in an invitation to a celebration ball at the *Stadhuis*. Whether it is a ball to celebrate our three days' presence or marking the city's relief at our departure tomorrow, I am unable to say.

Hauptmann Bauer and Fritz Dorn are also among the guests and I envisage spending most of the evening with him, feeling distinctly out of place in this glittering pillared hall with its food-laden, damask-clad tables along one side, and the cream of Bruxelles society teeming and chattering like a flock of exotic birds in their feathers and full finery.

For all I have mixed with nobility and even royalty in the

past, I have never been invited to a large society gathering such as this and am not familiar with the courteous niceties that govern such occasions. Fritz, too, is a novice in these affairs, though he can at least understand the language better than I.

Whilst our superiors mingle easily from the outsetting, he and I spend the first part of the evening upon the fringes of the room. Once or twice we are approached by matrons and staid burghers who quiz us about how we like their town and how it compares with our own home towns, to which we politely answer what we assume they want to hear: that it far excels any other town we have visited in the splendour of its buildings and the civility of its inhabitants.

In between such fulsomely courteous exchanges, however, are eyes are drawn to the numerous young ladies also sitting around the edges of the room upon velvet cushioned benches, invariably watched over by elderly female chaperons.

As the orchestra strikes up, I feel distinctly envious of the gentlemen who, with elegant bows and extended hands, invite many of their number to take the floor. But I am uneasy that my halting language skill may tarnish my gallantry a little. And I fear the glower of the matronly dragons even more.

I sense that Fritz is as fidgety as I and, as the first cohort takes the floor for a stately *Allemande,* he is stirred into action. 'Come, ve must ask de ladies, Jack. Stay vith me, I shall invite for both of us.'

Threading a careful course to avoid the circling dancers, we approach a pair of young ladies who have missed out upon the first sortie. They are not among the most prepossessing but are by no means ill-looking, and we are, after all, only in search of a dance-partner, not a wife.

With a stiff bow and (I note with amusement) a click of his heels, Fritz requests the pleasure of their company for the next dance. After some modest giggling and fluttering of fans, they eventually accept, persuaded in no small part by the quiet encouragement of their elderly guardian.

As the *Allemande* progresses, being unable to converse with my new partner as we await the next dance, I carefully observe the dancers and by the time it concludes feel I have a competent knowledge of the required steps and moves. It is with some confidence, therefore, that when the dancers re-group, I offer my hand to the young lady and we take our positions among them.

To my horror, the band strikes up with a sprightly *Bourree.* My confusion must be evident from my face for my partner's eyes widen in concern. She says something in German and I attempt, but fail, to mutter an apology in reply, by which time we are swept up willy-nilly in the twirling bodies. For the next excruciating minutes I essay a kind of jig in imitation of those around me whilst desperately trying to keep from colliding with them, and at the same time forcing my features into a grinning mask in the attempt to convince my unfortunate partner that I am hugely enjoying the experience.

It comes as no surprise when she declines the next dance and I retire, embarrassed and vanquished, to my post beyond the side pillars noting, with a small stab of jealousy that Fritz is still happily capering through a lively *Gigue* with his partner.

As I watch the skipping couples, a fan taps me lightly on the shoulder and a voice whispers in my ear, 'I can recommend a good dancing master, if you so wish.'

I turn to see Agnes Mayer, her eyes alight with mischief. A quick glance assures me that she is alone. Finn Kelly is not with her.

The *Gigue* coming to an end, she slips her arm through mine and says, 'Come, let us take a turn about the room, lest any forward maiden snaps you up for the next dance.'

'She must be deficient in sight and heedless of danger to her toes, then,' I quip in response.

'You do yourself an injustice, *Mr Weaver,* for you are not unpleasant on the eye, methinks,' she teases me, 'and I do not fear for my toes.'

'That is because I do not offer to dance with you.'

'Indeed, sir,' says she with a coy arch of her brow, 'and what would you offer to do with me?'

Having arrived at the vestibule doors and feeling a cool breeze wafting into the overheated room, I suggest we take the evening air where, in the encroaching dusk, we may stand less chance of being overheard, being able to converse without having to raise our voices above the clamour of fiddles and the stamp of feet. Also I do not wish to draw attention by being seen together.

'My friend, Fritz, may wonder who you are,' I say, 'and 'twould be unwise to excite his, or anyone's, curiosity.'

'My very thought,' says she, 'for I have news to impart.'

The news must wait, however, for, having emerged into the cool dark and finding the discreet shadow of a buttress, I press my lips to hers, savouring all the honeyed pleasure of her presence that has been denied to me for so long.

'Fie, Will, you are importunate,' she gasps as our lips disengage. For a moment I fear I have been too audacious, but then, pulling my face down to hers, she re-engages with increased ardour, her tongue eagerly seeking mine.

It is not long before her fingers are busy with the laces at my crotch, bringing my little soldier to immediate attention.

My hands, too, meet little resistance as I hitch up the silk of her gown to find there is no inner defence to deter my gallant warrior.

An encounter more different from that in her room at the van Andels' house is hard to imagine. On that occasion, in the warmth of feather pillows and white linen, all was soft cherishing and gentle murmurs of love that seemed to last for ever, but yet not long enough. But here, against rough stone with the dread of accidental discovery, all is over in a moment to the urgent refrain of breathless gasps and cries stifled by each other's insistent lips.

When all is done, we readjust our dress in embarrassed silence. I am ashamed to have been so overwhelmed with desire as to have lost all decorum, and I suspect that Agnes feels the same way.

When we are eventually able to speak, it is almost with the awkwardness of strangers. Something has changed between us, but there is a tacit mutual agreement not to mention it.

Offering my arm to continue our evening promenade, I clear my throat. 'Well, Miss Mayer, you said you had something to tell me?'

'That is so, Will. It will doubtless gratify you to learn that, in the interests of security, Mr Kelly and I are to go our separate ways. We follow the same route – that dictated by the army's movements – but henceforth merely as individuals who may occasionally encounter each other, not as travelling companions.'

'A wise precaution. And one of which I'm sure Sir William will approve. For all Finn Kelly may profess to seek the same as us, we need to remember that he is still our enemy. And I suspect that, whilst he has appeared open, there is still much he has not told us.'

'Before we parted, however, we agreed that Gerard should act as go-between.'

'Between you and Kelly?' I say, perhaps a little too sharply.

It provokes an equally curt reply. 'Between all three of us. I have informed Sir William, never fear.'

'And what says he?'

'He has not yet replied. But I have suggested to him that it may be more expedient to have Kelly with us than against us. I have said that Finn and I are no longer travelling together, but will remain in contact. Close, but not too close, by which means we may perhaps discover more of his purpose.'

'Well, I only hope Sir William agrees,' I murmur dubiously. 'And Gerard, you say, is to act as a go-between?

'Yes, to which end he has acquired a military uniform and will insinuate himself amongst the troops.'

'This is a highly risky stratagem,' I say with alarm.

'Not so risky, I think,' she replies. 'Can you honestly say

that you yourself would take note of one strange face among so many hundred? He, like you, has his orders to keep his eyes and ears open for anything untoward. '

'Am I no longer to be trusted, then?' say I, bridling.

'Of course you are,' says she impatiently, 'but "two heads are better than one" as the old adage runs. Gerard will pass on aught he learns to you, as you will to him. In turn he will convey information to me. It will be easier for he and I to remain in contact over the coming weeks, for he will be able to pass more freely than yourself.'

By now we have done a complete circuit of the building and are now almost back to the fringes of the light that spills from the entrance.

Pausing in the half-dark only long enough for me to inform her of my explanation of Josh Barley's death and how it has been received, she says, 'I think we must go in separately, do you not agree? It will not do for our companionship to be remarked upon.'

Much as I appreciate the wisdom of her suggestion, I cannot prevent a sinking of my heart. *Is this coolness the result of my earlier unbridled behaviour?*

I owe her an apology.

'I'm sorry, Agnes, if I...'

With a glance over her shoulder to see we are unobserved, she kisses me quickly on the cheek.

'The fault is mine equally,' she says. 'Now, wait five minutes before you come back to the dance.'

And with a tiny waggle of her fingers by way of farewell she sweeps elegantly into the entrance hall, leaving me more disappointed than reassured.

Eastwards

How to describe the next few weeks?

We march, we set up camp, we strike camp, we eat, we sleep – and march again. Through meadow and forest, on paved roads and rutted tracks, through villages and towns which all begin to look the same. Past shrieking, delighted children and awed townsfolk and dark-browed peasants, we tramp relentlessly as though in a trance. The sun rises in front of us and sets behind us, telling us that we march eastwards, but otherwise one day is so like another that we lose all sense of time.

Since setting out from Ostend all those weeks ago, I have seen the bare branches of trees burst into bud, the snow-laden ground give way first to mud, then to a swathe of green dotted with bright coloured crocus and pale snowdrops, with trembling bluebells and lent lilies. As we left Bruxelles, the may was dusting the bushes pink. It has blossomed and faded, and we now tread over a carpet of fallen petals.

There have been days of rain and days of sun, days when we have been soaked by mist or buffeted by wind.

And, while nature has marshalled its infinite variety around us, ambushing us one day and giving us free and glorious passage the next, news of our military manoeuvres continues to reach us in regular dispatches.

It is reported that General Stair's forces are assembled and keen to attack the French, commanded by the Duc de Noailles, but the bulk of the Austrian army are not yet arrived at the rendezvous and it is rumoured that Count d'Arenberg, their commander is having doubts about the wisdom of the undertaking. What effect our arrival with a thousand more men will have is yet to be seen.

Meanwhile, I receive dispatches of my own.

Less than a week after we depart from Bruxelles, Gerard makes his first contact.

Just as I leave Bancroft's tent, having served him his evening meal after a long day's march, Gerard is suddenly and silently beside me.

'*Guten abend*, Master Weaver,' says he in an undertone. 'A fine evening, is it not? Are you at leave to walk?'

'Aye,' say I, 'my supper may wait.'

The sun is setting, bathing the plain around us in a ruddy twilight. Men are erecting tents, exchanging the coarse, good-humoured banter which usually accompanies this daily task. Others gather together, tending fires for the evening meal or smoking pipes of tobacco, whilst platoon sergeants press 'volunteers' for latrine detail. As far as the eye can see, men are busy about their evening tasks. None will remark upon two more red-coated figures walking together.

All the same, we do our best to thread our way between the busy, vociferous groups at a sufficient distance not to be overheard.

I cast an eye over his dusty red coat, worn britches and muddied boots, a uniform indistinguishable from all about us. I do not venture to ask whence he procured it – it is not so much its provenance as its efficacy which concern me.

'None have questioned your presence?' I ask.

He laughs derisively. 'You English! Such lack of discipline in marching. You straggle here and there. I march to the rear of one platoon and in the van of another. The men in one take me as a member of the other. I would certainly not pass unremarked in the Austrian line. They march in formation always.'

'And how do you for food?'

'I befriend or scavenge where I may,' says he, and then, with a brazen leer at the small bundle of Bancroft's leftovers which I have in my hand, 'you invite me to share your repast tonight?'

I cannot but admire his impudence. Finding a secluded hollow in the lee of a hedge, we sit and I untie the napkin, laying it out upon the grass.

'Sure, your officers dine well,' he says appreciatively,

taking a large chunk of meat and a piece of bread.

'Feel free to help yourself,' say I ironically as I rescue some for myself.

We eat in silence for a few minutes, washing it down with a half bottle of wine that I smuggled out when Hauptmann Bauer produced his customary bottle of *Jenever*.

Then, lying back against the hedge, I ask, 'Have you any news? How does Miss Mayer? And have you seen any more of Finn Kelly?'

Gerard frowns. 'So many questions, Master Weaver. All the marching, it makes you impatient. But first, Sir William, he has a question for you. Or, rather, a list of names.' He reaches inside his coat and brings out a folded piece of paper. 'Have you come across any of these men?'

It is getting dark and I have to hold the paper close to my eyes. There are no more than a dozen names on the list and most of them mean nothing to me. But two stand out: Frederick Sebastian Ward and Edward Latham.

'I know these two,' I say. 'One is a Second Lieutenant in charge of a platoon that has travelled with us, the other our own platoon Sergeant. What would Sir William have me do?'

'Nay, I do not know. He lists them as persons of interest only, he gives no reason why, only asks that you take note.'

I shake my head in dismay. Used as I am to Hervey's enigmatic communications, this is more puzzling than most. *Does he suspect either of these of being the King's potential assassin? Or are they like to be connected with Finn Kelly's plans?* Whatever the reason, I know that there is no point in questioning Gerard further for he will be no wiser than I.

'Miss Mayer is in contact with Sir William?'

'Sir William has certainly been in contact with her,' he replies evasively before asking bluntly. 'Have you news of your final destination yet?'

'The order to rendezvous at Mainz has been superseded. We are now to continue on to Hanau unless we have orders to the contrary,' I tell him. 'How is Miss Mayer?'

'Well,' he replies tersely. 'She intends to find lodgings in a *gasthuis* in Bingen, about three day's march from here. If you discover aught about this Ward or Latham, I will pass it on to her there.'

'May I not tell her myself?'

'I am more free than you to do it.'

'But if we shall be in Bingen in three days' time, will it not be better that she hear it from my own lips rather than at second hand?'

'I am *der verbindungsmann* - the link-man,' says he in a manner that admits of no further argument.

'Very well,' I concede, 'but how shall I find you if I have

information to impart?'

'You won't. I shall find you.' He gets up to go.

'Wait,' say I, also rising to my feet and brushing flakes of pastry and wisps of grass from my britches, 'you have not told me aught of Finn Kelly.'

'There is *nicht* to tell. Since Bruxelles, we have not heard, not seen anything. Now, *auf wiedersein*, Master Weaver. Thank you for the supper.'

He becomes just one more shadow melting into the dusk, leaving me feeling distinctly uneasy about the manner in which he has blocked all my questions about Agnes.

Is it her choice, or his, that I am seemingly forbidden to see her?

As I make my way back to my tent, I determine that I shall not let surly Gerard stand in my way. Whether he likes it or not, I shall contrive a way to meet Agnes, come what may.

Sortie

Since crossing the Moselle at Treis Karden, our route has wound steeply up a thickly forested range of hills and the going has been slow. But breasting the summit on the second day we are afforded a spectacular vista across the tops of the trees before us and discern the distant sparkle of water on the horizon.

' 'Swelp me!' exclaims Tom Hooper, 'we ain't crossed the whole blessed continent and arrived at the sea again, 'ave we?'

Ben Woodrow laughs. 'There's no sea for thousands of miles in the direction we're travelling, Tom. That'll be the Rhine river,' he says.

Today, since dawn, I have been tramping alongside the two of them through the densely packed trees. Tom, pining for his farming roots, has for several weeks past taken upon himself the role of ostler to my horse and is presently leading it carefully through the tangled undergrowth.

Often, as I have ridden alongside the platoon or, as now, forsaken the saddle to walk with my friends, I have thought how Charlie would have loved to be in Tom's position – in sole charge of my mount, providing it with fodder, grooming it and checking its fetlocks and hooves after a muddy day, and wheedling the occasional ride. And the thought has once more made me sick for home, for Charlie's casual impudence, Susan's warm embraces, and the friends whose companionship I was so suddenly wrested from.

Will I ever see them again? And will they recognise this weather-beaten, unshaven and long-haired fellow as their former callow actor, Will Archer?

And, more to the point, will I know them again? Over the past months I have had no news of any further triumphs which Mr Garrick may have achieved. For all I know, Susan may have found another young man on whom to bestow her charms. And Charlie will be a boy no longer. Already, before I was abducted, his upper lip was dark with the down of adolescence, and he was well nigh up to my shoulder.

Such thoughts of those who were once dear to me put me in mind of she who is presently dear to me. Since talking with Gerard two nights ago, I have been gnawed by the fear that I might be losing her, too.

I have racked my brains to devise some stratagem whereby I might see her, but have come up with nothing. Now, as we weave our way through these interminable trees, my melancholy mood grows ever darker.

'How now, sober-sides,' says Tom, giving me a dig in the ribs after yet another long silence, 'a penny for your thoughts.'

I shake myself from my reverie. 'You would not get your money's worth, Tom. I was merely pondering if we will find a place to camp tonight. The ground is steep, the trees thick with no sign of clearings. For all we know, there may be bandits ready to set upon us round every damned tree.'

'Pshaw, Jack,' jeers Tom, 'you think a ragged band of outlaws would chance their arms against a thousand soldiers? No low pad German snaffler's going to pick me off in my sleep,' whoops Tom, 'not unless he wants my bayonet in his gizzard!'

'Aye, if you can rouse yourself from your snoring in time,' grins Ben, then turns to me. 'Why don't you suggest to Lieutenant Bancroft that you ride ahead and scout out the land, Jack? The day is yet young and if you keep to where the trees are thinnest you can cover a passable distance on horseback.'

I almost embrace him with joy for providing a solution to my dejection. Bingen, where Agnes resides cannot be more than half a day's ride away. I could be there and back well before nightfall.

'Best not ride alone though, Jack,' says Hooper. 'Think o' them bandits a'waitin' to slit yer throat.'

'Well said, Tom,' I reply as a another idea forms in my head. 'How would you like to ride with me – and bring your bayonet with you?'

We wend our way between the trees towards the main forest track, if the meandering path of slightly beaten earth can be called such. For the past two days it has been monopolised by the wagons and some Austrian platoons which, undeterred by the lumbering pace, still prefer to march slowly in formation rather than join the majority of troops who, more impatient, have fanned out singly or in small groups beyond the path, to thread their way amongst the thickets and tree-trunks.

It takes near quarter of an hour of elbowing past ambling bodies before I catch sight of First Lieutenant Bancroft and Second Lieutenant Ward leading their mounts on foot amongst the low-branched trees.

I explain my purpose to Bancroft who is at first reluctant. It is Ward who convinces him of the soundness of the idea.

'Your corporal speaks sense, Bancroft. Even a small clearing may facilitate our security. Let him reconnoitre the ground by all means, even if only for the comfort of our own platoons.'

Apart from serving him his supper, I have until today had little to do with Second Lieutenant Ward, though since his name appeared on Gerard's list, I have lingered a while after they have dined in hope of eavesdropping upon his conversation with Bancroft in the hope of learning more about him.

Observing him more closely, I judge that he, like Bancroft, comes from gentry, perhaps even the lower ranks of the nobility. His accent speaks of refinement and education and his appearance of privilege. But his after-supper conversation has been unremarkable and so far yielded nothing of interest.

Now, however, as he urges Bancroft to accede to my request, he seems interested in me for he scrutinises me closely.

'You are Weaver, are you not?' he asks

'Yes sir, Jack Weaver.'

'And a capital fellow,' adds Bancroft who then, to my discomfiture, proceeds to praise me in the most liberal terms. 'He used to be a jobbing actor, y'know, but a straighter, more honest fellow you couldn't hope to meet. In truth, Frederick, I know not how I would have fared without his aid and sage counsel these last weeks.'

Ward assesses me candidly. 'An actor, and now a veritable paragon! And here he is with another excellent idea, yet you, Henry, are reluctant to let him go. Does that not pique you, Corporal Weaver?'

'Lieutenant Bancroft overstates my merits, I fear,' say I modestly.

'Be that as it may, Weaver, I think you a fine fellow with more to you than Henry here appreciates. It is a pleasure to make your acquaintance.'

'Sir,' I acknowledge with a brief inclination of the head, momentarily discomposed by the intensity of his gaze.

To my relief, after a few moments, he turns his attention to Hooper who is standing respectfully behind me, holding my horse's reins. 'You wish this man to ride with you?'

'If I can find a mount for him, yes sir.'

'Look no further, Weaver,' says he with a radiant smile. 'You may borrow mine, she is but an encumbrance in this woodland and it would appear we will not be free of it before nightfall, what think you, Bancroft?'

'Very like,' agrees Bancroft, a little huffy at Ward's chaffing. Then, with an indulgent smile designed to re-assert his authority, 'You will be back by nightfall, Jack?'

'It is my intention, sir, if no misfortune befalls us.'

Ward takes my arm as he hands me the reins. 'I'm sure no misfortune will come your way with such a stout fellow by your side. Look you return my mare in good condition.' His eyes hold mine as he gives my arm a brief squeeze. 'Fare you well, Jack Weaver.'

Tom and I lead our animals towards the main path and, taking advantage of a gap between wagons, hitch ourselves up into the saddles.

'Danged if you ain't made a conquest there, Jack!' crows Tom as we urge them into a trot. 'Couldn't take his eyes off you. Too handsome for your own good, that's your trouble.'

'Nonsense, Tom, 'twas mere civility. 'Tis the way a gentlemen talks, that's all. Why, Lieutenant Bancroft, he's the same.'

'Aye, point proven,' he whoops. Then, leaning forward to pat his horse's neck, 'I'll lay odds this is the only mare that twiddle poop has ever ridden or is like to ride.'

I laugh with him but I cannot deny that the intensity of Ward's scrutiny has unsettled me - though I am not sure its cause was what Tom Hooper implies.

Once we have made our way past the wagons we make good progress, leaving behind the rumble of wheels and din of innumerable men. We are able to trot in relative ease, with only the sound of birdsong from the surrounding woodland to accompany the thud of our horses' hoofs on the winding forest path.

After an hour or so we light on a number of places where trees have been thinned out and the undergrowth cleared. A scattering of half-charred logs around blackened, hollowed-out patches of earth suggests that a charcoal burner may have plied his trade here fairly recently, but there is no sign of him now.

'Not been here for a while. Before last winter, I'll lay,' opines Hooper. 'See, there's shoots and saplings already half-grown.'

Sure enough, amongst the litter of dead and burnt brushwood, there are thin sprigs of green and, as we scour a little further towards the edges of the clearing, we find the remnants of an abandoned hut, its roof caved in and forest creepers already invading its walls.

'Well, dead or fled, there's one thing certain,' says Tom, 'he won't object to us campin' 'ere tonight.'

'You're right,' say I, 'but I've a fancy to press on a while. See how far the forest stretches. You need not come with me, Tom. 'Tis best you ride back and let them know they'll have fit ground within a couple of hours' marching.'

At first he demurs, 'Is't wise to ride alone, Jack? You know not what may lie ahead. Remember those bandits you were afeard on earlier,' he reminds me with a grin.

'Aye, well we have not met with any this last hour of travelling, so there is no reason to think there will be any ahead either. I think they were a figment of my melancholy mood. But fear not, Tom, I shall keep my wits about me,' I reassure him. 'There be full five hours before nightfall. I'll be back here before then.'

All the same, he insists on giving me the dagger he wears at his waist before he reluctantly turns his horse about and trots back the way we came.

* * *

Left to myself, I set off at a brisk canter, ducking beneath branches which overhang the path and within half an hour notice that the afternoon sun is beginning to make inroads into the forest canopy. Soon there are wide patches of blue sky visible between the treetops and a few minutes later, I emerge into open countryside, leaving the woodland behind me.

The Rhine lies before me, so wide and blue that I can quite understand why, from the crest of the hills yesterday, Tom took it for the sea.

Now, across verdant, gently rolling downland, I see that the river changes its course from due north to due east in a sharp, almost right-angled bend. From yesterday's vantage point, we saw the sun reflecting on width one way and distance the other, making it seem like one vast sheet of water. A pardonable error for, though only a river, it is a mighty one, so wide at this point that it makes the Thames back home seem like a mere stream in comparison.

I spur my steed into a gallop across the springy grass, slowing to a more sedate crossways trot as the ground begins to slope steeply down towards a paved road that runs along the bank.

Recalling the maps which I studied with First Lieutenant Bancroft, I surmise my direction must still lie eastwards so I take the road with the sun behind me, the river upon my left hand side.

Hailing a passing craft upon the river, I shout, 'Bingen, *bitte*?' and am reassured by the boatman waving his arm in the direction I'm going.

A mile or so further on I see the ruins of a fortress high on the far bank and then, after the road veers to the right along the bank of a side-stream joining the main river I cross a stone arched bridge and find myself at the city gate of Bingen.

Enquiring of the watchman about accommodation in the town, he directs me to the only *Gastehaus* which is situated in the town square, a matter of five minutes away.

The afternoon not yet past its prime and the narrow thoroughfares still a-bustle with the business of the day, I deem it more politic to dismount and lead my horse rather than ride through the crowded streets.

Arriving at the *Gastehaus* I enquire if Fraulein Mayer is in residence and that, if so, I would be honoured to attend on her.

A menial is dispatched and I am asked to wait in a dark panelled parlour enlivened with faded tapestries of hunting scenes. In one, a wide-eyed stag is beset by a crowd of horsemen all armed with bows and arrows in a contest that seems not only unfair, considering there can be no more than five feet between hunter and hunted, but also distinctly dangerous as the bowmen all appear to be aiming directly at the back of the man in front.

It is while I'm examining this bloodthirsty scene that I hear footsteps in the corridor outside.

I turn in joyful anticipation.

But my smile of pleasure turns rapidly to a look of confusion.

It is not Agnes who enters, but Sir William Hervey's disdainful factotum, Nathaniel Grey.

Information

Grey gives me a thin smile. 'I am sorry to disappoint you, Master Archer. I see from your face that I am not who you were expecting. You will, I'm afraid, have to make do with me, however. Miss Mayer is presently indisposed.'

'Is she ill?' I ask in alarm.

'Not ill,' says he, as equally unforthcoming as Gerard was, 'but not at the moment able to see you. Now,' he continues, signalling that the matter is closed, 'I take it your unexpected arrival here signifies that you have matter of some urgency to impart? If so, you may impart it to me.'

My mind works quickly. I can hardly tell him that I have no news, urgent or otherwise, to relay but am come purely on impulse simply to see Agnes.

He notes my confusion. 'Well, Master Archer, have you anything to report or not? Pleasant as it is to renew our acquaintance,' he says with thin-lipped distaste, 'I do not have all day.'

'Is Sir William here?' I ask, to gain time.

The thin mouth purses yet tighter. 'I believe that, at your last meeting, Sir William made it clear to you that, whatever may appear to the contrary, he is not here. Therefore you must accept my word that he is not.'

The sardonic curl of his lip makes it patently obvious that he is lying. Nevertheless, I play along with the pretence.

'That is a pity, Mr Grey, for I come not with further information, but with a request for clarification of his instructions.'

'Did Gerard not pass those instructions on to you?'

'He showed me a list of names which he told me were persons of interest to Sir William, but gave me no indication of why they should be so.'

'That is because Gerard did not know. His job was merely to show you the list. As you well know, Master Archer, it is often wise in our business to ration information according to an individual's function. In this instance, Gerard's function was merely that of messenger.'

'And my function?' I inquire, irked by his supercilious tone.

'Is to observe and discover what you can about the persons whose names you recognised. Surely Gerard made that much clear?'

'Indeed so, sir,' say I, trying to keep calm, 'but am I not to be given some indication of *what* I am supposed to be looking for? You, of all people, Mr Grey, must know. Are you not the person who compiles such lists for Sir William, the person who provides all the intelligence upon which he so much relies?'

I know full well that Grey is Hervey's fount of knowledge and information – and that he is proud of the fact, so I have no hesitation in appealing to his vanity.

With a self-satisfied inclination of his head, he accepts the compliment. 'Very true, Master Archer.'

'So I may ask my questions?'

'You may ask, Master Archer. Whether I shall answer depends upon what I consider it meet you should be told. But first,' he says, bringing out a small notebook and pencil to note down what I say, 'tell me what you have discovered of those whose names you recognised. This fellow Latham, to start with.'

'Sergeant Latham is, as far as I have observed, experienced, unswerving in military discipline and loyal...'

'Loyal, you say?' interrupts Grey with a piercing look. 'Where would you say his loyalty lies?'

It is a shrewd question which I take my time in answering. 'Loyal to his country, for sure,' I reply thoughtfully, 'but his loyalty to his superiors is, I think, inspired more by duty than by inclination. His true loyalty, I would judge, belongs to the men under his command.'

'Hmm,' murmurs Grey, tapping the pencil upon his chin. 'That accords with what we know of him. He was involved in the Shoreditch and Whitechapel riots, back in '36.'

'That was against Irish immigrant workers, was it not?'

My passing knowledge of that disturbance was gleaned mainly from the gossip of clients at Mother Ransom's molly-house where I was at that time, but it seems to impress Grey.

He shows a modicum of grudging approval. 'Indeed, Master Archer. There was an allegation that the contractor who was building the new church of St Leonards at Shoreditch had dismissed his labourers and taken on Irishmen who were prepared to serve for a third less wages. This inflamed the weavers who had long nursed resentment against the Irish migrant weavers for driving down wages in their trade. The result was five days of anti-Irish riots.'

He relates it all with the accustomed dry regard for detail, which makes him so invaluable a servant to Sir William Hervey.

'And Sergeant Latham, you say, was caught up in this?'

'He was not a sergeant then. It was not only weavers and disgruntled craftsmen who were protesting, there were one or two soldiers, too. Latham was one of them. No charges were brought against him, his activities confined apparently to shouting and torch-bearing with perhaps an occasional stone thrown. But, as a soldier, it was enough to bring him to our attention as a trouble-causer.'

'There are many amongst whom I have been travelling these last few months who may share his support for the working man, Mr Grey,' I suggest. 'There is, for example, a band of evangelicals in our platoon who preach that all men are equal, and though Sergeant Latham and I are not on the best of terms, I cannot say I have observed any greater propensity to revolution in him than in them. All accept their lot, however inequitable it may seem.'

'Aye, Master Archer, and wolves may be adept at donning sheep's clothing,' says he enigmatically before consulting his notebook once more. 'But what of this other fellow: Frederick Sebastian Ward?'

'Second Lieutenant Ward and his platoon joined us at Ghent and until today I have had no real cause to note him, except at meals which I have served to my commanding officer, First Lieutenant Bancroft, where he neither did nor said anything out of the ordinary.'

'But today...?' prompts Grey.

'He interceded with Lieutenant Bancroft to let me come on this mission in a manner which I found somewhat unsettling. My companion, Tom Hooper, joked about sodomitical intent but I sensed there was something else. Something in Bancroft's account of my supposed talents that piqued his interest. But what, I could not say.'

'Mayhap he recognised an ambition in you that reflected his own, Master Archer,' says Grey, acidly, 'for he, too, has aspirations that belie his humble origins.'

I express surprise. 'He gave every impression of nobility, sir.'

'Aye, he has the manner and the speech to perfection, I believe, yet he was born a humble merchant's son. He has been assiduous in ingratiating himself into society these last few years. We know he purchased his Lieutenancy three months ago, but we have no idea why, for he previously showed no military inclinations. He did, however, associate with one or two of the gentlemen who frequent Prince Frederick's circle at Leicester House.'

'You suspect he is working for the Prince's faction?'

'It is a possibility. As Sir William told you, it is unlikely the Prince would act against his father. But those around him might – or even against the Prince's younger brother, the Duke of Cumberland, whom it is well known King George would rather have as heir to the English throne and ship Prince Frederick off to rule over Hanover.'

'The Duke is coming with his father, is he not?'

'He set out two days before the King, newly promoted to the rank of Major General. The two of them, it seems, intend to take command in the forthcoming battle.'

'And what of Field Marshal Stair?'

'His advice has so far gone for naught, ignored or countermanded. There is no sign that things will change in that respect. It is likely that His Majesty and his son, the

Duke, will want to be at the heart of the action which, of course, will make them an easier target,' says Grey, tucking his notebook away in his waistcoat pocket. 'Your instructions are therefore changed. Whilst we suspect both the King and his son to be in danger, we are no nearer to identifying the actual assassins. Your task, therefore, is not only to continue observing but to keep as close as you may to His Majesty or the Duke of Cumberland and, in the event of any unusual threat to their safety, to act in the most decisive way possible to avert the danger.'

'Decisive? You cannot mean - to kill?' I ask, aghast.

'Sir William is instructing you to do whatever is necessary, Master Archer,' says he, coldly. He rises, signalling that our interview is over. 'It is unlikely that there will be opportunity for you to contact any of us again before hostilities commence. It is a measure of Sir William's trust that he now leaves you to your own devices. Now, good-day to you.'

He opens the door to usher me out, but I have one last question.

'May I not see Miss Mayer before I go?'

'As I told you, Miss Mayer is at present indisposed. If all goes well, there may be opportunity for the two of you to see each other when this business is over.'

* * *

I ride back through the forest at a more sedate pace, considering what Grey has told me.

Learning of Sergeant Latham's history has modified my opinion of him somewhat. *But is he potential assassin or potential victim?*

His support for the Shoreditch workers serves to emphasise that same loyalty to the common man and contempt for the over-privileged that was implicit in his warning to me that I would sooner or later be abandoned by Bancroft and his like. *But does it necessarily follow that he would act against them?*

On the other hand, he was protesting against the Irish, which would certainly not endear him to Finn Kelly. *Might he be in danger from the Irishman?*

As for Ward, I can more easily understand Sir William's interest in him. His links with Prince Frederick's faction at Leicester House and possible Jacobite connections make him a more plausible threat.

Darkness is falling by the time I arrive back to find camp already being set up. But in my mind, the new information vouchsafed by Grey has, I think, thrown little more light upon my purpose.

River Main

For four more days we march.

Past Bingen, we follow the Rhine on our left until we reach the town of Mainz where it is joined by the River Main. Then, following the Main, a mere stream compared with the mighty river we have left behind us, we continue eastwards until, passing the small town of Seligenstadt we come within sight of the vast army encampment.

Because we arrive at evening I am unable to comprehend the true extent of the forces marshalled there but my first overwhelming impression is one of noise.

Constant marching for weeks on end has accustomed me to the regular thump of feet and crunch of cart-wheels. It has become the rhythm of the daily round. But here are all the sounds of a city, the hum and yell of voices, the clatter of carts, the neighing of horses and, in place of the bells that regulate the days in cities, the harsh bray of trumpets.

The combined English, Austrian and Hanoverian camp is a huge metropolis, grown mushroom-like along the narrow plain between the river and the encroaching hills and stretching further than the eye can see. It has its own thoroughfares criss-crossing the serried ranks of tents, its own districts of little Austria, little England, little Hanover, each with their own disparate languages.

Weary with the day's march, we can only search out where the bulk of English troops are encamped, lay our claim to whatever stretch of turf affords us space to lay our heads and, without even troubling to wrestle blankets from our packs, slump exhausted to the ground and go supperless to bed.

In truth, we have gone supperless for the last two nights. The supplies we brought with us have been well-nigh exhausted. The carts that started laden with supplies have been rattling ever emptier over the past week because the cost-conscious commissioners back in London have underestimated the duration of our journey. Any hope of supplementing supplies as we passed through the countryside has also been dashed. Pillaging by the first forces to arrive has alienated the populace and caused the inhabitants to drive away their cattle and shut their doors against us.

For the last two days, stomachs have been empty, the men scouring the woods in hope of snaring a rabbit or wood-pigeon, searching for berries or fungi, or reduced to plucking leaves or stems of grass to chew on. Even our officers have had only black bread to eat.

Men and beasts alike are in a critical situation. It is a measure of our desperation that all eyes look hungrily for the least sign of what might prove a fatal stumble in our debilitated animals. By the time we sink exhausted on to our patch of hard ground, death in battle seems as welcome a prospect as death from slow, lingering starvation.

I wake in the dawn light to the sound of birdsong and the growling ache of my empty stomach. My neck is stiff from using my back-pack as a pillow and my uniform is damp with dew. Every bone and sinew protests as I roll over to harvest what moisture I can from a ragged tuft of grass, pushing my face deep in its broken fronds to suck what goodness I can before it evaporates in the growing light.

The sweet freshness on my tongue, meagre as it is, nevertheless triggers an urgent need to empty my bladder. I drag myself to my feet and stagger over to a nearby tree. Unlacing myself, I support myself upon the trunk and let go a dribbling, steaming stream.

Around me, others are also stretching themselves from their uncomfortable slumbers, greeting the new day with groans and grumbles.

'Another fucking foodless day,' growls Tom Hooper as I rejoin him and Ben Woodrow. He nods in the direction of a slovenly group of soldiers bickering over scraps. 'They bin out overnight, thievin'. Damned if I ain't tempted to join them tonight if we 'ave to sit on our arses 'ere for much longer.' Then, casting a bleary eye up at the wooded hillside above us. 'mind you, there'll be coneys or squirrels a-plenty up there, I reckon. If we're not fighting Frenchies today, who's up for a bit o' vermin hunting?'

Ben Woodrow rubs his eyes. Exposure to sun and the accumulated grime of the last few weeks have made his facial wine-mark less conspicuous.

' 'Tis a fair enough occupation for a Friday,' says he, 'if we've naught better to do.'

Both Tom and I shake our heads, laughing.

'Sure, Ben, what would we do without you,' snorts Tom. 'Old Moore's Almanack has nothing on you! So finical about days and dates whilst all about reck nought what year it be, let alone the months and days! So come on, tell us what date it is today.'

'Ah, but there lies the problem,' replies Ben, 'for the date here is not the same as it is back in England. Would you have English time or Flanders time?'

Tom turns to me in mock exasperation. 'Is this not typical of an equivocating lawyer, Jack? Cannot even give you the time of day nor the day of the month without quibbling!'

'I think what Ben means is that here in Europe they work upon the Gregorian calendar, whereas back in England we still reckon the days on the Julian system.'

' 'Swelp me, I am beset by bloody scholars!' Tom groans. 'This is all gibberish to me. Enough of the argle – what bloody day is it?'

Ben permits himself a smile. 'Here, in the Electorate of Mainz, as in most of Europe, it is Friday June 21st. But back in England it is Friday June 10th for we English, being of a stubborn nature, stick with the old ways and do not accept the Gregorian manner of reckoning, which is seen as a Popish invention.'

'June 21st, a straight answer at last!' exclaims Tom. 'Though not without a bellyful of twattle and riddle-me-ree along the way. And speaking of bellies, who's coming with me to see if we can catch some dinner?'

Going with Tom on the hunt for food, I am impressed not only by his skill in setting traps but also by the efficient way he dispatches his prey with a swift but humane twist of the neck. He catches a couple of good-sized rabbits which, will later stew up nicely with a handful of mushrooms and wild garlic bulbs.

Whilst he lies in patient and silent wait, I survey the area from our vantage point. Between the River Main and the steep, thickly wooded hills where we are seeking our dinner, there is a margin of fairly flat ground. As far as I can see to either side, I judge this narrow plain betwixt river and foothills to stretch about nine or ten miles.

To the east where the hills retreat northwards, the river winds in a great arc at the apex of which I discern the dwellings of a moderately sized township.This, I learn later when Bancroft shows me a map of the area, is Aschaffenburg.

In the opposite direction, to the west, the hills advance in a sort of peninsula, causing the river to skirt them in a southern flowing loop. On the opposite bank of its southernmost bend, just visible from my vantage point, lies the small town of Seligenstadt which we passed on our march hither.

In surveying the lie of the land, I also begin to appreciate the true size of the army. Our encampment stretches nigh on two or three miles along the plain. Arriving here the other night, I realised there must be many thousand soldiers, but now it is apparent that there are not just thousands but tens of thousands.

It is a huge army – and a huge number of mouths to feed. All the wildlife of the woods behind us would go but a little way to sating such an appetite.

Which is why the small villages and isolated farmsteads which lie between the two towns of Seligenstadt and Aschaffenberg at the extreme ends of the plain have become prey to nocturnal plundering raids by some of our more desperate and less scrupulous colleagues.

Our contingent arrived but a couple of nights ago but many have been here for nigh on two weeks. Hungry and fatigued, chafing at prolonged inaction, they have become undisciplined and fractious. If we are to stay here much longer, there might well be mutiny.

The simmering atmosphere of revolt is not helped by the fact that the French camp is easily discernible on the far bank of the Main opposite Aschaffenburg, where the countryside is flat and open. Rows and rows of tents occupy most of the area, more orderly than ours, restricted as we are by the narrowness of the plain and the forest encroaching from the hills behind us.

Shading my eyes against the morning sun, I can pick out innumerable colourful pennons fluttering in the breeze and see the glitter of arms and harness. I can even hear the distant sound of occasional trumpet-calls.

I have no doubt the French are in better shape than our troops for, although they have also been here several weeks, their supply routes are not cut off and they are not starving.

They, in fact, are the ones who are causing us to starve. General Noailles, their commander, so Lieutenant Bancroft informs me, has blocked our supply route from beyond Aschaffenburg and has positioned a regiment of his troops to cut off supplies from Hanau in the opposite direction.

Bancroft is in as low spirits as I have ever seen him. In meetings with other officers who have been here longer than us, he learns that things should never have come to this pass.

Some weeks ago when Sir John Stair first arrived here, the French army under General Noailles was still many miles away, in retreat before the Austrian advance. Stair's plan had been to take up position on the flat, open plain on the south bank of the River Main and, when the French army arrived, join battle. But orders came from King George in Hanover to withdraw to the northern bank and await His Majesty's arrival.

'Aye, the King wants all the glory for himself,' was Sergeant Latham's comment upon being apprised of this. 'General Stair may be an old man, but he's a seasoned campaigner and I dare say has forgotten more military strategy that His German Majesty ever knew. Now here we are, starving and hemmed in on all sides while the damned Frenchies on the south bank have had time to recoup and only bide their time to pick us off like sitting ducks.'

Needless to say, this treasonable sentiment is not expressed in Bancroft's hearing. But I doubt even he would have the heart to reprimand Latham's bitterness, for there is no denying that our situation is perilous. Here, on the north bank of the River Main, we are caught like mice in a trap.

The hills close us in from the rear, the river from in front. The French control the bridges at Aschaffenburg five miles to our left and at Seligenstadt, as many miles to our right.

We have a choice between sitting still and starving to death, or trying to break through their lines to open the road to Hanau where our magazines are stationed.

It is, in truth, no choice.

Our commanding officer, be it General Stair, the Duke of Cumberland or the King himself must sooner or later make the decision. But while they ponder, we starve.

In the meantime, I think of my master, Mr Garrick and hear his voice:

"The poor condemned English
Like sacrifices by their watchful fires
Sit patiently, and inly ruminate
The morning's danger."

I can only hope that, like Henry V's army at Agincourt, which was also vastly outnumbered by the French forces, we too will be neither condemned nor sacrificed.

Raising the Spirits

Next morning, as the camp stirs wearily to life, heavy eyed and heavy limbed, something appears at last to be happening. There are trumpet calls from the far end of our encampment and, from the same direction, we can hear the faint sound of cheering.

Sergeant Latham is almost immediately hurrying amongst us, barking commands, marshalling our sluggish men into something like order. We are a sorry bunch, haggard, gaunt-faced, our coats besmirched with grass and leaves from sleeping on the ground, boots holed from months of marching, our appearance so unkempt it is hard to know where hair ends and beards begin.

First Lieutenant Bancroft and Second Lieutenant Ward hasten to take their place in front, smoothing down their uniforms which, thanks to my efforts, are still in far better state than those of the men around them. Bancroft gives me a brief look over his shoulder and Ward, turning to see the object of his companion's attention, gives me such a complicit smile that I wonder if Tom Hooper can have been right after all in suggesting he has taken a fancy to me. I do not smile in return.

Meanwhile the whisper has come down the line, 'It is the

King himself and his son the Duke of Cumberland.'

'Come to breathe life into our flagging spirits before we all die of ennui,' mutters Ben Woodrow.

'Be not such a crab,' chides Tom Hooper, 'at least something's happening at long last. And it's not everyday you see the King close to.'

Aye, think I to myself, *though not as close as I have seen him, sitting with his daughter and his German mistress, Madame von Wallmoden, watching Mr Garrick, Mrs Woffington and myself play* 'Twelfth Night' *in the King's Chamber at Kensington Palace.*

But even at the distance of a hundred yards on this river bank in Germany there is no mistaking his portly figure as, white-wigged and red-coated, he trots upon a solid Sussex grey, regally waving his gold braided hat towards the cheering troops.

Nearly every time I saw King George at Kensington, he was either lugubrious or irritable but today he essays a smile. Playing the soldier, he is in his element, far more so than at Court where he seemed perpetually in a fit of the grumps.

Behind him, resplendent upon a gleaming black stallion, rides a man whom I presume is his second son, William, Duke of Cumberland.

During my brief adventure at Kensington Palace, I once

caught sight of his elder brother, Prince Frederick, the heir to the throne. I remember him as lame, straw-haired and plain-faced.

This is the first time I've seen Prince William, for he was not resident during my time there, and I can understand why he is his father's favourite.

About my age, the Duke of Cumberland cuts a fine figure astride his proud charger. Fuller bodied than myself – but then I doubt he has ever had to exist on short rations – he has the Hanoverian nose and fleshy features of his father. His eye is lively and his stance erect and the cheers that greet his passage are more wholehearted, less dutiful than those accorded to his sire.

Tom Hooper is cheering with the best of them, waving his battered tricorn and huzzaing until he is hoarse.

It is not until the King and his son have passed along the line that he is able to speak again. 'A bene swell, the Duke, don't 'ee think? Some would have him the next King, they say.'

'Aye, so I've heard,' I agree, recalling Nathaniel Grey's words about King George wishing to make him heir to the English throne whilst dispatching his elder son, Prince Frederick, to be Elector of Hanover.

'God save us from that,' interjects Ben Woodrow, 'for he's more a warmonger that his sire. A fine face but little sense and less morality.'

' 'Slife!' booms Tom, cuffing him playfully on the shoulder, 'what's eating you today? For all the world 'tis like you've lost a sovereign and found sixpence.'

'Aye, and a sovereign may be the least we'll lose before long,' retorts Ben with grim humour. 'Can there truly be a sorrier sight than starving men cheering their throats sore for two royal nincompoops who tomorrow will lead them to their deaths. The world's gone mad I think!'

'Nay 'tis you who will run mad, my friend,' jests Tom, clasping him in a bear-like embrace and tousling his hair. 'You think too much and it makes you queer as Dick's hatband. Aye, 'tis true we may all die tomorrow, but is that not all the more reason to enjoy today? Come, cheer up, you old grumbletonian!'

The King and the Duke having now passed out of sight, the ranks of men around us are dispersing. The general mood is more buoyant, spirits lifted by the fact that His Majesty has shown his appreciation, however fleeting, for the assembled troops.

In the general stir I am momentarily separated from my friends and I become aware of someone at my shoulder. 'Your friend expresses some seditious views, Corporal Weaver,' murmurs a voice confidentially. 'You do not share them, I trust?'

I turn to see Lieutenant Ward with a smile on his face. But it is only his mouth which smiles. His eyes are probing.

'I would pay them no heed, sir, ' I reply, making light of it. 'The parlous times affect his tongue, I think. He is a good fellow at heart.'

'Many a good fellow may be hung for loose talk. A man of parts should put his tongue to better use, and be able to grasp the outcome of his actions, do you not agree, Jack?' he enquires in an insinuating tone.

His smiling gaze is fixed on me in a manner which makes me uncomfortable.

'I am not sure I follow you, Lieutenant,' I say ingenuously.

By way of reply, he simply holds my gaze, unflinching, for several moments. Then, in the most honeyed tones, he almost purrs, 'Oh, I think you do, JackWeaver. I think you know exactly what I mean.'

The suspense is broken by First Lieutenant Bancroft coming up. 'Why, Fred, here you are. Come, we are summoned for further orders.' Then he notices me. 'I am not interrupting anything, am I? Have you concluded your business, the two of you?'

Ward becomes all affability. 'For the moment, yes. You have a fine young squire here, Henry. I swear I shall steal him from you one day,' he laughs. 'I do not think you truly appreciate his merits.'

'I assure you, you are mistaken, Frederick, and Jack knows just how highly I value him. Come, Frederick, we are waited for.'

'Thank you, sir,' I say as he turns on his heel.

Before following him, Ward holds back for a moment. 'Farewell for the present, Jack Weaver,' he says in an undertone. 'Be assured, matters shall be resolved between us anon.'

As I ponder the import of the remark, I am near catapulted forward by a hearty thump between my shoulder blades. I am only prevented from falling by a sturdy arm across my chest.

'Tryin' to get into your britches again, is he?' booms Tom Hooper. 'Come, Jack, stop pining over your mincing lieutenant and join us in more manly pursuits. The boys and I have a dice-game afoot.'

Four more days of inaction.

Of scavenging what bare sustenance we can from the surrounding countryside. As the supply of larger forest creatures decreases, my companions and I are obliged to supplement our diet with voles, shrews and rats, even snails and earthworms. Boiled in river water and mashed into a paste they at least take the edge off our gnawing hunger.

Four days of finding things to occupy our time. Of brushing coats till they are near threadbare, polishing boots and buckles till they are near worn away, of endlessly checking and oiling our muskets in preparation for the battle which, it seems, will never come.

To break the monotony of military drills and needless cleaning, some of our number take advantage of the noontime warmth to gambol in the river shallows, snatching brief moments of carefree play. A couple of times, my friends and I join with them, laughing and relishing the cool sparkle of water on our naked skin.

But even in such light-hearted frolicking, the war is never far from us. We occasionally glimpse squads of French soldiers on the far bank, sometimes simply observing, but sometimes cantering in formation, harness glinting. On occasion they even shout greetings – or more likely insults – which we return in kind. But our high spirits suffer a setback at the unmistakable sight of cannon drawn behind the horses.

All too easily during these days of enforced indolence, disagreements explode into arguments, scuffles into full-blown fights. Quickly inflamed and equally quickly extinguished, stifled by the torpor of constant waiting and the weight of unfulfilled foreboding.

How easily we wrung hope from the King's brief

appearance among us, a fresh feature on the horizon – and how quickly that hope disappears as the tedium of pointless routine once more takes hold.

Every morning we wake in anticipation, albeit fearful, that today will see us go into action. And every evening we fall into a fitful, restless sleep of non-consummated expectation.

Another manifestation of this suspenseful tedium is the rise of Seb Williams' small band of evangelicals who now hold services twice a day, drawing an ever increasing crowd. Perhaps it is the sound of voices raised in song, or the novelty of someone speaking with passion in this interminable monotony that attracts them – or perhaps day after day of waiting for the unknown brings with it a sense of mortality that craves comfort.

I stand at the periphery of one of their meetings one morning and confess myself stirred by the ardour of their devotion. Williams, so humble and reticent when last I met him as Brogan's reluctant witness, is a very different man in front of this congregation. He preaches with eloquence and zeal, the light of the Lord shining in his eyes. His words inspire the men with a sense of their own worth, with hope for the rewards of a good life.

As my gaze travels over those who have gathered to hear him, it is suddenly pulled up short. There, in the crowd, is

Sergeant Latham. I did not have him down as being of a religious turn of mind. Yet here he is, rubbing shoulders with the men under his command, and raising his voice as fervently as they with cries of 'Praise the Lord!' in response to Williams's exhortations.

I do not see Bancroft, Ward, nor any other of the officers attending these occasions though I am sure they are not without religious beliefs. I have no doubt they attend church back at home every Sunday. But theirs will be the comfortable creed of an Anglican establishment which supports the idea that every man should know his place in society. Williams's evangelical fervour, which preaches that all men are equal in the sight of God, is much too radical for them.

For my own part, I prefer to rely upon myself rather than upon any divine being to shape my destiny.

And it transpires that I shall have to do just that within a matter of hours.

The evening of June 26th 1743 (reckoned, as my friend Ben Woodrow reminds me, according to the Gregorian calendar) promises to be no different from any during the preceding week.

The camp fires glow in the darkness while the drums and cornets sound the last call of the day along the line, signalling that the camp is secure. We crawl under our blankets, positioning our muskets by our sides in the state of constant readiness that we have been ordered to maintain these last three nights, and resign ourselves to another restless night.

Next to me, Tom Hooper is soon asleep, mouth open, snoring deep and raucous. On my other side, Ben Woodrow tosses and turns, uttering occasional incomprehensible mutterings. Beyond and all around, the slow, heavy breathing darkness settles like a thick pall, pierced only by the distant shrieks of night hunting owls.

It seems that I am the only one in the entire camp who is finding it impossible to sleep. Thoughts crowd unsought into my mind. Images of three dead men: Scatchard lying in a pool of blood; Brogan, idly swinging from a tree branch; Barley's broken, bleeding body hauled from the canal.

Each death has been explained. Yet, to my mind, each explanation gives rise to yet more questions.

With his dying breath, Josh Barley admitted to killing Scatchard. But was it of his own volition or did someone set him on to do it? And why?

Similarly, Finn Kelly admitted to killing Brogan because his threat to accuse me of spying would expose Kelly's plans. But what are those plans?

And, although I witnessed Barley's death with my own

eyes, I still have no idea why he was following me in the first place.

Then there is the matter of the potential assassin, the main matter Hervey has assigned me to discover, to which I am no nearer now than I was at the beginning.

Is it someone yet unknown? Not a French assassin, if Finn Kelly is to be believed. It would not serve their ends.

A supporter of the Jacobite cause, then? But I have not come across any such.

Or have I? According to Nathaniel Grey, Second Lieutenant Ward has connections with Leicester House, and there are Jacobite sympathisers there.

Equally, he could be of Prince Frederick's faction. If either King George or his younger son, the Duke of Cumberland, were to die, the throne passes immediately to the Prince.

Or is it not the succession which is at issue - but the very existence of the monarchy itself? In which case someone with such anti-authoritarian views as Sergeant Latham might become a suspect.

Is there a link somewhere which I am missing? Puzzle as I may I cannot see it. Thus, bemused and bewildered, I eventually succumb to a sleep which is to prove only too short.

Dettingen

In the blackest part of the night I am shaken awake by a rough hand upon my shoulder. 'Rouse your fellows,' whispers a rough voice.

Rubbing my eyes as I drag myself from the depths of sleep, I see the man who awakened me, a blacker shadow against the blackness of the night, winding an erratic path amongst the huddled, sleeping forms, bending every so often to wake others.

Gradually the sleepers stir and roll over. Slowly, the solid ground becomes a roiling, heaving sea of mumbling bodies. And by degrees the bewildered mumbling gives way to discontented grumbling which, in its turn, becomes an agitated murmuring.

Is this it, at last? Are we going into action after all these weary days of enforced lethargy?

Still fuddled and disoriented from sleep, the men stagger to their feet. Blankets are rolled, packs shouldered and muskets taken up. The training that has been drilled into us takes over and within a quarter of an hour we are lined up, rheumy-eyed and yawning still, but ready to receive our orders.

These orders are delivered to our platoon by First

Lieutenant Bancroft. His heavy-eyed, gaunt features, lit by the flickering lantern that Sergeant Latham holds aloft, seem to hover, suspended on the darkness, like some bodiless wraith.

'We are marching to Hanau, men. Once re-united with supplies and provisions, we shall be better disposed to face the enemy. It is now an hour and a half after midnight and I enjoin you to silence as we march. Thus we may hope to cover much ground before the enemy are aware that we are on the move.'

'Some bloody hope!' mutters Tom Hooper in my ear. 'Ten thousand horses and forty thousand men tiptoeing away like thieves in the night – do they think the Frenchies are deaf?'

It is near four in the morning before we are fairly on the move, however, and in the waiting hours of pre-dawn the sounds that drift from the far side of the river suggest that Hooper's glum prediction is right.

There is no way the French are going to allow us to make an ignominious retreat to Hanau to replenish supplies. Though largely unspoken, the feeling is that we shall see action before the end of today.

At a little after one o'clock, there comes the sound of galloping hoofs heading west towards Seligenstadt, but whether of one or more horses is difficult to tell.

Then, at the same time as our platoon, with stealthy movements in response to hushed commands, begins lining up with others in preparation to march in the same direction, the noise of similar, but less secretive, activity is heard in the darkness beyond the river. The French, too, are preparing to move and they are making no effort to keep their voices down or mask the lights which bob like a swarm of fireflies in the darkness.

As dawn starts to lighten the sky behind us, we are finally in motion, our English Cavalry leading the way, with the Austrian Cavalry in their wake. We, the foot soldiers follow on, first the English regiments and then the Austrian.

My friends and I are amongst the rear ranks, the first of the Austrian infantry just behind us. I glance back several times to see if I can catch a glimpse of Fritz Dorn, but with no success, and I wonder if I will ever see him again.

As daylight brightens and the confused and shifting shadows gradually take solid form, we can clearly see French troops marching on the opposite bank.

'What the deuce are they playin' at?' exclaims Tom in amazement. For they are moving in the opposite direction, towards Aschaffenburg.

'My guess is that they're going to cut off any possibility of our retreating,' observes Ben Woodrow. 'They'll cross the river and follow us. They know as well as we that the land between here and Seligenstadt is narrow and boggy - do you not remember it on the way here? As we flounder, they'll come up behind us and pick us off.'

'Right bloody Job's comforter you are, Ben Woodrow!' scolds Tom. 'In that case, why not just sit down and wait for 'em. "Here, Froggy, Froggy, here's an English chicken all ready for the plucking!"'

I laugh. 'They're in for a nasty shock if they think to ride roughshod over us,' I tell them, 'for according to Lieutenant Bancroft an assault is anticipated from that direction. There's three battalions of English Guards together with four of His Majesty's German allies and most of the Hanoverian cavalry and artillery left behind to act as rearguard. His Majesty himself intends to be there with them.'

'Aye, with his precious Hanoverian troops,' says Ben bitterly, unwilling to relinquish his pessimism, 'whilst we, his English subjects, may go hang!'

By now, the early morning mists have cleared, the sun has risen and is sparkling on the water with all the promise of a fine summer day ahead.

But, even as the morning light enables me to distinguish the colours of the uniforms around me and the forested hillside rising on our right hand, there comes the sudden boom of cannon and the river bank to our left explodes with plumes of flying earth and great fountains of water.

Taken unawares, everyone involuntarily ducks, raising arms as a shield against the clods of earth and stones raining down around us. For a moment, all is a chaos of foul oaths and swerving bodies as we scramble to avoid the hail of flying dust and fragments.

Here, as we tramp slowly along the narrow riverside plain we present an open a target to French batteries of 12 pounders that have been set up on the opposite bank. These are the cannon we've seen being towed along by horses two days ago whilst we were frolicking in the water. General Noailles has obviously anticipated that sooner or later we would be obliged to make a break for it, and positioned them to fire upon us from across the river.

Hardly has the order come down the line to wheel right into the outskirts of the wood than another volley screams through the air ripping the ground apart again. Fewer fountains of water this time. The enemy have adjusted their range of fire.

For the next two hours, we march on in fits and starts, pounded by shot which shakes the ground and raises clouds of drifting smoke and dust, obscuring the trees which loom with such suddenness out of the murk that we have great difficulty in avoiding unlooked for collisions in addition to all our other woes.

At about ten, judging by what I can see of the sun's position through the thick air, we are called to halt. Word comes that French soldiers have been sighted ahead and that we shall see action before the afternoon.

With Bancroft's permission, I take the opportunity to climb further up the hill to see if I can espy the disposition of the enemy.

We have traversed, by my reckoning no more than three, or possibly four miles. Scanning the countryside to my left, I make out plumes of smoke back in the direction of Aschaffenburg. Our artillery must be returning the French fire.

Also, slightly nearer, the drifting smoke allows brief glimpses of a confusion of blue and red uniforms with the occasional flash of sunlight on helmets and breastplates. And I can hear the distant whinnying of horses and crack of muskets. The French troops which we saw at dawn heading east must have crossed the bridge at Aschaffenburg to pursue us on this side of the river and are now engaging with our cavalry.

Just as I begin to wonder if King George is really there in the rear-guard, urging on his Hanoverian troops, a flurry of activity down by the river attracts my attention. A small band of riders, braving the continual French cannonade, is galloping apace from the direction of Aschaffenburg towards Seligenstadt.

By the abundance of gold braid upon their coats, they are high ranking officers, and unmistakable in their midst is the King himself. Clearly he has been apprised that the French are offering a threat to the front of us as well as in the rear and is come to set our forces in battle order.

Suddenly a gruff voice mutters in my ear, 'Your King has had word that le Conte Grammont awaits him with a force of twenty-eight thousand on the road ahead.'

I turn to see Gerard at my shoulder, his dark features more saturnine than ever with three days growth of beard.

He gives me a twisted smile. 'You think to avoid the confrontation and stay alive by hiding up here among the trees?'

'Not at all,' I reply indignantly. 'I came to see the lie of the land, that's all.'

'Nay, rail not at me,' he scoffs. 'It is the duty of a spy, is it not, to stay alive. There is no shame in it. Especially when faced with such overwhelming odds.'

'Twenty-eight thousand, you say? How do you know this?'

'My eyes and ears, they are everywhere. Look there where the river bends.'

He directs my attention to a point some two miles away

where the hamlet of Dettingen lies upon the banks of a shallow ravine spanned by a single, narrow bridge.

'Grammont, he is stationed just beyond that bridge since eight this morning. As soon as General Noailles saw you moving, he gave orders for Grammont to cross the river. I watched the horsemen urge their beasts into the water where it was shallow enough to ford. Others crossed by the bridge they have erected at Seligenstadt. Now they champ with impatience at your tardiness.'

I look in dismay at the river plain between us and Dettingen remembering how we passed along it a week ago on our way here. Below where we stand it is at its narrowest, little more than a mile between the river and the trees, but relatively firm underfoot. A little further on, it becomes boggy again. And then there is the ravine with its narrow bridge.

No need of twenty-eight thousand troops. A party of twenty marksmen could just as easily pick us off as we pass in enforced single file across that bridge.

But now I hear our officers shouting us back into line to continue our march.

Gerard slinks off between the trees, one more red-coated figure to sidle amongst all the rest - or pursue, incognito and unremarked, his own separate way.

As I rejoin my friends, it is clear that we are being lined

up for battle. Outriders have confirmed that the lines of French foot soldiers spotted this side of Dettingen is no mere rumour.

It is undoubtedly the case that Count Grammont has advanced his troops over the twin obstacles of the bridge and the ravine which would have undoubtedly proved our downfall and is now mustering his forces on the narrow plain.

I turn to my friends in amazement. 'Why, when they have the advantage upon the other side of a narrow bridge and a ravine, would they advance to meet us?'

They are as bewildered as I, but in one respect at least this incomprehensible manoeuvre proves a blessing. The bombardment of artillery from the far bank has become more intermittent, fearing, perhaps, to wreak as much havoc upon their own army as upon ours as it takes up position.

As a result, the pall of smoke and dust is clearing somewhat and when finally, after a great deal of marching and counter-marching, our position in the line has been decided, I am able to see exactly what we are faced with.

I am in the second rank, almost midway along our front line. From within a furlong of the river, a solid block of red, three ranks deep and with muskets at the ready, stretches for near three quarters of a mile towards the forested hills. Immediately to our right is a further brigade of Austrian foot, then, encroaching at the far end into the outskirts of the wood, four regiments of cavalry: the Blues, the Life Guards, the Sixth Dragoons and the Royal Dragoons.

A hundred yards behind us, in the second line, are another six regiments of foot and seven of cavalry, and another hundred yards behind them a smaller contingent in reserve.

But, when we think all is arranged, there is yet one more burst of activity. General Clayton has surveyed the enemy lines through his spyglass and calls for a regiment of cavalry to take up its position in the two hundred yards between the river and our first regiment of foot in order to bolster our left flank.

He has seen that the flower of the French forces, the *Maison du Roi,* the French Household Cavalry regiment, has taken the place of honour at the right of their front line, directly opposite our foot regiments. The French have chosen to deploy their infantry in the centre, with cavalry on both flanks.

Nor is everything ready yet. The King, who for the last half hour has been capering about on horseback giving orders in great excitement whilst staff officers have galloped to and fro, is now engaged in heated discourse with his son, the Duke of Cumberland and a handful of Generals.

From my position near the front I catch snatches of the

argument. His Majesty, it seems, would be in the thick of the action with his son, the Duke, upon the left flank. It is only with extreme difficulty that he is prevailed upon to have more regard for his own safety, but eventually he concedes and, after riding along the line waving his sword and shouting words of encouragement in his strong German accent, takes up a position between the rightmost regiment of foot and the Blues.

Which, by good fortune, happens to be within a few yards of my position in the line. In my task to keep an eye on His Majesty's safety, Fate could not have arranged matters better.

Now, however, the time has finally come.

All we await is the order to advance.

I cannot remember any other minutes in my life when I experienced such apprehension and such unnatural silence. It is as if all the thousands of men around me are holding their breath.

In the bright summer noonday, the air hangs heavy with anticipation. Suddenly the gentle plash of the river shallows over pebbles, the distant cooing of wood pigeons, the snuffling of horses and the soft jingling of harness take on a hitherto unnoticed clarity and resonance in the expectant quiet.

And, mingling with all these, a low, fervent whispering

of innumerable murmured prayers.

At just gone noon, the King raises his sword and, bringing it swiftly down to point at the enemy, finally gives the order to advance.

Action

No sooner have we started moving than the battery of the guns starts up again aiming directly at our left flank.

Exhausted, light-headed from lack of food, we trudge doggedly forward. My limbs seem to move of their own accord, like a sleeper in a nightmare from which I cannot awaken. And we trail our own hell with us in the form of the yells of mortally wounded men and the terrified whinnying of horses from the direction of the river where the Third Dragoons are suffering the brunt of the cannons' onslaught.

The rest of us press on relentlessly, trying to blank out the chorus of destruction where each thudding impact of artillery is followed by fresh cries of agony and the splashing and thrashing of floundering bodies in the river shallows.

But the going is slow, for some of the regiments along the line are once more mired up to the knees in the morasses and when we are still a few hundred yards from the enemy, the order is given to halt, that we may take breath.

A feeble, derisive cheer arises from some of the British line, quickly stifled by outraged barks from the officers. Sergeant Latham passes on the reprimand, yet I would swear that he himself had but a minute before lent his own voice to the jeer of exhausted discontent.

Once the line is re-dressed, the advance resumes in better order. The ground is firmer now, the pace more eager as if we are seized with a reckless lunacy, a desperate determination that, if death lies ahead, we are determined to rush rather than stumble towards our fate.

A full-throated roar bursts from every throat, adding to the clash of arms and drowning the cries of the dying as I, together with all around me, am caught up in the wholesale madness and break into a run with the hooves of the cavalry to our left and right drumming in my ears.

In the forefront of French line we see the *Maison du Roi* prancing and fleering, which provokes some of our men to forget the discipline of their training and open fire before being ordered.

Such wild firing serves only to enrage the enemy and our own commanding officers who scream at us to halt, resume ranks and restore the order of fire.

We obey from force of habit, forming into our three lines, creating a solid wall in face of the charging line of horses bearing down upon us.

In front of us, the King rides up and down the line, waving his sword and exhorting us to uphold England's honour.

I load my musket and stand ready as the row of men in

front of me fire a volley exactly as we have been taught in our innumerable drills.

Or at least, not quite.

Someone in the front rank mis-aims, for at the very moment the men in front drop to their knees to reload and I raise my musket to fire, I catch in the corner of my eye the last spatter of a divot of earth thrown up immediately under the hooves of the King's horse. The beast rears in fright, scattering soldiers immediately behind it like ninepins, and bolts to the rear.

My shot discharged, I and all my line drop to our knees in turn but, rather than reload in the manner I was taught, I scramble between the legs of the men behind me and set off in pursuit of the King.

Whether anyone notes my flight I do not know. A brief glance back, a few moments later, shows that the second rank has only just had time to discharge its second volley before the *Gens d'Armes* are upon them and all is a confusion of scattering bodies and careering horses. The din of yelling, screaming men and beasts surges like a tidal wave behind me as I hurtle, headlong, after the King's runaway horse.

His Majesty, with purple face and eyes starting out of his head, is pulling desperately at the reins but with little effect as his mount dashes pell-mell towards the woods.

Eventually, whether by the King's own horsemanship, by the obstruction of the trees - or, more likely, by the intervention of several horsemen of the King's Dragoon Guards who, waiting in the second line, see the situation and ride aside from their fellows to impede the animal's flight - the errant steed is brought, snorting and sweating, to a halt.

I am still some distance away, my speed being no match for that of the King's horse. I come to a standstill, bent double, heaving for breath. Only as I recover do I realise the foolishness of my precipitate action.

A nameless soldier claiming to have broken ranks to save His Majesty? I'll be lucky not be shot on the spot as a deserter!

The continuing turmoil behind me, however, may prove my salvation. Pausing only to satisfy myself that His Majesty is no longer in any immediate danger - two Staff Officers have ridden up and are now escorting him back towards the right flank of the front line – I scurry back to where my fellow soldiers are regrouping.

The French cavalry have retreated, repulsed by a flanking charge from the Blues and the gaps in our infantry lines are being repaired. No heed is paid to original platoons, we are all part of one army now.

Nevertheless, Tom Hooper's burly frame is easy to pick out and I elbow my way through to stand by his side.

Looking about me, I see that Ben Woodrow is missing.

'Where's Ben?' I ask of Tom. 'God forbid he has not fallen?'

'Nay, I know not. He was right in front of me when the damned Frenchies charged, but was upended and flung aside like the rest of us. He'll have come to no harm, I'll lay, not if the Almighty wants to avoid being sued for breach of contract!' he guffaws.

The line repaired, we are brought to order. This time I am in the front rank and am able to see that the King has dismounted, clearly placing more confidence in his own two legs rather than a skittish horse to carry him in the right direction.

As the order is given to load, I am reassured to see many familiar faces from both Bancroft's and Lieutenant Ward's platoons. Bancroft and Ward stand together a dozen or so men to my left and I note that Sergeant Latham is in company with Seb Williams and his band of Christians.

The King takes up his position in front of us, closely flanked by several staff officers both on foot and on horseback, preparing to give the order for a second advance.

Count Grammont, the enemy commander, seeing that a brigade of French cavalry has failed to rout us, now faces us with several regiments of infantry. Cheering loudly, they open a fitful and disorderly fire which raises more derisive jeers from the English side.

'Silence!' shouts an old soldier imperiously, galloping up. This, I guess, must be Sir John Stair, the Commander in Chief of our forces.

There is, I know, little love lost between him and His Majesty. The rumour has gone round that this morning King George gave the order for the army to move without informing Stair which resulted in the old General quitting the Berlin in which he was travelling and racing on horseback to arrange the disposition of troops when we were unexpectedly faced with Grammont's forces this side of Dettingen.

Now there is a frostily polite interchange between him and the King which results in the King deferring to the veteran soldier, who takes up his position before us.

'Now one and all together when I give the signal.'

Certainly this appearance of amity heartens the troops for as Stair raises his hat, we stand firm as a wall of brass and, as his arm descends, pour out volley after volley, deadly and unceasing, which tears great holes in the lines of the enemy. Seeing them topple, we give vent to another great roar of triumph which seems to cow them. Turning tail, they flee in disorder through the close-packed horses of the cavalry to their rear, suffering as much damage under the hooves behind as from bullets in front.

As soon as our officers see the French infantry retreating, they give the order to dress by twos so that gaps are opened for the cavalry behind us to advance in orderly fashion through our ranks to meet the enemy.

Weary as I am, I cannot but feel a sense of pride in how we have comported ourselves. The French may have by far the greater numbers, but they have not shown our discipline. I hear in my head the words of the Austrian soldier on the road from Bruges: 'Die Fransozen? Pah!' Dey are better dancers than soldiers.'

But now the battle becomes the province of the cavalry. We foot soldiers at the right flank disperse into the outskirts of the wood, fighting only occasional brief skirmishes with any isolated groups of the enemy we chance to meet, whilst down on the plain the rival horsemen clash.

During one of our periods of respite, Tom Hooper grabs my arm. 'Look there,' says he urgently, directing my attention to a point some four hundred yards away down on the plain. 'Is not that Ben, scurrying about like a mouse among cornstalks?'

Now that French and English are engaged in close combat, the artillery bombardment from across the river has ceased and, with the infantry fragmented, smoke from musket fire is largely dispersed, leaving the afternoon bright and clear.

There, sure enough, in the midst of the fighting, swerving his way round unhorsed troopers fighting hand to hand, and skirting the rearing, towering horses, the hurrying figure looks mightily familiar. Though begrimed with the stains of battle, it is still possible to make out, even at this distance, the dark patch of his disfigurement.

'Come on, Jack,' says Tom, 'let's catch the bugger.'

I am hard on his heels as he sets off at a lumbering trot, half running, half sliding down the slope, and soon we ourselves are dodging the sword-blades of riders and hooves of horses as we try to keep our quarry in sight.

As we weave an erratic path through the mayhem and the hubbub, we are as often confronted by dead bodies in our path as by live combatants. They lie scattered, limbs twisted, the gashes of open sabre wounds mangled even further by the trampling of iron-shod hooves.

In the midst of all the shouting, the braying of horses, the thud of hooves and the clash of steel on steel, they lie wrapped in eternal silence.

We have covered no more than half a mile and are come into an area where the conflict is slightly less when I am suddenly brought up short.

'Hold hard, Tom,' I cry. 'Is that not Lieutenant Bancroft?'

I run to the side of the prostrate figure and kneel beside him, bending my ear to his lips.

'He lives, Tom, he breathes still. Here, help me,' I say, attempting to raise him.

The front of his red coat is stained a deeper crimson, but as I lift him up, he opens his eyes and groans in pain. 'Jack, is it you?'

'Aye, sir. Are you badly hurt?'

'Shot, I think,' he whispers with an effort. His breath, drawn with difficulty, wheezes within his chest.

'Come, we will get you to safety,' I say, draping his arm around my shoulders and urging Tom to take his other side.

Together, we carry him, bravely stifling groans and gasps of pain, to a place of greater quiet and lay him on a grassy mound where I can examine his wounds with greater security.

Carefully, I remove his coat and waistcoat and roll up his shirt. The bullet has pierced his side and likely punctured his lung but has, as far as I am able to see, passed straight through and is not lodged inside his body. He has lost a deal of blood but it is a clean wound and he will live, given the right care.

I tear away a short strip of his shirt and fold it into a pad to staunch any further loss of blood. Then a broader, longer strip which I bind tightly around his chest to hold the pad in place.

He smiles weakly. 'Sure, Jack, you are quite the surgeon,'

he murmurs. 'Is there no end to your talents?' He attempts a laugh, but is overcome with a coughing which causes him great pain.

I grip his hand tightly. 'Peace, sir, do not attempt to speak. We will take you to safety.'

Loosely re-fastening his waistcoat and draping his coat around his shoulders, I once again enlist Tom's aid to raise his arms about our shoulders.

'What, and risk dislodging your handiwork? By your leave, Lieutenant Bancroft, sir, you'll not object to carrying?' says he, and proceeds to pick him up and cradle him across his arms as if he were no heavier than a child. Indeed, to a strapping fellow like Tom Hooper, Bancroft's slight frame poses no more challenge that an errant sheep or bags of grain that he grew up with on the farm he has left behind

That thought suddenly brings an overwhelming sense of what I myself have lost. Here, with the smoke and confusion of the battlefield raging but a short way off and surrounded by the clash of arms and groans of dying men, the image of my mother, my family and my friends back in Yorkshire unexpectedly flashes across my mind. Companions with whom I am only recently reacquainted, yet whom I may never see again.

But in the present circumstances I have no breathing

space to dwell upon a life twice lost.

In pursuing Ben Woodrow, who has now disappeared in the mayhem, we have come closer to the river where the devastation caused by the persistent bombardment of the French artillery is too hideously apparent. But it is here where the fighting is now getting fiercer as the enemy advance in earnest against our weakened left flank.

Tom Hooper and I have to fight against a surge of fusiliers in their characteristic mitred caps coming at a fast run, called forward to reinforce the front line. Within minutes they have formed the defensive wall and commence a rapid and rolling fire against the oncoming French cavalry which brings men and horses crashing down in turmoil and confusion.

Preceding Tom as he carries Lieutenant Bancroft towards the rear of the line, I glance back and see that the French horsemen are still coming on, pistols in both hands, their swords dangling from their wrists. When in range, they fire their pistols and, once among our forces, dash the empty weapons in our soldiers faces and lay about them with their swords. But the fusiliers fight back like devils, holding the line, their platoon fire continuing to thunder out as regularly as on drill parade.

By the time we have reached the rear and the comparative safety of the baggage wagons, a hearty cheer from behind us signals another French retreat.

We leave Lieutenant Bancroft with the scores of wounded who have crawled or been carried hither. With no qualified surgeon or physician to hand, and every able-bodied soldier being called to the thick of battle, they must shift for themselves, the lesser injured tending to the greater, until the fight be lost or won.

As Tom and I make our way back to the action, we are accosted by Lieutenant Ward who looms suddenly out of the smoke.

'Get back to the line, you scum. Do you not realise that while you cower your comrades die?' He emphasises his order by bearing down upon us waving his pistol.

Only as he comes closer does he recognise us and his manner changes. 'Jack Weaver, I did not see it was you. What are you doing here?'

I explain about Bancroft.

'Shot, you say?'

'Aye, but like to recover. Now Tom and I are returning to continue the fight.'

'Follow me,' says Ward. 'We must fill the gaps where the need is greatest.'

All this time we have not ceased our steady trot towards the continuing smoke and din.

Now we increase our pace to a run.

Death on the Battlefield

We head for the left flank of the front line nearest the river where the fighting is fiercest and arrive just as the Third Dragoons are mounting another charge against the *Maison du Roi.*

Already heavily depleted by the artillery bombardment and repeated assaults from the French, they are now well-nigh annihilated. More than thrice the number of men and horses litter the hundred yards or so of trampled and cratered wasteland than are left alive. But such is the survivors' determination and gallantry that, weak and weary as they are, they are essaying a third charge into what must be ten times their number of French, valiantly cutting their way through them.

Meanwhile, the line of British infantry and fusiliers, now supplemented by numerous Austrian foot soldiers, still forms a solid wall, men moving forward to fill the gaps in the front rank when comrades are felled by enemy fire.

So great is the noise of clashing arms and musket fire that Ward must needs gesture where we are to station ourselves, for even his shouts cannot be heard over the din.

Tom and I insert ourselves into the back row of the infantry, whilst Lieutenant Ward takes up position five or six men away to our right, and immediately we fall into the pattern of rolling fire that has been instilled into us.

Scarcely five minutes pass before there is an urgent trumpet call followed by a general scattering of the men to our right. Then, to the thunder of hooves, a vast surge of cavalry crashes in from the right flank.

We fall back rapidly as two more regiments of British Dragoons gallop within a few feet of us, riding to the aid of the beleaguered Third.

Shaken, we line up once more to be ready if our fire power should be needed again. In the jostling for places someone slaps me on the shoulder. I turn to see Fritz Dorn edging himself in beside me. He puts his mouth to my ear, to be heard above the tumult. 'JackWeaver, is good to see you. Ve survive, *ja?* De damned French, ve are too good for them.'

I give him a comradely hug, my face wreathed in smiles. 'Good to see you, too, Fritz.'

His hat is gone and his fair hair matted with dried blood, which also streaks his face. Seeing my look of concern, he leans close once more. '*Eine Kugel,* a stray bullet,' he says, tapping the side of his head. '*Nur ein gras* – a graze only.'

But now the order comes for us to stand ready. The English Cavalry are being driven back, their swords and bullets being no match for the heavy breastplates and helmets of the French Household Cavalry.

The shout is passed along the line, 'Aim for heads and horses!' and once more we open fire and are rewarded with the sight of many Frenchmen toppling with bloody faces as their steeds are shot from under them.

This gives time for our repulsed cavalry to re-group and, learning the lesson of our targeting heads and horses, they close in on the enemy from the sides and shoot them down in scores.

Gradually the enemy is forced back and it seems we may yet have prospect of winning the day. But just as a cheer goes up from the English and Austrian foot soldiers, it is stifled in our throats.

A large contingent of French horse breaks away from the main body in front of us and gallops away between the continuing interchange of infantry fire along the centre of the line to make a dash against the British Royal Dragoons which is the only cavalry regiment left guarding our weakened right flank.

I am filled with misgivings that the enemy may regain the initiative, but beside me, Fritz almost dances with glee. '*Französische idioten!* Dey have no sense. While dey attack the British in front, Marshal Neipperg will bring our Austrians behind and all vill be done!'

And so it proves. The foolhardy breakaway French

regiment, which I later learn were the vainglorious Black Musketeers, are surrounded and cut down.

We do not see it from where we are. What we do see a few minutes later, however, is the triumphant British and Austrian cavalry bearing down from our right, routing the remaining French infantry at the centre who take to their heels and flee, and thundering along before us to complete the humiliation of the *Maison du Roi.*

In the midst of the confusion, one figure on horseback stands out. It is the Duke of Cumberland in the thick of the action.

And, at the same moment as I recognise him, I also see Ben Woodrow.

He is heading directly towards the Duke with a pistol in each hand.

Without thinking, I break ranks for the second time today and hare off in pursuit.

Fending off arms outstretched to grab me and buffeted by the milling horses, I fight my way through, reaching Ben just as he raises his weapon.

I leap forward, striking down his arm at the moment the pistol discharges. In the general melee, one more gunshot attracts no notice. But I have seen where it was aimed. And I also see the Duke suddenly bend double over his horse's neck, as if poleaxed. His mount, whinnying with alarm, takes flight directly towards enemy ranks.

Ben Woodrow, his face a mask of fury, rounds on me, his other pistol raised, but seeing who has thwarted him utters a cry of distress. 'No, Jack. Not you, I cannot.' His weapon droops in his hand.

Suddenly, all is clear. 'You are the assassin,' I say.

We are shouting at the top of our voices, because all around us is bedlam. I grab him close, as much to prevent us being crushed by the cavorting beasts all around us as from any desire to arrest him for his treachery.

We grapple, simultaneously supporting and fighting each other in the midst of the confusion,

'Why?' I ask.

'Need you ask?' he yells in my ear. 'A rotten tree bears rotten fruit. I did only what I had to do. Now, if you are my friend, let me go.'

'You know I cannot do that, Ben, friend or no.'

He struggles yet harder, managing to wrest himself from my grip as we are struck by a stumbling horse which knocks me off balance and throws me to the ground

He staggers back and raises his pistol. 'I'm sorry, Jack,' says he standing over me, 'but you give me no choice.'

I shield my eyes with my arm, bracing myself for the fatal shot.

But it does not come.

I open my eyes, expecting to see him gone, but he is still there. No longer threatening me with a pistol, for it has fallen from his nerveless hand.

Tom Hooper has him pinioned from behind with one brawny arm around Ben's slim chest.

As I scramble to my feet I see Tom take our friend's head in his other huge paw, just as he took those of the rabbits he captured and, with one swift flick, twist it round to the side. Even above the clamour around us I hear the sickening crack of Ben's neck breaking.

Tom releases the body, letting it fall to the ground, just one more casualty among the hundreds. Then, he grabs my arm and pulls me away.

'It's for the best. Quick and clean. Better than torture and public gutting for treason. He doesn't deserve that. He was our friend, in spite of everything.'

We try to push our way back towards the infantry line against the general flow of bodies, but our efforts are futile and we have no option but to be carried along with it.

The defeated French forces are being pushed back, their army, on horseback and on foot, in headlong flight towards the fords and bridges of the River Main.

I see scores, if not hundreds, of men plunging madly into the stream, being engulfed or trampled by floundering horses, escaping being killed on the battlefield only to perish in a watery grave.

In truth, the horror of it all washes over me as surely as the water of the River Main washes over their luckless heads. For since the revelation of Ben Woodrow's treachery my senses are numb. I feel strangely disembodied, as if I am a wraith, a facsimile of myself with neither will nor volition of my own. Observing myself as unemotionally as the floating dead.

And all is not over yet.

As Tom and I stand in silence, watching but not really seeing the carnage before us, a voice penetrates my consciousness.

'Turn, Jack Weaver. Lay down your arms. I am arresting you for deserting your post.'

Beside me, Tom Hooper swears under his breath, 'For fuck's sake!'

We turn to see Second Lieutenant Ward with Sergeant Latham at his side.

'I am not armed, sir,' I reply with weary resignation.

'That's it, lad,' says Sergeant Latham in a surprisingly approving tone as he comes to bind my wrists behind me. 'Best come quietly,' says he in my ear as he bends to tie the cord. 'I warned you this day would come, did I not? That they'd cast you aside.' There is no triumph in his tone, only regret.

Tom Hooper steps forward holding out his arms. 'Best tie me up, too, sergeant. For if Jack's guilty, then so am I.'

'Stand aside, soldier,' replies Ward. 'My business is with Corporal Weaver, not you. Report back to your platoon.'

Tom looks as if he would protest, but in face of a direct order and the implacable presence of two senior officers, he has no choice but to obey.

'Never fear, Jack,' says he in an undertone as Latham urges me onward, 'I'll go to Bancroft immediately. He'll put an end to this nonsense.'

'Enough,' snaps Ward, though I am certain he has not overheard Tom's promise. 'Bring him along, Sergeant Latham.'

So dejected am I with all that has transpired that I allow Latham to lead me along without demur and it is only when the three of us are entering the outskirts of the forest that I begin to realise that, wherever we are going, it is not back to the line.

Latham, too, has noticed and seems uneasy.

'Lieutenant, sir,' he calls to Ward who is striding rapidly ahead, 'where are we taking the prisoner?'

'None of your business, Sergeant. You are required to obey orders, not question them.'

I sense Latham bristle at Ward's peremptory tone, but

discipline is too much ingrained in him to object.

We are now some way up the hill where the trees cluster more thickly. Outlined against the sky at the top of the rise, at a distance of about half a mile, I can just see, in between the trunks, a line of coaches, the Berlins which have carried all the high-ranking officers hither and from which government officials, including Lord Carteret, the Secretary for War, have observed the progress of the battle.

But it is not to them that we are heading, for now Ward stops and waits for us to come up with him. Once we are within a couple of yards, he says, 'Untie the prisoner, Latham. Then you may return to your men.'

Latham unties my wrists. In the distance, the noise of battle is lessening, becoming more subdued as the victors regroup and begin to count the cost of the day.

Up here in the wood, there is no-one but us. Though, as Latham worries at the knots, I could swear I see a shadow flit between the trunks beyond where Ward frets impatiently at Latham's slowness.

Surely Tom Hooper has not had the rashness to follow us?

I sense the sergeant's delay is more to do with his own indignation than with the tightness of the knots, however, for when he at last undoes the cord, he protests, 'This is most irregular, sir. I cannot in all conscience leave you alone in company with such a desperate fellow.'

Dutiful as ever, he cannot find it in himself to question an order - only to profess himself mindful of his superior's safety.

But Ward is not to be so cajoled. 'Do as you're told, Sergeant. I am more than a match for this fellow. See, I am armed and he is not,' says he, drawing his pistol.

By now, my despondency has totally evaporated and my every nerve is jangling in alarm.

I know now who Ward is and what he is about.

I speak up boldly. 'This has nothing to do with desertion, has it, Lieutenant? This is to do with things back in London.'

'Silence, Weaver,' spits Ward. 'Sergeant, make yourself scarce if you know what's good for you. Corporal Weaver and I have business of our own.'

But Latham is not to be so cowed. His face is a picture of disgust. He, like Hooper, probably suspects some lecherous motive. 'No sir, I will not. This is against all military discipline. Weaver is one of my men and I will not have him used so.'

He gets no chance to continue, however, for Ward, swinging his pistol towards the Sergeant, fires.

With an exclamation of disbelief, Latham staggers back, blood pouring from his thigh.

Ward pays him no heed. He now has the pistol pointing

squarely at my head. 'I don't know what you have done, Weaver, but my orders are to eliminate you. Believe me, I bear you no personal grudge, but you have offended people more powerful than I and you must pay the price.'

As he cocks the weapon, I consider my best course of action. *To run – and die with a bullet in my back? To stand – and meet death full on?*

As his finger presses the trigger, I take a third course. I throw myself bodily to the ground, knocking all the breath from my body in the process, but luckily hear the bullet whizz harmlessly an inch above my head.

Quickly as I can in my winded state, I roll over and start to stagger to my feet.

Ward is re-loading and coming towards me. But as he raises his pistol, I feel myself pushed aside and thrown once more to the ground.

Latham limps heavily past me, bayonet fixed on the muzzle of his musket. As Ward redirects the pistol at him, Latham brings the blade down in a sweeping arc. The gun drops to the ground, the Lieutenant's hand still curled around it. With a scream of pain Ward, clutching the bleeding stump, turns tail and flees.

Latham, panting, slumps down next to me.

'You're a jumped-up jackanapes, Weaver, but rules is rules,' he gasps. 'What that bastard intended – 'tain't soldierly nor Christian.' Then he falls unconscious on the ground beside me.

Looking to where Ward has fled, I see a shadow run swiftly from between the trees and, with a swift blow to the head with the butt of a pistol, fell the running man in his tracks.

Hanau

When I see Ward fall, my first thought is to cover the two hundred yards to accost his assailant who even now is dragging him away.

But a groan from Sergeant Latham, whose leg is bleeding profusely from the wound in his thigh, alerts me to my main priority. Using his belt as a ligature, I fasten it tightly around the top of his leg to act as a tourniquet.

It takes me fully twenty minutes to get him back, for though our way lies downhill and I am sturdy, he is a big man and his weight near exhausts what little reserve of determination I have left. Besides which, his hurt has made him delirious. He babbles nonsense and seems to have no memory of what has brought him to this pass.

As we emerge from the woodland, I feel the first heavy drops of rain which, by the time I lay him amongst the other wounded, has become a downpour of such force that I am drenched to the skin within seconds.

By now the day is well-night spent, the heavy-bellied, leaden clouds pre-empting the encroaching dark of evening only by an hour or so.

Unfortunately it is not just a temporary cloudburst. It promises to be set in for the rest of the night. Already it is turning the torn ground into a quagmire through which bedraggled figures plod, counting and collecting the dead from river and plain, though by now it is difficult to tell where one ends and the other begins. Burgeoning rivulets weave in ever greater profusion through the mud, creating islets and peninsulas in once solid ground. The heavens seem intent on expunging all evidence of the battle that has been fought here, intent on erasing all memory and washing away all blood.

Makeshift shelters of tarpaulins have been erected by the baggage wagons to protect the injured from the elements and, now the battle is done, one or two surgeons have appeared, shipped hither, I guess, by the fleet of Berlins carrying those who have observed the day's events and which now will be transporting the generals and government ministers to drier accommodation.

As I surrender Sergeant Latham into the care of a physician, I notice that there are French as well as Austrian and English amongst the incoming wounded. In the aftermath of the conflict, it appears that enmity is forgotten and humanity is the one true victor.

I search out First Lieutenant Bancroft to see how he does and am cheered to find him on his feet, albeit treading slowly and charily, doing what he can to assist those in more desperate straits than himself.

'I am glad to see you well, sir,' I say.

'And I likewise,' he replies. 'Private Hooper brought some story of you being in danger – I could make no sense of it – something about Lieutenant Ward and Sergeant Latham?'

'It was nothing, sir. A misunderstanding. But Sergeant Latham is injured. I have just brought him in.'

'Not seriously, I hope? Can you bring me to him?'

I do as he requests, hoping that Latham has not yet recovered his wits enough to tell what happened.

As we make our slow progress amongst the sprawled and groaning bodies, Bancroft tells me of an incident he observed earlier.

'The Duke was brought in, shot, it is said, by Austrian soldiers mistaking him for a French officer – his horse had bolted into the enemy lines. When the surgeon came, the Duke insisted he attend first to a French musketeer who lay beside him. "Begin with the French officer," I heard him say "he is more wounded than I am, and I shall be certain of assistance, which he is not." Truly, he is a noble young Prince.'

We find Latham conscious, thanking God for his deliverance, but luckily with no recollection of events which led up to it.

I leave the two of them together and squelch my way to

find Tom Hooper, assure him I am safe, and that no further mention need be made of Ward's peculiar behaviour.

We agree that explanations can wait until tomorrow, our only aim for tonight being to find what shelter we can from the pelting rain and fall into the profound sleep of the unutterably weary.

The next morning, it is still raining, but it is decided that whilst seriously wounded casualties will be left here to be cared for, the rest of the army will march on to Hanau.

'At last,' says Hooper who marches beside me, 'some decent food and a dry bed!'

Progress is slow as the walking wounded are marching along with us. First Lieutenant Bancroft has nominally resumed command of both our platoon and that of Ward who has not reappeared. In the absence of Sergeant Latham, whose fever keeps him still at Dettingen, and with Bancroft's continued weakness, it falls to me to relay commands.

It takes us a whole day to cover the distance from Dettingen to Hanau. Mercifully, the rain eases a little after eight in the morning and the skies have completely cleared before noon. We trudge through the sodden countryside, the clothes on our backs steaming in the heat of the sun.

'So,' says Tom Hooper when we are well on our way,

'what happened to that bastard Ward?'

I give him an abridged version of events, professing myself as much at a loss as he about Ward's motives in acting as he did.

Tom nods his head sagely. 'Unhinged by the stress of battle, probably. Well, he's no great loss, I dare say. Shame about Ben, though...'

'Aye, well we'd best keep that as our secret, don't you think – for the sake of Ben's memory?'

'True, 'twill do no one any good to stir the shit on that one, you never know who'll get covered in it.'

This, as it transpires, is to be my last exchange of any consequence with Tom Hooper. Hungry and weary, we both relapse into a moody contemplation that lasts for the rest of our journey to Hanau.

We set up camp between the walled town and the River Main and our first thought is to fill our bellies that have been empty for so long.

For a brief hour, it is almost like old times with Fritz Dorn and I waiting upon Lieutenant Bancroft and Hauptmann Bauer. The absence of their erstwhile companion, Ward, is speculated upon, his disappearance eventually attributed to being drowned and carried away in the river amongst the many nameless dead.

After we have served them their meal, Fritz goes off to

attend to some minor task, promising to meet up with Tom Hooper and myself later.

But I see neither of them again

Return

He comes as silently as ever, and with the inevitable irresistible demand, leading me towards the Hanau city gate where a coach stands waiting.

'Is it Sir William Hervey?' I ask Gerard as we approach.

'Use your eyes,' he replies, mounting upon the box. His surliness has not improved.

I unlatch the coach door.

It is not Sir William.

'Agnes!' I exclaim in delight. I scramble inside and make to kiss her but she pushes me away, her nose wrinkling in distaste.

'Faugh, Will, sit further off!'

I retreat, mortified, to the far corner of the coach as Gerard urges the horses into a trot. 'I'm sorry, Agnes. I am so used to being in this state these past weeks that I forget how it must seem to one of more delicate sensibilities. Being deprived of food and sleep, and the rigours of combat do not conduce to wholesomeness.'

'No, Will, it is I who should be sorry. I did not mean to offend you, but oh...,' she breaks into a tinkling laugh, 'you do stink so! Pray, let down the window.'

Soon the fresh evening air is gusting into the carriage.

'Where are we going?' I ask.

'Home, Will. You are going home. But first we are going to a guest house where you may bathe and wash away Jack Weaver for good.'

The next week is one of the happiest in my life, for every moment is spent in Agnes Mayer's company.

It does not matter whether the countryside we travel through by day is lashed with rain or bathed in sunlight. Or whether the hostelries we lodge in overnight be sparse or comfortable. In truth, I hardly even notice. To be with her is enough.

From Hanau, with Gerard as our coachman, we travel back the way we came. What took months on foot across country takes but a few, all too brief, days in horse and carriage on well-maintained roads.

Returning to Ostend, Mijnheer and Mevruow van Andel are delighted to welcome us back, though somewhat surprised to see me in the clothes of a gentleman rather than soldier's uniform. I do not know what story Agnes tells them, but she convinces them with as much ease as she provided me with the apparel and wherewithal to become Will Archer once again back in Hanau.

Indeed, so joyous has been this last week that I have all but forgotten Jack Weaver. The pangs of regret I felt on deserting my new-found friends - Tom Hooper, Fritz Dorn and, yes, First Lieutenant Henry Bancroft - have lost their initial sting. But, nevertheless, I still occasionally feel sad that I could not properly say goodbye to them. Though, on reflection, it is better they puzzle for a short time over the ingratitude of my inexplicable departure than that they know the full duplicity of the imposture that I unwillingly had to practise upon them.

Whatever disappointment they may be feeling, however, is nothing to that which is now visited upon me as my present felicity is brought to a harsh end and my future hopes are cruelly dashed.

With a passage to England booked for the morrow, Agnes and I spend one last clandestine night under the van Andel's roof.

It is only after we have made love, that Agnes tells me this will be our final time together.

I stare at her, aghast.

'The passage is for you alone, Will,' she says sadly. 'It grieves me as deeply as I see it grieves you. But Sir William wants you back in England whilst I must stay here.'

'But...' I say helplessly.

She puts a finger to my lips. 'There can be no 'buts', Will. We are his creatures and have no say in the matter. You know what he does to those who disobey him. Perhaps in some future time we may...'

Her eyes start with tears which I brush away and, enfolding her once more in my arms, we make love with a passion made all the sweeter by the regret for an Elysium denied that infuses it.

Reunion

At first I do not recognise the young footman who answers the door of 6 Bow Street. Almost as tall as myself with a slim body and broad shoulders, his dark hair neatly brushed.

But he recognises me straight away. 'Fuck me!' he exclaims, his voice breaking in a most un-footman-like way. 'Will – is it really you?'

He throws his arms around me in delight, hugging me so tightly as almost to stop my breath. Then, holding me at arms length, he surveys me and pronounces, 'You look older – and sadder, somehow. Foreign parts ain't done you much good, that's for sure!'

The voice veering betwixt bass and traitorous treble, and the new-scrubbed cleanliness have momentarily confused me. The unkempt, tousle-haired urchin that I left behind is almost become a presentable young man.

'Good to see you, too, Charlie – or should I call you Charles now?'

With a familiar cheeky grin and a punch to my shoulder, he croaks, 'Stow it, Will.' and drags me in to be reunited with the rest of the household.

It is nearly the end of July, four weeks since Gerard plucked me from the camp at Hanau, and I have sent no prior word of my coming, hoping that surprise at my return may cancel out whatever disappointment was caused by my involuntary disappearance nearly a year ago.

And so it proves. In the kitchen, Mrs Wiggins is so overcome with amazement that she near faints away and must needs resort to her bottle of 'restorative'. Susan laughs and weeps by turn. Unsure whether to slap me or hug me tight, she does both in profusion.

Upstairs, my reception is less effusive but no less heartfelt, Mr Garrick clasping my hands in welcome and demanding to know all that has befallen me during my absence.

I spend the evening giving the assembled household a suitably abridged account of my adventures.

They listen in open-mouthed wonderment and, when the time comes for us all to retire to bed, I am not surprised when Susan gives me a 'come-hither' wink.

She clearly wants to make up for lost time and is eager to reacquaint herself with my little soldier. But tonight he is not playing and remains lethargic despite all her coaxing.

I do my best to apologise and she says she understands – it's been a long day, I'm exhausted after my journey – but I can tell she is disappointed and also a little suspicious.

I cannot tell her the real reason – that, even though I may

never see Agnes Mayer again, I feel I would be betraying her.

I settle back into life at 6 Bow Street, but things are not, perhaps can never be, the same as before. In some ways I have become a stranger, remote from the life of the theatre which dominates the household.

And that life is showing signs of unrest. Garrick and Macklin's relationship with Fleetwood, the manager of Drury Lane where they are nearing the end of their season, has never been less than fraught, but is now at breaking point.

Over the next few days I frequently come across my master and the Irish bear in close conversation, planning how they may get all the Drury Lane company on their side to confront Mr Fleetwood at the end of the season.

After my experiences of the last few months, these squabbles do not engage my interest as once they did. Having been in the heart of battle and slaughter, I find it hard to set much store by such petty matters.

It is as if a melancholy has seized me that I would fain throw off but lack the will to do so and it is affecting my relationship with all about me.

Therefore the inevitable summons to Westminster, which arrives less than a week after my return, comes as an unexpected relief. It will, I hope, help me unburden myself of much that afflicts me and allow me to return to the regularity and order of the life I once loved.

'I hate to say "I told you so",' says Sir William Hervey genially, 'but I remember cautioning you about that Woodrow fellow.'

'You did, Sir William, and I regret to say my friendship with him blinded me to his true intent, despite him sharing his views quite openly.'

'His opinion on the rights of the common man and the evils of supposed tyrants were not uncommon in the company you found yourself in, you say?'

'When face to face with death, doubt about the established order of things may be excusable, I think,' I reply, not wishing to incriminate anyone else.

Seated in his Westminster chambers with a glass of ruby wine in my hand, I have already related my conclusions about Ben Woodrow.

That he was, indeed, the assassin we sought. That he probably made an attempt on the King's life at the commencement of the battle but mis-fired, resulting in His Majesty's horse bolting.

'Or,' I suggest, not wishing entirely to damn him, 'it may be that he had no intention of killing the King at all.'

Sir William raises a sceptical eyebrow. 'You betray your partiality, Will. Admit it, Woodrow was a scheming murderer. He had no qualms about aiming directly at the Duke of Cumberland. It was only your timely intervention that hindered him from killing the Prince. And,' he continues, driving home his point, 'you cannot now doubt that he used that simple fellow Barley, playing upon his gratitude and dog-like devotion, to compass the rogue Brogan's death? 'Twas only because Barley was a simple soul that he mistook his quarry and killed Scatchard instead.'

'We have no proof of that, Sir William,' I protest mildly

'Nor are likely to get any now,' agrees Hervey, 'but we may assume that, seeing Brogan in conversation with Finn Kelly when you were in Ostend, roused Woodrow's suspicions and made him fearful for his own safety.'

The conclusion seems inevitable. 'So Ben must actually have stolen Brogan's knife. But it can only have been only to protect himself, I cannot think he would have used it on Brogan.'

Sir William shakes his head regretfully, 'Still you would defend him? But do you not see, that makes him yet more despicable? He had not the courage to act directly but must coerce a gullible simpleton to achieve his ends.'

'Well, he has paid for it now,' I say despondently.

Hervey signals for Gray to replenish our glasses. 'Tell

me, Nathaniel,' says he briskly, 'what think you of this Tom Hooper's action in twisting the assassin's neck?'

'I'd say 'twas an act of impetuosity and not very conducive to due process, Sir William,' replies Grey drily.

'Nevertheless, he sounds a sensible fellow. Able to assess a situation quickly and act decisively. He has saved us a deal of trouble. Perhaps we should try to recruit him?'

I start to protest but Hervey breaks into laughter.

'Nay, Will, I do but jest. Sleeping dogs are best left to lie. You're sure he will not blab?'

'He, like me, regarded Ben as a friend. As no one is hurt, he will not want to sully his memory.'

Hervey assumes a look of mock amazement. 'No one hurt, you say? The Duke of Cumberland is hurt. His leg is like to give him trouble for the rest of his life. Fortunately both he and all who were present regard it as an accident, an unfortunate instance of what I believe is termed *friendly fire*! Though how a bullet in one's thigh can in any way be construed as friendly, I fail to see.'

I smile in response to his good humour, but there are still things that puzzle me. 'It seems Ben Woodrow acted out of personal motives, Sir William. He was not a French spy, he detested King Louis even more than King George. Are we any nearer to discovering who the French spy is?'

Hervey purses his lips. 'We are not, Will. Indeed I begin

to doubt if there really was one. And now that the French are defeated, it is not a matter of immediate importance. Any more than our friend Finn Kelly is.'

'Is he our friend, Sir William?'

Hervey grimaces. 'I doubt it. He is an annoyance, certainly. But I think we have discovered his game. The army is still encamped at Hanau and about a week ago a certain Major Powerscourt met with a tragic accident. Shot himself whilst cleaning his pistol. Unfortunate business. Only heir to a family with large estates in Ireland, absentee landlords, not very well liked.'

'And you think Kelly killed him?'

'I think nothing. All I know is that security is very lax in Hanau following our glorious victory at Dettingen, and that the path the bullet took was – shall we say – inconsistent with a self-inflicted wound.'

'Kelly has not been apprehended, then?'

'No, and as far as I am concerned at the moment, I shall not be expending a great deal of thought on him. There are matters nearer to home and of more interest to yourself.'

I catch my breath, thinking he is about to speak of Agnes and his veto upon our being together. But I am mistaken. That clearly is a matter which he regards as settled, and which I am prudent enough not to question.

'After Gerard witnessed Frederick Ward's attempt on

your life, he apprehended him, as I believe you saw. Unfortunately Gerard, in his usual ham fisted manner, was over zealous in rendering him senseless, so that he never regained consciousness. Therefore we are, I regret, no nearer to discovering who it is at Leicester House that seeks to do you harm. I think, however, that they will think twice before mounting another such attempt. In the meantime, whilst you would do well to remain vigilant, I do not believe you to be in any immediate danger.'

As I walk back to Bow Street, I am struck by the general air of jubilation in the streets. It feels almost like a public holiday, the houses adorned with bunting, and ballad singers adding their ditties to the usual cries of hawkers and pedlars.

Curious, I pay a penny for one of the broadsheets and read the ballad there printed:

> *Our noble generals played their parts,*
> *Our soldiers fought like thunder,*
> *Prince William too, that valiant heart*
> *In fight performed wonders.*
> *Though through the leg with bullet shot*
> *The Prince his wound regarded not,*
> *But still maintained his post and fought*
> *For glorious George of England.*

Carelessly I crumple the paper.

'If only they knew,' I think to myself.

Historical Notes

The War of the Austrian Succession

Charles VI, Emperor of Austria, died on 19th October 1740, leaving his imperial throne to his daughter Maria Theresa. During his last years, Charles, fearing that the powerful states of Europe would upon his death seize chunks of the empire, persuaded the monarchs of Europe to subscribe to the Pragmatic Sanction of Prague, a convention that would guarantee the integrity of Maria Theresa's imperial dominions.

On the death of Charles VI, Frederick, the ambitious new ruler of Prussia reneged on his commitment and seized Silesia.

Maria Theresa declared war on Prussia and invaded Silesia, precipitating wars that would rage for a quarter of a century.

The first period of fighting from 1740 to 1748 was known as the "War of the Austrian Succession" or in England as "King George's War".

George II sent English troops to join the Pragmatic Allies. Ostensibly the army was to fight for Maria Theresa, but George's concern was that the French intended to pass through the Low Countries and invade his beloved Hanover.

An English force was dispatched to Flanders in mid-1742 and remained there until the end of the war in 1748, fighting the four battles of Dettingen, Fontenoy, Rocoux and Lauffeldt.

In 1742, England had not fought a European war since the time of the Duke of Marlborough. In the intervening twenty years of peace, the army had been neglected by governments reluctant to spend money on the armed services.

The first British commander-in-chief was John Dalrymple, Earl of Stair. He was hampered by the refusal of the Dutch, Austrian and British commanders to co-operate in a plan of campaign. An additional embarrassment was George II's fear of provoking the French to outright war.

In 1743 the Pragmatic Army marched South to the Frankfurt region of Germany. There it was joined by George II and the battle of Dettingen was fought against the French Army commanded by the Duc de Noailles.

The Battle of Dettingen

The Battle of Dettingen took place on Thursday 27th June 1743 (Thursday June 16th back in England, which was still working on the Julian Calendar) and was the last time a British monarch led his troops into battle.

Fought on a narrow plain between the River Main and the Spessart Hills, it was a a battle we seemed unlikely to win. Hemmed in by French forces which far outnumbered the combined Allies and with King George at odds with his commander-in-chief, the Earl of Stair, the outcome might be attributed more to happy accident than as a result of any coherent military strategy by the allied commanders.

Two things contributed to the victory.

First, Count Grammont, in charge of French forces at Seligenstadt, who had been ordered to wait beyond the ravine and single bridge at Dettingen, decided instead to cross it, thus squandering his undoubted advantage. His excuse was that, having waited so long, he thought the bulk of the Allied army must have passed him and that only the rearguard was left.

The second was that the Allied forces, both Infantry and Cavalry, were much better disciplined than the French. Whatever the inadequacies of their Commanders, the English and Austrian soldiers stood their ground and fought tenaciously.

Bolting Horses

Both King George's and the Duke of Cumberland's horses bolted during the battle.

Early on, the King's mount, startled by musket fire, carried him off to the rear, but he returned on foot and bravely urged on his troops.

The Duke also lost control of his horse later in the battle. It was said that two Austrian soldiers, mistaking him for a French officer fired upon him, wounding him in the leg and causing his horse to carry him towards the French lines.

Whether apocryphal or not, the story of his deferring to a more severely wounded French _mousquetaire_ called Girardeau when being attended to by a surgeon did much to create his reputation as a brave, generous and noble soldier. A reputation which was later irrevocably tarnished by his ruthlessness in putting down the Jacobite Rebellion of 1745 when 'Sweet William' became 'Butcher Cumberland'.

Unrest

Whilst the victory at Dettingen did much to temporarily improve King George's reputation, there was still much unrest. The Jacobite threat continued to simmer, eventually erupting in the 1745 Rebellion, two years later.

The rise of evangelical Christianity whose preachers found a ready audience among labourers and working men also fuelled social unrest as it began to challenge the establishment of Church and temporal rulers.

And, finally, in the narrower field of the characters within this story, the relationship between Garrick, Macklin and Peg Woffington was on the verge of breaking up – but we may hear more of that during Will Archer's next adventure!

Acknowledgements

A Collision of Giants: The British Army during the War of Austrian Succession and Seven Years' War in Europe 1740 – 1763

J. W.Fortescue   www.leonaur.com

Redcoat: The British Soldier in the Age of Horse and Musket

Richard Holmes   Harper Collins 2001

Soldiers Richard Holmes   HarperPress 2011

All the King's Men: The British Redcoat in the Era of Sword and Musket

Saul David   Penguin 2013

William Augustus Duke of Cumberland: His Early Life and Times (1721-1748)

Evan Charteris   Edward Arnold 1931

also the Internet for contemporary accounts of the battle.

25205978R00197

Printed in Great Britain
by Amazon